# DARING TO SHARE

## A Collection of Memories and Imaginings

By 35 Wichita, Kansas area authors

All proceeds of this book go to
Senior Services Inc. of Wichita, KS
A not-for-profit charity.

Starla
ENTERPRISES, INC.

For information regarding permission, write to Starla Enterprises, Inc.

Attention: Permissions Department,

9415 E. Harry St., Ste. 603, Wichita, KS 67207


First Edition

ISBN: 978-1-0878-1199-4

Editor & Cover Design by Starla Criser

Printed in the U.S.A.

# Contents

## From a Child's Eyes

## Inspirational and Spiritual

## Stories from Challenges

# Writing Challenges

Many of the authors in this collection belong to a group of senior adults who get together monthly for writing classes, to network, and to support each other. Some authors have used part of the exercises we do in the creation of their project(s). See if you can figure out who used the exercises and which ones. The words do not all have to be used or can be used in another form.

WORDS: snow – sky blue – cautious – cactus – foot

PROMPT: Write from the viewpoint of a cactus – what's it like to live in the desert or have a "prickly personality."

WORDS: sunny – orange – excited – mulberry – tooth

PROMPT: Write about finding a scrapbook and think about the memories it contains.

WORDS: windy – black – suspicious – sunflower – elbow

PROMPT: Write about an old, abandoned house.

WORDS: freezing – salmon – stubborn – corn – leg

PROMPT: Sit outside and write down the sounds you hear.

WORDS: curiosity – cake – brooch – freedom – lighthouse

PROMPT: Write about your happiest childhood memory.

WORDS: angel – queen – mouse – gun – thrill

PROMPT: She/he studied her/his face in the mirror.

WORDS: school – table – crow – spider – forgiveness

PROMPT: If I could change one thing about myself...

WORDS: holiday – pencil – hammock – attic – fortune

PROMPT: Imagine that you are an animal in the zoo.

WORDS: tree – necklace – gossip – rope – car

PROMPT: Finish the thought: If I were invisible, I would...

WORDS: cheese – slippers – club – stool – garlic

PROMPT: Write about a special summer's evening.

WORDS: sword – butterfly – water – justice – school

PROMPT: Write about a strange experience that you'd had.

WORDS: hope – train – flute – computer – castle

PROMPT: Write about a train journey

WORDS: gondola – monkey – sun – man – watch

PROMPT: Finish the thought: There was a strange wailing sound coming from the next room...

# THOUGHTS ABOUT LIFE

# Harbinger of Hope!

## Rochelle Boster

Look to the crocus, a tiny, pale yellow flower dusted with the most delicate sunset purple. All for hope and renewal. This optimistic little flower whose fragile existence defies the calendar, sings of a glorious spring to come. Knowing the bitter winter winds with their icy chill soon to be a longed-for distant memory.

Look to the crocus, as more than a harbinger of spring, but a lesson for life. Just like the crocus struggling to push up between the dull brown blades of grass we can realize beauty, our lives filled with optimism for hope and renewal.

Look to the crocus, a small, gentle insignificant plant turns the human's heart from thoughts of loss and despair to thoughts of what can be. The crocus makes a difference in the dreary scenic landscape of winter tipping into spring. While the crocus is small, it lights a spark in all who take in its beauty.

Look to the crocus, warmed by the sun and nourished by the gentle spring rains. The crocus is short lived. We must look quickly to gather our memories of its beauty and its promise.

Remember the crocus! We once again dry our tear-filled eyes and smile. Our sad hearts will beat with laughter instead of anguish. The warmth of the spring sun lightens the burden of winter. Our stagnant minds overdosed by too much reality will turn into wellsprings of positive thoughts and optimistic action. In place of the crocus, hope and renewal will bloom.

# Yesterday, a White Gander Goose

## Martha Williams Prentice

Yesterday, a white gander goose
  with a deformed wing
    walked up from the pond
      and into the yard
        while I was potting geraniums.
He stood there, so regal, head held high,
  his eyes straight at me,
    bold, inquiring, wise.
      In stillness I welcomed his presence.
A quick turn of his head,
  first left, then right,
    and we acknowledged each other
      with an air of acceptance.

Today, the white gander goose
  came up from the pond
    and marched into the yard
      right to the edge of the patio ...
        my beautiful new acquaintance.
A tilt of his head,
  slight spread of wing,
    a twitch of the tail,
      gave a simple sense of knowing.
He lingered there, with little nods,
  and seemed to say,
    in his way,
      "Here I am. I came back."

## When I Get Too Old to Dream

### C. Holden

Sometimes a thought is out of the blue or in a dream,
Or just a vision of places near of faraway.
We dream of things both real and fantasy
When we get too old to dream life is over.

## Life

Life is full of rough and bumpy roads with many muddy detours,

Many forks in the road, sometimes we take the shortest one, but it may not be the best one.

Do the best you can with what you have to work with.

I was told at a young age to HOE THE ROW YOU WERE GIVEN AND DO THE BEST YOU CAN.

# Feelings

## Misty Colbert

A smile is spreading happiness.
Laughter makes the body jiggle with joy.
A hug embraces love between two people.
Holding hands is enjoying being together.
To cuddle, is not wanting to let go; just yet.
A kiss is just one intimate moment shared.
Someone checking on you, is comforting it shows that you care.

# Cool?

You tell me I'm cool, but why?
My blood pressure is high.
My self-esteem is low.
We are all watching my waist, behind, and legs grow.
My hair has gotten thinner.
Somehow, my ego has gotten bigger.
I am no use to anyone, yet I sit on a pedestal.
I'm poor in health and spirit.
Tell me, how that's cool.

# A Breeze Weaved Through the Leaves of the Trees

## Martha Williams Prentice

A breeze weaved through the leaves of the trees,
   it showed me the path it had taken ...
   stirring within me a forgotten dream,
   a look at a new destination.

I had laid it aside, allowed it to drift,
   turned my back to what could be;
   new insight, new perspective, new purpose,
   a gift had returned to me.

# The Table

## Sherry A. Phillips

A library is my soul-filling place. Atmosphere is heavy. Quiet embraceable. Easy chairs face solitary spaces and wait. The order of shelves and books contradict chaos. Desks ready for writers. The Card Catalog full of directions.

I walk straight to the big as a church door solid pine table in the Ghost Ranch Library. From the light tan tabletop, I push aside evidence of earlier visitors. The Complete Fairy Tales of the Brothers Grimm left alongside Trees of North America.

Dropping my pack to the floor I sit down and scoot up close. I rub my hands over the well-used two-inch-thick pine surface. My fingers feel the smooth but rough texture of the annual rings of life in the wood.

As I think of the tree growing year by year when the pine tree stood tall in some unknown forest, I admire the content way in which it fulfills its purpose now. I trace cup rings and pencil scratches. My eyes linger on ink blotches. Marks mingle with oil stains from the hands of others who have sat in this place and taken time to enjoy the table's presence and purpose. I sigh and smile, put pen to paper now I am ready to write.

# It's Free

## C.A. Lemont

Would you bother to listen if I tried to explain?
Or would all my efforts just be in vain?
You know nothing in this world is really free.
Except of course advice from fools like me.

If I could tell you in one little song;
In all of life where I've gone wrong;
Of the mistakes I've made, and the lessons I've learned.
Of the price I've paid, and the wisdom I've earned.

I'd tell you to live your life as you see fit.
Do what you have to, it's your life, live it.
Why let others choose the path you take?
That's one choice you get to make.

You get to dance to your own song.
Whether you're right, or whether you're wrong.
It's too hard to dance to someone else's tune.
That's like eating spaghetti with a spoon!
Why do anything the hard way?
Just be who you are... it's okay.

# Signs of Aging

## Jean Welle

My skin has become much more puckered,
And age spots appear now with flair.
My joints seem to be a bit stiffer,
And color's abandoned my hair!
This body exhibits my aging,
Yet my spirit is vibrant and strong.
For Jesus communes with me daily
His truth from God's Word and with song.

# To Bake a Cake

To bake a cake all you will need
Is the basic mix or recipe.
From that point on it's up to you;
Create the same or try something new.

A cup of that, of this a nip –
A tidbit more; now give it a whip.
Cupcakes? Layers? Loaf pan or Bundt?
Melt in your mouth or chewy with crunch?

To bake a cake all you will need
Is the basic mix or recipe.
From that point on it's up to you;
Create the same or try something new.

# My Amusing Muse

## Mary McKay

Compelled to write is the hallmark of a Muse. Does it come from a galaxy far, far, away? Is it possible to identify one and if so, what does it look like? How do you find one?

My experience is that your Muse finds you. You are powerless and it is in control. Forget figuring out its business hours because it comes when it wants to, day or night. Many the time while night was in the midst of her course, my Muse has arrived and compelled me to get out of bed and write. No consideration has been given to the temperature, if it is cold, you'd better grab your heavy robe and put on a pair of socks.

It might be a one-liner, or it might be an outpouring that is almost impossible to keep up with. It could even be the title of your next book. What comes out of your pencil is what the Muse wants to have you write. I am always curious about what will come out of my pencil and, when it is finished with me, I can go back to bed and wonder what has just happened. I have learned not to ignore it! Why would I? Even if it is uninvited and unexpected, it is always welcome and full of certainty.

So far, I can find it safely on the shelf, patiently waiting for me to call upon it. It has been kind enough to allow me to take care of those responsibilities that life has required of me. Raise my children, keep a job to support myself and my children, as best as I can, and keep a home together for us. Writing has been a great luxury that I couldn't afford to indulge in until after I had finished my work. It just felt too selfish and nothing in my life prepared me to think I could make it my life's work and make a living from it. It was too much fun to be work. Something to enjoy when my work was done.

When time allows me to sit down at my computer and play, I am always tickled when my Muse returns and does the heavy lifting. It is smarter than I am, has a better imagination and can find the perfect words to convey what we want to share with others. From time to time it throws in a schmecken gut! Or a Mon Dieu! It has pushed me to take classes in Español and to learn enough Japanese to at least say Konnichiwa. Sometimes I have to get out my foreign language dictionary to satisfy my Muse with the perfect word or phrase to communicate with Habibi.

My Muse has been with me since early childhood. Before I was old enough to go to school and learn to read and write, my Muse had me making marks and trying to infuse them with meaning. I can remember a lovely white ash tree in our yard that I could pull leaves from and with a small stick I could scratch the white surface and the green juice would surface and satisfy my need to make a mark and write a story. A few marks on a leaf and I could pull another and another and stack them into my little books. My mother was wise enough to get old discontinued wallpaper rolls from the store for me to roll out on the kitchen floor and tell my stories on long reams of paper with my crayons and pencils.

That same need to make a mark may explain my love of painting. My oil paintings tell a story with everything from gypsy encampments to cattle drives and family castles in Scotland. I appreciate my Muse and will take this opportunity to thank it and praise it and invite it to stay with me always.

# Life in General

C. Holden


We have to work with what we have to work with. However, sometimes we can't find the time or the resources to do the job.

We do so much with so little for so many and please so few. It is no wonder we are in the shape we are in.

Seems like the further I go the behinder I get.

We don't always have the right answers, but we have answers.

We do the best we can in life. We have certain hurdles to cross. Some are small and some are large. You have to make the most of what you have to work with.


# Life is Like a Piano

Life is like a piano

What you get out of it is

What you put in it.

# Train of Thought

## Julie Lovelace

The idea of train travel begins a hopeful journey. I just get out my computer and it's quickly arranged. With tickets purchased and bags packed, I can climb aboard. The train cars are atop parallel rails and the engineer is ready to chug down the tracks. What a great reliable way to travel.

Less reliable is my "train of thought." I shudder to think that my sharp intellect is a thing of the past, but where do those thoughts go? Do my thoughts simply jump off or does the train completely derail?

Maybe my thoughts never actually bought the ticket. Perhaps, my good ideas couldn't latch on to enough gray matter to complete the trip. I'm not a young princess playing my flute in the castle anymore. I'm more like the queen mother who still looks good but isn't asked to chair committees for important events.

Could it be that I get distracted? As my thoughts are enjoying the train ride, maybe I spied a lovely creek running along the tracks and I decide I must jump the train, kick off my shoes to splash and wade in the clean, fresh water. You never know.

Frequently, I lose my train of thought when I walk from one train to another, It's that "threshold phenomenon" that happens when you must have an object in another place, but when I get to that other place it is impossible to remember what I went to retrieve. So, I have to walk back through that threshold to recapture the original thought. With any luck, I will remember. If not, I can always take a nap.

Occasionally, I'll get back on board my train of thought! It's quite dramatic when the train comes roaring down the tracks, stops in time for me to climb aboard and my thought journey streams all the way to its destination. My hope is restored that I can ride that train of thought.

## The Flashing Sign Read:

Martha Williams Prentice

The flashing sign read:
     "American Legion – Post #_____
        Marines – Budweiser Salutes You!
     Jim and Christie now playing
        June 15, 16, 17   8:00 – 12:00

The two-piece band wore black and white—
   he in leather-like black jacket and black pants,
     silver metal tips on his black boots;
   she in too-tight sparkled white with fringe,
     hair lightly pink and sprayed with glitter.
Jim played bass, Christie acoustic,
   both played quite well actually—
   their voices pleasant and well-matched.

One man and two women
   walked onto the dance floor,
   swaying and keeping time to "Kansas City."
   He left his cap on the table,
   where beer cans stood in a long row
   and cigarette smoke spiraled up
   in blue swirls from crowded ashtrays—
     a good-time silver-set threesome.
And to think, some men won't go after one woman.

# Peace

## C.A. Lemont

Children of the sixties, here we are at last.
The world of our parents has now become the past.
The vision as I recall, was love and peace.
Violence of any nature simply must cease.

Humanity requires a new sense of ourselves.
Climb out of your own private little hells.
Elevate your eyes to envision a better place.
Do what you promised for the human race.

Universal love, it can be achieved.
Once realization is, you are no different from me.
We watched the sixties on the evening news.
The brotherhood of man, our common view.

United, together, we can all survive.
The dawn of an era is standing by.
A revolution begins with but a simple cry.
Freedom and peace for you and I.

# A Perfect Day!

## Rochelle Boster

Morning announced in the garden with a
shy sun peaking between giant cumulous clouds and
earthy smells of turned soil drifting on cool breezes.
Gardener's thought: never a more perfect day!

Daily exercise, bending, tugging at stubborn weeds,
watering thirsty plants, feeding hungry roots.
Joy to the body and satisfaction to the brain!
Gardener's dreams coming true.

Peaceful reverie of this fine day interrupted.
From the trees, rushing feet crushing brittle leaves.
Sticks breaking with staccato cracks and pops.
Gardener's thought: what could it be?

Armed with metal bucket and trowel,
the gardener spread her feet to stand her ground!
Footfalls too heavy for rabbit or fox.
Wisp of fear alerts the heart, curiosity holds the mind!
Gardener's thought: what can I do?

In a split second the answer bounding out of the trees,
ebony colored, young canine. Red tongue lolling and drooling.
Legs strong, but brown eyes wide and searching.

The gardener thought: oh no, make lots of noise!
The concussion of trowel on bucket did not discourage
the travel-worn part Labrador/Pit Bull? Rather she took
it as welcome, belly flopping on the garden's soft, tilled soil.
Gardener's thought: now what?

The guest had obvious needs, food, water, and grooming to
lift the burden of ticks and burrs acquired on the journey's path.
The gardener's new grateful companion matching her every step.
Gardener's thought: what do I name her?

Days progressed, bonding grew deeper between human and canine.
Names were bandied about and Jessie the choice!
Jessie's search to find a safe haven a success.
Gardener's thought: never a more perfect life!

# Guilt Speaks

## Rochelle Boster

Do you really know me
>    You wear me like a badge
>    Use me as an excuse
>    Count on me to spoil your day
Do you really think
>    You have the right to take the blame
>    What business is someone else's life to you
>    How could YOU have changed things
Who are you
>    To be omnipotent
>    To be so selfish
>    To take responsibility
When he didn't answer
>    Did you want to check
>    And when they found him
>    Was it enough to be by his side
Don't use me
>    As a crutch
>    As a reason to bare a bigger cross
>    To be more holy than Thou
When will you learn
>    You are not in charge
>    If not today
>    Then tomorrow the same outcome

# Pre-Judgement Days

## REBrown

Carl Jung once declared the lack of a guiding mythology to be a major problem for modern cultures, yet there are and have been alternative lore to serve that function if one just looks for them.

Cases in point: stories told within our family, some of them pre me.

Around 1929 a black choir sang before a white Oklahoma congregation, parents and older siblings in attendance. After the performance they were politely thanked and applauded, but when they were gone, the minister stated that "we all know these folks sing beautifully, but we also know they're just not as good as we are." He then asked all who agreed to stand up. Our dad noticed one of my older brothers, perhaps four years of age, innocently moving to stand and quietly sat him back down in the pew.

A Mexican family was treated badly when it moved into that town, but when the man drowned trying to save a sixth neighbor in a flash flood, having already saved five, he was given a very nice funeral by his former tormentors.

After our dad left, our mother's wisdom and strength shown through. Never a bad word about our dad. (He was the only mechanic General Tinker would allow to work on his aircraft. He once bought five old car engines, disassembled all of them and built one good engine out of the best parts.) Mom moved to Wichita and served as a riveter throughout WWII, building Boeing B29s while sister Clarice and I were shepherded by our extended Chapman Kansas family. So many aunts, uncles and cousins, all having attributes worthy of emulation. I could not have gone astray if I wanted to.

And in small town Chapman there was a lone black student, the son of a sharecropper and a star high school footballer. After a victory over Junction City the team was to be treated to a steak dinner. When the owner refused to serve Chauncey White, the entire team stood up and walked out in protest.

Then, on the first day roll call of seventh grade in Planeview, just outside Wichita, one student named Roy Brown was absent. He showed up the second day. He was black, and several classmates laughed, saying their expectations had been that we were brothers. We laughed along with them, saying "we are."

Graduating second in senior class was an unexpected downer for such a smarty-pants, but beaten by a girl? he fact that she was black was entirely incidental. But, by a girl??

(She deserved it. I didn't.)

Four of us had formed a vocal quartet, aptly called "The Four Seniors," hoping to go professional. Booker T. Washington, Kenny Jones, Pinky Woosypiti, and me. Two black students, one Comanche and one well mixed Caucasian. Already serving in the Kansas Air National Guard, I introduced them to the First Sergeant, who apologetically burst my first balloon. The Guard would accept the Comanche, but not the blacks. Embarrassed to tears does not adequately describe the emotion.

On to college!

On the way to engineering school in '55, a VW Beetle going south almost caused a dangerous double-take. A black man driving a VW! Not a Cadillac? Not a Buick! Was there an unwelcome "stereotype" lurking somewhere? But it was a fact. Much later a realtor opined that the phenomenon was real, yet partly prejudicial. A car is very easy to repossess. Not so a house, and the labor market was sharply biased toward whites. One could only observe the forces in play and hope.

Three of us were about to graduate from college and had discussed at length the possibility of hitchhiking through Europe. One attorney patron of the Cedar Lounge overheard our frequent discussions, looked at me and said simply, GO! Quit talking and GO! He had considered the same prospect on approaching graduation from law school. Pragmatism struck. He planned to work two years, save his money and then take the tour. But two years showed promise of higher income—and he never took the tour.

So, we WENT!

And during that adventure another small bubble burst. An exceptionally attractive young Italian lady, a newspaper journalist, gave us a ride.

It is a fact that under casual circumstances a person can rationalize almost any absurdity or prejudice.

Take the example of the young lady in the Commons Cafeteria the first day at the University. On learning I was an engineering student she uttered a stifled oh! When asked to explain, she claimed that most engineers are "fade-outs," which after several challenges she defined as one who doesn't know the difference between Bach and Beethoven. After learning my enjoyment of both she could only retort that "most engineers were fade-outs." Unable to resist the temptation I asked how many engineers she knew. A stifled "three" followed.

Back to the young Italian lady! When she revealed she was a communist, the façade crashed. I saw myself before I saw myself seeing myself. No rationale possible.

It could not be! Communist women are dumpy, wear black shawls, lace-up work shoes, and push wheelbarrows.

SELAH!

Please note: I cannot recall the word "prejudice" ever being used in our home, only illustrative stories, or lore. No labels or epithets. Our mother gets full credit for that, and for the literature she championed, such as Rudyard Kipling's "If" and "Gunga Din."

"Though I've belted you and flayed you, by the living God that made you, you're a better man than I am, Gunga Din."

## Today = Tomorrow = Yesterday

### C. Holden

Work hard today, do the best you can, strive to achieve.

Plan for tomorrow.

Planning will make better and more prosperous tomorrows.

Remember the past.

Don't forget those who have taken the time to teach all you have learned.

Share with others your wisdom.

Sharing is a gift that is priceless.

When you are gone all that is left are memories

## The Rainbow

All our lives we hear there is a pot of gold at the end of the rainbow.

All our lives we try to get ahead, sometimes it is like chasing rainbows.

We work hard and save, plan, and do the best we can.

And at the end of a rainstorm we look up to see if there is a rainbow,

And wonder if there really is a pot of gold at the end.

We go to church and we hear of a city with streets paved with gold,

And wonder if this is the pot of gold at the end of the rainbow.

# A Writer's Love of Language

## Rochelle Boster

Love in twenty-five words or fewer.

It can't be done, I say. Language doesn't allow it.

Language sees that in English alone we are confused, bemused, used, and even abused by words that look harmless and innocent. The challenge of Language is to tame those words and sprinkle them here and there in the most interesting and appropriate places. Making sure that their definition matches their use with no fear of misunderstanding.

Who is responsible? The writer!

Language can bring about embarrassment when a bear cub, bares it all. Language can be strong and opinionated. Manipulated it can influence people poised on the razor's edge of decision.

But lest we forget, the writer is in control!

Language conveys all emotions, and can sooth a savage beast, mend a broken heart, or stir a hornets' nest. Language can confuse with hyperboles, similes, idioms, metaphors, and puns, lovely puns!

It is the writer's choice!

Language is guiltless when it comes to abuse by words. Language does not choose to demean, denigrate, or demonize in 140 or fewer characters. Language is at the mercy of who is using it and in what context.

It is the writer who holds Language hostage!

Language is malleable, immaculate, and rarely humdrum. Language can bring you to fits of hysterical laughter, gut wrenching screams, and tender moments or romance. Language has the power to put you into a mindful reverie, or not.

The writer lays the black and white path!

# The Big Man

C. Holden

He is big and burly and unshaven.

Only bathes on special occasions.

His clothes are well worn and faded with a rip and a patch here and there.

His hair is always a mess.

His language is something to be desired.

He only speaks when he is spoken to.

Sometimes the words don't come out like the thought he was thinking.

But he is just a good old boy with a big heart.

No one knows his education background.

But when he speaks, most folks listen.

His eyes are soft and sincere.

This simple man keeps to himself most of the time.

But he has another side few know about.

He is a writer.

He writes with a solid and true meaning.

He writes of life in general, hopes and dreams, and of the past.

Some of which is his own.

# FUN AND HUMOR

# Don't Mess with Me, Buster!

## Starla Criser

Zelda lay in the hammock stretched between fake trees in her oversized cage at the Sedgwick County Zoo. It was low enough she could dangle one leg over the side and touch the straw-covered floor. She gave a small nudge and sent the hammock into motion.

Basically, she was bored. What she needed was to go on a holiday trip somewhere. But she didn't have a fortune to spend on anything lavish. Okay, she had no money. A simple problem like that would not stop her from at least dreaming about a vacation.

If she had a pencil and some paper, she could write her thoughts down. Except she couldn't actually write... or read. Again, those were problems she didn't care about.

Maybe she'd go where it was warm with lots of sand, like a beach. From time to time, she'd overheard zoo employees talk about their vacations. One veterinarian that checked on her and the other orangutans had liked Maui. That might be okay. The woman had told her assistant about going zip-lining. They had fastened her to a heavy line, and she slid on it from one high-up landing to another. But then Zelda could swing from tree to tree without being secured.

Or she could go where it was cold, maybe try snow skiing. When two caretakers had talked about a trip to Vail and skiing, that had sounded intriguing. Except she didn't like cold weather. So maybe that wasn't a good idea.

Hmm. This dreaming of a vacation away from here was harder than she'd thought it would be.

Attica—a stupid name for an orangutan, she thought—bellowed for her attention from across the cage.

When she glanced in his direction, he tossed a huge ball at her. Surprised she grabbed for it and ended up losing her precarious balance. The hammock tipped over.

Just as a young family stopped to look at her in the observation room, she toppled out and plopped on her stomach. How humiliating!

Attica would pay for this embarrassment.

Ignoring the family, she stood, snatched up the ball, and tossed it with all her might at the annoying male. She grinned in delight when the ball hit him in the chest. It hit him with enough force fell backward onto his fat ass. She chuckled.

He sat up and blinked at her. "What was that for?"

Sometimes he could be so dense. "For interrupting my daydreaming," she snapped. She bobbed her head toward the big windows. "And for making me look clumsy in front of visitors."

Attica glanced at the kids pointing and laughing at Zelda. He had the good sense to appear remorseful. There was even a tinge of red embarrassment on his huge cheeks. He mumbled, "Sorry" and looked down at his big feet.

Oh, he looked adorable. She forgave him in an instant. Besides, she'd rather play ball with him now than do anymore daydreaming.

# Fear's Friend Garlic

## E. L. Morrow

Thomas Onion raises garlic. His is not one of those big corporate operations, but a family-owned, business offering the personal touch. In fact, that was their slogan for years: "Onion's Garlic all the flavor with the personal touch." It didn't catch on.

Their current marketing uses the phrase, "The seasoning you trust from the people who love their work so much they take it home with them." A veiled reference to the garlic odor clinging to the workers' clothing. Like the other, this slogan is not catching on.

It's a family operation. One of their workers and best customers is a Cousin Fear. No one can remember if Fear is his real name or a nickname that stuck. In fact, no one seems to know how he is related to the Onion clan. But no matter, after all these years he's Cousin Fear.

Cousin Fear is afraid of almost everything. He doesn't drive, because that's dangerous. In fact, he never rides in cars (buses or trucks either) because he read somewhere passengers are more apt to be severely injured or killed than the driver. He fears many things including, water, bridges, shadows, airplanes, and especially shadows of airplanes flying overhead. His primary list also includes shellfish, cracks in sidewalks, people who smile at strangers, people who don't smile at strangers, those in uniforms, doctors, undertakers, and cab drivers. But most of all, he is afraid of vampires.

This is where his obsession with garlic comes in. He wears a cluster of fresh garlic around his neck, changing it every three days to be sure it is stout enough. He also has garlic in his pockets, as anklets above his shoes, and in his hair.

The power of the herb also protects his house. There is garlic under the seats of his furniture. It's placed around each mirror and in front of each air vent and window. Over the entryway to any room where some would place mistletoe during the Christmas season is—you guessed it garlic. As extra insurance the last time his house needed exterior painting, he insisted the painters stir in a pound of garlic powder for each gallon of paint.

One day Fear realized he was spending a lot of time avoiding or protecting himself from those things that might undo him, and he had a horrible thought. "What if there is something I should be afraid of—but I'm not? It could sneak up on me and take me unawares. But how can I find out what else I should be afraid of?"

Then he had an exciting idea. "I'll form a club of people like me. We can compare notes and help each other with our obsessions."

He put an ad in a local paper: "If you are afraid of anything, come to share your wisdom. We will listen."

He secured the sorting shed at the garlic fields and set the time for late afternoon. That way, they would all get home before dark. Everyone knows what terrible things can happen after dark.

There was some confusion at the first meeting. Three people thought it was a support group to help overcome their fears. They were informed "No indeed! We must respect all fears as real— we want to be sure we are not missing out on anything we should be afraid of."

The three left deciding to have coffee and watch a few episodes of "Mom." They talked about forming a twelve-step group of their own. They were never heard from again—a clear sign to the remaining fearing group that some unknown evil had pounced on them (probably vampires, or werewolves, or maybe just wolves). Another theory revolved around them killing each other over the question of which coffee shop to use. No matter, they met their demise because they did not take fear seriously enough.

The group decided to refer to the three who departed as "The Unfortunates." The "unfortunates" untimely ends became a major topic of discussion at the next several meetings. In their fifth meeting, they passed a resolution of "Condolences to the Families of the Lost." Of course, they knew nothing about their families. They weren't even sure the unfortunates had families. In fact, no one knows the names of the three people presumed lost. None of the group introduced themselves by name, since giving your name provides the other with power over you. With someone's name, you can find out where they live, and work, even their birthday, if they own property, and lots of other things. There simply was not enough trust to share names yet. In the group's resolution, they express "... true sadness that we could not convince the unfortunate ones of the seriousness of the dangers that lurk everywhere...." After many more words, phrases, clauses, "Where-Ins," and "Therefore Be it Resolves," the resolution concludes with a statement of continued dedication to their purpose. "Despite our sorrow, we must protect ourselves, and others, so their sacrifice will not have been made in vain."

They were so pleased with their Resolution. So much so they published it in the newspaper. The group placed it on the obituary page, which caused significant befuddlement through-out the county.

This resolution was the third action taken by the group. The only decision of the first meeting was setting a date to meet again.

Of the six members remaining, after the unfortunates departed, one proclaimed his fear of numbers loudly. The group decided to meet only on days that are prime numbers. Reasoning prime numbers can only be divided by themselves or one, and everyone knows division is the root of all problems. They also agreed never to mention a number when they were together.

They avoided the 13th and all Fridays because everyone knows how unlucky Friday the 13th is. No one could be sure the bad luck didn't rub off both ways.

So, unless the date falls on a Friday, they meet on the first, second, third, fifth, seventh, eleventh, seventeenth, nineteenth, twenty-third, twenty-ninth, and thirty-first. If the month has fewer days, they wait until the first of the next month.

The second decision the group made is the name. The name is like a secret password. They will only use it if someone suspects an evil possession. It took until the end of the fourth meeting to agree upon their name: The Knights of the Unknown Unknowns.

After naming their group, and writing the resolution, they delved more deeply into their fears.

The only woman in the group declared she was afraid of slippers. She believed she had been a dog in a past life and either chewed up her owner's slipper, getting it caught in her throat and choking to death. Or her owner was so angered by the damaged slipper that she (the dog) had been beaten to death. Either way, slippers are to be avoided at all cost.

Another man, who calls himself Harry, saying that's not his real name, expressed fear of wooden stools. He believes he had been a circus lion in a past life. The "trainer" tormented him with his whip and the menacing bar stool with its four-legs poking at him. He dreamed of eating the trainer but could never get past the stool and whip. So, now when he sees a wooden stool of any kind, he picks it up and bites each of the four legs, leaving teeth marks behind. Then he kicks it across the room and snarls at it.

This behavior has landed Harry on the street or in jail more than once. After hearing from Harry, Fear realizes, "I have spent my whole life around stools and never knew how dangerous they are. Thank goodness for this group."

The only other member of the group who wasn't afraid to speak in public said, "My greatest fear is cheese. You can't trust cheese. It looks harmless enough, but it's sneaky; sometimes it's yellow, sometimes it's white. Occasionally it bears warning labels like "sharp." What is that—does it have little razor blades in it? If I eat it, will it cut my throat? And what if someone mislabeled some sharp as mild—you can't trust cheese. They say it's made from milk, but why would anyone make cheese when they could make ice cream out of the same stuff? It must be some terrorist plot.

Fear was having a great time learning what others feared. But at the end of the tenth meeting, he listed all the new things he had discovered to fear. While making his notes, he thought, "Some of these fears seem silly." Then he began to wonder, "Do my fears seem silly to others?"

# Dumbbell

## Don Boldea

On vacation in Italy a few years back, my wife and I were enjoying the sights, sounds and food of Venice. Everyone we met kept insisting that we must not miss a water tour on a tradi-tional Venice gondola.

There were so many of these beautiful water taxis, we just couldn't decide which one would be the best for us. Luckily, standing on one of the many bridges crossing the canals, was the stereotypical Grinder man and his monkey with the proverbial tin cup.

I addressed the Grinder man as I dropped a few liras in the monkey's tin cup. I asked if my wife and I wanted to tour this wonderful city by water, what gondola taxi should we select.

After a quick glance at me, without hesitation the mustachioed fellow said, "The 'Signori-na Amore.'"

I thanked the gentleman and dropped a few more liras in the monkey's tin cup as I went to rejoin my wife.

The Grinder man had said the gondola passed at this very bridge every two hours. As we reached the steps, where we were told to watch for the Signorina Amore, the gondola pulled to the dock.

We knew that it was the correct gondola because emblazoned on the raised tail portion of the boat was the gold-filled insignia "SM." Hmm! We inquired hesitantly and suspiciously if this was the two-hour tour gondola for the city of Venice. The gondolier smiled and assured us it was. We climbed aboard.

It was a bright, sunny day in the low nineties. Mary was wearing a white pair of capris, white Italian sandals and a light blue scooped neck blouse with a white, wide-brimmed hat. Her beautiful olive skin color made her look like a glamorous model.

I was wearing white slacks, white boat shoes, no socks and a red Polo shirt but no hat. I al-so had a slight spray-on tan to cover my fair complexion. Yet, I still looked like a pudgy, middle age man who didn't belong with this beautiful woman.

After we finished the tour, we disembarked from the gondola and walked to our hotel. On the way, I felt like every man, woman and dog on the streets was watching, muttering, laughing and pointing at me.

Arriving at our room, I felt warm; no, hot and a bit crispy. I went into the bathroom to shower. I disrobed and as I passed the large mirror over the vanity, I saw a burnt matchstick. Oh my God that's me! My face, arms and feet were sunburned to the color of a cast-iron skillet.

After a long two hours of standing under a soft spray of cold water, the hot, crispy look and feeling were subsiding, a little.

Boy was I stupid. I'm a dumbbell. That's what my mother used to call me when I was eight years old and I did the same thing, except all I had on was a bathing suit.

She'd say I was a . . . "Dippy, dappy, dopey, disconnected, dark complexioned dumbbell!"

"Sweetheart," my lovely wife began, "I don't care if they point, mutter, laugh and think you're a dumbbell, you're my dumbbell and I love you."

That was all I needed to feel good again. However, it took about another two weeks for my body parts to return to my fair skin state with a slight spray-on tan.

# Writer's Block — The Wichita Race

## Tom Elman

"Here we are once again, fans. Right here on Main Street in downtown central Kansas. Welcome to the 11th Annual Wichita Iditarod Snowshoe Race. This gentleman on my right is the former Indiana University basketball coach, the one and only 'The General' Bobby Night. On my left is the beautiful Ms. Sparus Hilton. And of course, all of you know me from all the past ten snowshoe races. But for those of you who don't hail from the Land of Oz... I'm Gov. Sam Brokeback. Fans, don't forget that Dillons is celebrating Fiesta Days at all area stores this week. We'll be back in 60 seconds after this station identification.

"Dammit, Sparus, put those buffalo hot wings down for a minute you're getting that sauce all over our equipment..."

"She's a pig, Sam, and I think your mic is still on..."

"Is this mic still on?"

"Welcome back to the finish line, fans. The excitement is mounting. But before we get started here, I have a few announcements to make concerning this year's race. Because of the new budget cuts I just agreed to... this year's race will be shortened to only two blocks instead of the usual twenty-six miles."

"Hold on to that thought for a moment, fans... reports ae starting coming in from one of our spot reporting crews. The first report is just in from KEYN's Don Haul and the crack, up-to-date, broadcasting team from the starting line down at Douglas and Broadway. Come on in, Don."

"Good morning, Sam. We would like to report that we have our first estimated count of these rabid fans lined up between the starting line here at our broadcast booth and the finish line where you are on Main Street. The early exit poll projections have just been shattered by an unusual influx of fans created by a young mother and her two children who just came out of Pasta Pizza to add to the maddening throng."

"Can you give us that count, Don? We're on the edges of our seats up here in the broadcast booth at the finish line. This booth has been furnished by Cox Communications. Don't forget, you can upgrade your internet service for just $19.95 a month for the next two years. Make that call right now folks. Back to you, Don."

"Thanks, Sammy. I'll give you what's just been placed in front of me by one of the many volunteer runners always so much help to make things go so smoothly at this great sporting event. The preliminary count is now 13 fans, but there seems to be heated discussions going on about a man or woman lying next to the curb at the corner of Market Street. Wait a minute, Sam... this is hot stuff just in from another runner. They have confirmed it is a man. His face is all blue and his tongue is frozen to one of the metal rods on the drain cover. They have turned him over so that the sun will thaw out his tongue. We're sending you the video now."

"Oh My God shut that off!"

"Just look the other way, Sparus, the public has a right to see this."

"What do you mean by look the other way, Sam? This is the only way I look."

"Ah ... back to you, Don."

"Some bad news, Sam. The two EMC guys have officially declared the man dead. They are saying he probably had a fatal heart attack or maybe too much hooch. So, I guess the official count will stay around 9 or 12. Oh crap the lady and the two kids... who were taking pictures of the dead guy, are headed north on Market."

"Well, there you have from street-side. I will turn this over to our color commentator for a little out-side the box analysis. Take it away, Bobby."

"It's Coach Night, Sam. Or Mr. Night will do. How much did they say I was getting paid for this? And how long does it take to get to Eisenhower from here?"

"All right then. Thanks for that timely and informative comment. I see our two entrants are at the starting line. Which one are you putting your money on, Night, the one in the donkey outfit or the one in the elephant get-up?"

"That's it. I've had enough disrespect from you, Sam." Coach Night throws his folding chair out in the street and turns back to

Sam. "I'll bet this ding-bat blond will be at the top of the teacher crop after what you did to the school system's budget here in Whichaway. Hey you! You in the Play Angry Shocks hoody. Get me a cab punk."

"Take it away, Don."

# Flip-Flop

## Caroline G. Contreras

Flip-flop, flip-flop, what is it I hear?
The sound of flip-flops drawing so near;
everywhere I go or whomever I meet,
that sound of flip-flops coming down the street;
in the office or at the big game,
flip-flop, flip-flop—it's always the same!

Flip-flop, flip-flop—please take a seat;
I don't want to hear your flip-flopping feet.
Flip-flop, flip-flop, the sound is not cool;
the louder the flip-flop, the bigger the fool.
From the time that you're born 'til the day that you die,
flip-flop, flip-flop—please pass me by.

They look like shoes Samson wore in his day,
you can't wear them at work, you can't wear them to play.
You can't keep your feet clean and you can't keep them dry,
you can't run in them, either, so don't even try.
They flip if you walk; they flop if you scoot,
so why don't you trade them in on a good pair of boots?

# The Fourth of July Party

## Gwendolyn Eldridge Gandy

With summer into full swing, I love having my family and friends at my home for our annual Fourth of July party and fireworks. I had already penciled in this holiday on my calendar a few months ago. So now it's time to start bringing some of the decorations down from the attic and put my plans into action.

******

We are now in countdown mode with only two days left until the party. The menu is set, food and drinks have been purchased, signs have been made for all the different games and activities, even a banner for live music. The yard decorations will be placed around the house the morning of the party. It seems that everything is going as planned, even the weather will be on our side according to the TV weatherman.

I hope no one brings up last year's party when Granny's dentures got stuck in Emma's special extra sticky gumdrop cake. All of the younger children were frightened and crying at the sight of the tooth hanging onto a piece of cake sitting on the table right in front of them. With all of the screaming and crying, someone called 911, which only added to all of the chaos. It took the police, firemen, a fork and pliers to get the gumdrops off of the dentures. Once cleaned, we put some Poligrip on them and put them back in her mouth. She was good to go and rejoined the party.

******

As our family and friends arrived, they marveled at the transformation of our yard and house. This made me feel good about all the work I put into the decorations this year. Once the food, drinks, games and music were underway, I even started to feel more at ease about everything. The highlight of the party would be the fireworks later this evening.

Everything seemed to be going great. Then my son, Adam, ran into the kitchen looking for me. At first, I couldn't quite understand what he was saying because he was talking so fast. I made him slow down and start over slower.

He said Uncle Charlie had climbed into my brand-new hammock and thought—with his fat butt—he really was too heavy to have been in it anyway. But he had. He told the children to push him from side to side, as hard and as high as they could. Well, he flew off the hammock and fell over and landed in my flowering cactus bed and was screaming for help.

When I got outside, some of the men along with my husband were helping him to his feet. He had spiny needles all over his backside. I said to myself, "Another one bites the dust."

It was not a pretty scene pulling out the needles of an eighty-year-old, 300-pound man's buttocks.

I am thinking next year I might set an age limit—no one over sixty, at least that would take care of Granny and Uncle Charlie.

# Jingle Bells

## C. Holden

Dashing through the snow in a one-horse open sleigh

through the fields we go laughing all the way.

It has to be cold because of the snow on the ground,

and with a wind chill very cold,

and the horse running will make it an even colder wind chill.

You must have a lot of cheer to enjoy the snow

the horse is kicking in your face with the cold wind chill.

Bells on bob tail ring.

Why would anyone bob a horse's tail just to keep the snow out of its tail?

The poor horse will need this tail for a fly swatter this summer.

And why the bells on the tail?

It must be great looking at the backside of a horse

with the cold wind chill.

You are full of cheer, with rosy red cheeks and a frozen nose.

If you have too much cheer, the horse knows the way home.

Oh, what fun it is to ride in an open sleigh tonight.

In a few days you say, Doctor, I hope it isn't pneumonia again.

# Gondola

## Mary McKay

Now, I don't usually go to the county health department, but this was their annual, free skin cancer clinic. I had stood in the long line outside in the hot sun and filled out the lengthy questionnaire. Next, they placed me in an examination room. They left the doors open in anticipation of a doctor's visit. There was a strange wailing sound coming from the next room.

A man entered the next room and I couldn't help but overhear the conversation that followed.

"What on earth is going on?" he said.

The noise had stopped long enough for the woman in the next room to inform him that they had instructed her to call all the people she had been sexually involved with in recent months and insist they join her at the health department immediately. Then the sobbing resumed.

"Stop that bawling and tell me why," the man demanded.

"Oh, Bill, I have what they called an STD," she said.

"An STD?" he said. "What kind of STD?"

"Gonda..." she muttered. "Maybe it was gondola?"

"What the hell is Gonda?"

"Well, it started with a G and ended with an A, but it sounded more like diarrhea."

"Do you mean, Gonorrhea?" he questioned.

"Yes! That is it!"

"Holy Shit!" he shouted. "How did you get that?" he asked. "You sure as hell didn't get it from me!"

About that time, I saw another young man enter the next room and the crying began all over.

"Brenda, what is going on?" the new fellow asked.

"Oh, Charlie, I'm in an awful mess!"

"Hi, Charlie. What are you doing here?" the first man asked.

"Brenda called me and told me to get down here right away."

Now things were making sense to me. The health department is also the place all sexually transmitted diseases are tested for free. They not only keep track of them, in addition, to control the spread of STDs, they notify the partners of those infected. Sounded to me like Brenda had come to be examined and was found to have one of the more common sexually transmitted diseases. The health department was informing all her recent sexual partners.

That two different men had appeared as her partners, apparently made it a bit embarrassing. Before I could hear any more conversations, a third fellow entered the next room.

"George, what the hell are you doing here? Don't tell me you were monkeying around with her too?" asked the first man.

"I don't know what you are talking about," said George.

George had a high almost feminine voice, and all involved seem to know one another. It was getting more interesting by the moment. I was wondering how many more might show up for Brenda's gathering. Do you suppose she had a different fellow for each day of the week?

I looked at my watch and saw it had taken no more than ten minutes for all this drama to unfold. What had begun as a strange noise had turned into a really curious occurrence. I was hoping so many had come for the clinic that I might be a witness to more of this story. I hate it when I don't get to hear the end of a truly intriguing tale. Indeed, truth is always stranger than fiction.

# We All Have Fears of Some Kind

## Starla Criser

Matilda paced back and forth on top of the worktable in Farmer Sam's utility shed. This was ridiculous! Embarrassing!

If I could change one thing about myself, I would not be such a darn scardy cat.

She plopped down on her butt and heaved a disgusted sigh. Except for this business of being a tad bit terrified of spiders she was as perfect as a cat could be. At least in her unbiased opinion.

What was she going to do? She couldn't stay here much longer. Blossom, Steve and Priscilla were probably wondering where she was. They were all supposed to go out to the field and visit their bull friends Ferdie and Hamish.

She'd already been at their meeting spot by the side of the barn. But she'd got bored waiting for them and decided to explore the shed for a few minutes. Now here she was, stuck on this stupid table. All because the massive eight-legged beast easily as big as a crow had lunged out at her from behind a tall toolbox. She'd been forced to leap up here to safety.

Enough of this nonsense! She crouched low and inched on her belly toward the table's edge. She peered down, holding her breath. Hopefully, her foe had run off by now.

Nope!

He stood boldly glaring at her with enormous eyes. Then the evil tormentor moved.

She screeched and lunged to her feet. The hair on her back bristled. Her heart pounded. Trapped. Forever and ever.

"What are you doing in here?" Priscilla asked from the doorway.

Matilda wanted to cry out for her nearly blind goose friend to save herself, to run for her life. Instead she kept her gaze focused on the devil's eyes. If she kept its attention…

But the spider turned toward Priscilla. Oh, no!

Forgetting her fear, she leaped off the table with a war cry. Rrrrrr! She flew through the air to pounce on the beast before he could attack Priscilla.

By the time she landed, he'd disappeared. She crashed into Priscilla at the same time Blossom and Steve walked into the shed.

"What's going on?" Blossom asked, gaping at Matilda laying across Priscilla's back.

"I…uh…" Matilda scrambled off the goose. "There was a…"

Priscilla blinked at her in confusion. "It was the spider, wasn't it?" She eased to her feet. "You were saving me. I forgive you."

Steve the rooster giggled and looked toward the toolbox. He pointed with a wing. "That spider? The one just bigger than a speck of dirt?" He giggled again.

Blossom frowned at him. "Be nice. We all have things that frighten us."

Even Priscilla scowled at the rooster. "Blossom is right. You need to be schooled in manners. We don't make fun of our friends."

He hung his head in shame. But a second later he glanced at Matilda, nodding toward the spider still watching them. "Want me to—"

Matilda raised her chin, pranced by him, slapping him with her tail. "Drop it, buster! Or I'll tell them about when that worm…" She let the threat die away. He got the point.

Just in case that fuzzy, eight-legged fiend might come rushing out for her, she hurried from the shed.

# Saguaro as I Know

## Don Boldea

Okay, okay! Yes, I'm a cantankerous old prickly Saguaro cactus. I have a gosh darn right to be. You know why? Do you? Look, I was born here, in the desert, between Phoenix and Tuc-son, Arizona over ninety years ago. And I have a very large number of little Saguaros standing around. They just don't want to leave home.

I want to move to some other place, where it's green, has seasons and maybe some rain a little more often. It's all about the environment, and peace, and quiet.

My doctor said it wouldn't be conducive to my health to uproot and move to somewhere else. Those are his words, not mine. I'm not the kind of cactus to take his words laying down. I want an explanation for "Not conducive to my health." Those were my words.

Oh, I guess I do like it here in the desert though. I like the sky-blue sky. Most of the time, I even like the low humidity. I enjoy watching the animals, except for those darn birds. They sometimes build their nests on top of my head or bore into my side for water. That always gives me a tall headache and most of the time a pain in my side.

Here was the doc's explanation, "Your anatomy does not have a system by which to pro-tect you from the cold. The best temperate zone for you is between 1,000 feet and 4,000 feet ele-vation. At this elevation range, cold temperatures and a light dusting of snow for a short period is okay."

The doctor continued, "The annual monsoon provides necessary moisture when absorbed through your roots. The low humidity of the desert protects your system from too much mois-ture, which if it didn't you would drown. Finally, your system balances these factors to keep you healthy, but only in this environment."

My comment to the doc went this way, "You mean to tell me this is in my genes, my he-redity?"

The doc answered with a smile on his face, "Yep. Saguaro as I know," he smirked. Real funny doc. He concluded his depressing summary by saying, "You're so healthy you'll probably live another twenty to fifty years."

"Oh no, Doc!" I blurted out. "The Misses and I can't afford anymore Saguaros standing around!"

Then it came to me, "Say, Doc, can Saguaro cacti have vasectomies?"

# Cholla

## Mary McKay

My name is Cholla. While spelled Cholla, it is pronounced "Choy-yah." It is a Spanish word so the ll's sound like yy's. I think it is a pretty name, and from the many comments I have overheard, a lot of humans think I am pretty too when I am in bloom.

I am just covered with beautiful spines that are hollow and so thick I almost appear like a fuzzy cloud. When I bloom, it is just extraordinary the number of "Oohs and Aahs," that I have heard from my many admirers. Sort of makes me want to reach out and connect with them in any way I can.

They have accused me of being a "jumping cactus," and I am probably guilty of it. Nothing makes me happier than to prick a bare foot or just about anywhere else that has a bit of moisture to it. When I get damp, the tip of my spines curl and makes them like fishhooks. Then I hang on tight.

Living in the great southwest deserts of North America, I don't get a lot of rain to enjoy. The very rare snow that I have witnessed in my lifetime is just a fluke of nature and not to be counted on.

My favorite kind of weather is a sky-blue day, when the sun is so bright and hot, that humans sweat and remove as many of their protective clothes as they can. I can smell the sweat a mile away and try to be as attractive as possible to lure sightseers to my side. My great, great, grandfather is a big attraction as he is close to eight feet tall. I am just a short distance from him. In fact, my whole family is nearby and stretches out as far as I can see. We are natives of Sonora, perhaps you have even heard of the Sonora Desert Museum, where I live.

I overheard a very learned sounding gentleman explain that there are at least thirty different kinds of cacti. He said, "You can even spell it cactuses." I don't know Latin, so I wasn't able to understand all the technical information that the group of humans following him heard. I think he was a tour guide. I sure have had plenty of experience with them.

I get a lot of respect. Tour guides sound very serious when they announce to their groups, "Stay clear of the chollas!" I don't think they mean just me, but all of my particular family.

There is an old saying, "If you wear out a pair of boots in the desert, you will never leave." Be cautious when you walk about in the desert, because I am not the only painful, even poisonous element to be encountered. Rattlesnakes enjoy my shade. Now there is a nasty piece of work, if I ever saw it. Skin, dry as a bone. Not only are rattlesnakes plentiful, but Gila Monsters, scorpions, and lots of other critters that can make us uncomfortable or even dead.

I am very sociable. I get a few birds who have learned how to find safe harbor in my limbs, but they are nimble and covered with those darn feathers, so I can't even get a good grip on them. Did you ever try to bite into a feather? Not good!

Speaking of feathers. Birds have feathers, I have my spines and humans have all those protective clothes on them. Far as I can tell, humans are the only ones able to remove their coverings. My Aunt Charlotte said one moon-lite night a couple of humans came so close that, seeing them, she just bloomed on the spot. They were talking softly.

"You are so beautiful!" the man said. Aunt Charlotte thought he was talking about her, but come to find out the woman was removing her protective clothing.

"It is so warm I just had to remove those hot clothes," the woman said.

"All the better to see you, my dear!"

The man grabbed the woman and before long the smell of sweat and slobbers from their mouths, which were working furiously against each other, filled the night air. Aunt Charlotte said she just couldn't help herself, she reached out and caught the side of the woman's naked thigh.

"Aye yi yi!" the woman cried as she danced around the clearing where they had spread a nice Navajo blanket on the ground. It was a very romantic location. The sound of pain in the woman's voice set the man into immediate action. He yanked out his wallet and pulled out a credit card and scrapped it across her thigh, dislodging the hollow spines that had curled, as the tips pierced her skin.

"This is the only way to get them out!" he shouted as he continued to swipe away at her thigh.

"It's already started to welt up," she cried.

"I will pour some of our whiskey on it, to disinfect it, and take some of the sting out. It will burn like the very devil!"

"Blow on it, please!" the woman pleaded.

Suddenly, the lady jumped up, dressed, and started throwing things into the center of the blanket.

"Let's get out of here," she said.

Once they had departed, I was aware of the murmuring of my nearby relatives. In fact, I could even hear the laughter and chatter of those across the arroyo from me. My cousin Pasquale said, "That was more entertaining than a meteor shower!"

# My Birth

## Don Boldea

I've been six months in my mother's belly (by the way, this is a G-rated story). I'm bored. Another three months floating in this water balloon I will be severely wrinkled and bored out of my mind. However, it is kind of fun floating around in this somewhat cramped space.

I'm curious, am I going to be an adorable baby or a long-haired hippie looking Musk Ox? You know the kind, like an eight-hundred-pound hair ball.

My dad was a good looking fellow, and my fraternal grandfather and grandmother were a gorgeous looking pair. My mother was gorgeous, but my maternal grandfather and grandmother, well, they were okay. So, what will I look like?

Hey out there! It's a little cramped in here! How about a little kick in the bladder; will that help let you know that I'm ready to come out? How about some pressure on all parts of your body innards? How does that feel, gotta go to the bathroom?

Good, here comes the doctor. I ask you now, how can a person with just one long eyebrow instill any confidence in his doctoring skills? Go figure. Anyway, he says, "It's time for the birth of your child. All the planets are aligned." What the heck does that mean? Then he loudly asks, "Ready? Thumbs up, that's an A Okay in my books."

There's my poor mother, in a chair like thing elevated at a 45-degree position with her feet in those things called stirrups, five miles apart. And me, I'm uncertain if I'm up or down. Since this is my first time, I'm not sure what's next. Oh, oh! What was that whooshing water sound?

Let me tell you what happens next. I hear someone say push! Have you ever felt like you've been dropped into a very large black hole and expected to come out alive? What's worse is a cord (they call an umbilical something or other) that keeps trying to pull me back to where I want to escape from. I've made it through that stage, well almost.

Next I hear, "There's the head, get ready, push!"

I was blown out into the world like photon torpedo fired from an interstellar star ship. I flew through the air and through the hands of both the doctor and his nurse assistant.

I soared across the room at light speed, sliding across the cold tile floor, bouncing off the opposite wall, rebounding like a Yoyo, the umbilical effect again. I finally landed in the doctor's hands. He must have been a fan of astronauts returning from space because he yelled, "Touchdown!"

After all of that, he had the audacity to hold me upside down and slap my butt. I didn't know that I supposed to cry and so I didn't. Well, that pervert slapped me again.

If my arms had been long enough, I would have slapped the doctor's face, skunked him and with a twinkle in my eye made a cute baby-like cooing sound.

This traumatic birth experience could have had a devastating effect on any typical human being's psyche. But neuuu, it only made me a very unique individual.

I am now married; I have two children and my wife's family has adopted me as part of their family. Every other year, they visit us here on Earth and then we visit her family every other year on their planet.

My parents tell our Earth family that I, and my family, am on a secret research assignment in a far-off land to cover for our lengthy time from the family

Now, telling the true story of my birth may seem to have been outrageous. However, you must admit that many of the physical references are correct.

But I must also remind you of what the comedian Lily Tomlin's Edith Ann character would say, "And that's the truth... thuuuuupppppps!"

# Trauma at the Zoo

## Jean Welle

"Oh, look, kids! There's a bobcat, and she has kittens."

"Where, Daddy?"

"Next to the hut. They're hard to see. She's sitting very still watching us, but her kittens are lively. See them?"

"Aww! They are so cute!"

"Cute but wild, nevertheless. Notice how their markings vary—one has brown and black stripes and the other two kittens have spots like their mother."

"I see them, Dad. Why are their tails cut off?"

"They're born with stub tails; that's why they're called bobcats. It's rare to find them in a zoo."

******

Rare, indeed! And why am I the fortunate one? Humans! Their endless gawking and babbling around this cramped confinement every day is enough to drive a cat mad! This is no place to raise my kittens.

How did I let this happen? I thought I had found the perfect habitat to give birth. The weather-beaten shack had been abandoned at least three years. The wood frame remained intact except for a few missing boards. The open portholes in the attic and its elevation were advantageous to spot deer, rabbits, birds, or other prey living within the dense foliage as far as I could see. And of course, there was the farm just three miles to the north with lambs and chickens to consider for food if wildlife became scarce.

The only annoying noise was the flapping of that raggedy hammock that clung to a tree with fraying pencil-thin twine. How different here in the zoo. No privacy. No space to roam nor coverage to teach my kittens how to stalk, leap, and pounce adeptly. And the strangest noises never cease in this wretched place? Whatever is that clanging sound?

What kind of future do my young'uns have now, growing up in captivity? What will they think of me—the mom who got captured; the mom who wasn't able to develop their survival instincts; the mom who withered away for want of fresh kill?

Was it the farmer who noticed my sanctuary? Was it a hunter that spotted my hideout? Did the thunderstorm prevent my hearing abductors sneak up with a stun gun? Racket…like that annoying maddening sound. Who is doing that? Will it never stop? No critter can nap with such a racket, especially my kittens. And I will get no rest with their pouncing on me all day.

******

"Mom, wake up! You're making weird sounds."

"Mom, I'm hungry."

"I'm sorry, Honey. I forgot to take my cellphone to the kitchen to brew your morning coffee. Son, shut off the alarm for me. My hands are full."

******

Ah! Sweet reality. Two little ones pouncing me awake who need to be taught better manners, and the wonderful aroma of hot coffee, lovingly offered to me from the man who captured my heart.

The dog is barking, the cat's meowing, roosters are crowing, goats are bleating, the geese are honking…my life is a zoo! And I love it!

# Thoughts from a Sloth

## C.A. Lemont

Yep, yep, hanging in my hammock here at the zoo.
Big ol' sloth, staring back at you.
Look at all you kiddies, on your holiday vacation.
Your little faces, lacking any emotion.

You look lost, not hooked to your precious net.
Pay attention! You might have a future yet.
Hey! Got a pencil? Oh, I guess not.
No one does these days. I forgot.

See, I've been around a lot longer than man.
Seen many, many things in the palm of your hand.
Rocks, spears, guns, and now cell phones.
ODD ... how the danger has grown.

It's you little people that will suffer the most.
When the natural world is but a ghost.
Animals, fish, plants, nowhere to be found.
Except on a screen you can't put down.

# FROM A
# CHILD'S EYES

# Fly and Caw

## Jan Koelsch

I sat at a picnic table in the park across from the elementary school. The children seemed to enjoy the freedom of escaping the classroom. Running, swinging, climbing, and hopping were on the agenda for the short 15 to 20-minute recess. "Children, it is time to go in," called the teacher. "We have lots of things to learn about insects like a spider. You have 30 seconds to get in line starting now."

"Do we have to go in, Teacher? Just one more minute, please!" the children pleaded.

"Time is wasting, children. If you do not get in line right this minute, you will need to be asking forgiveness of the bus driver or your parents when they find you will have to remain 15 extra minutes after school. Your 30 seconds is down to 10, 9, 8, 7, 6, 5, 4, 3, 2, 1."

As the countdown started each of the boys and girls slowly made their way to the line that formed behind the teacher. There were no smiling faces. The quietness of the children was almost deafening. I heard one little boy say, "I wish I was like that crow in the park."

"Why is that?" his friend inquired.

"Because if I was a crow, I would caw."

"Silly. Crows say Caw, Caw, Caw."

"That is not what I mean by caw. I would caw, you know. Choose Another Way rather than getting in line and following our teacher inside."

"Yeah," responded his friend, with a grin. "You might as well FLY – Feel Less Yucky. When your parents come to pick you up after school, they will CAW for you, help you see they have a better way. You might even get grounded."

The little boy thought for a moment. "You make a good point. Guess I'll just straighten up and FLY."

The line moved. Fly and Caw was another lesson learned that day at school, not from the teacher but from the mouths of babes.

# A Ducky Bear Story

## Caroline G. Contreras

It was a fine summer evening and Duck was sitting in his favorite perch on a chair by the bathtub. He was watching the three little bears as they took their bath. Duck lived in a pretty white house with the Bear Family. He went almost everywhere with Bo who was the youngest.

Duck could tell that this particular evening would be different. He would not be going with Bo. In the country where the little bears lived was a fast-flowing creek. It was in a parklike area just below their house and the little bears liked to explore there. They often begged to go swimming in the little creek, but their parents wouldn't let them go there alone.

Duck knew that whenever it was possible the little bears would slip out the bathroom window and go to the creek without telling anyone they were going. The little bears could all swim very well, but their parents still wouldn't let them go alone.

Duck knew also that Daddy Bear and Uncle Sam were police officers and they often were on patrol at the creek. One worked the day shift and one worked the night shift so that left very little time for them to sneak off to the creek without getting caught.

Duck listened intently as the little bears were talking.

"Come on, little bears, let's go swimming in the creek. Mamma and Papa are working on the car so they will never even miss us. We can play the radio loudly and they will think we are still taking a bath," said Kerry, who was the most adventuresome of the three little bears.

"We will never get away with it," said Bo. "Besides, I am enjoying my bath, so I don't have to go to any old creek to have fun. Look, we have a lot of soap bubbles to play with right here."

"Oh, you're no fun. You always want to stay at home. You never want to try anything new or different," said Bandy. "I will go with Kerry."

It took only a few minutes for the little bears to get outside as they crawled through the bathroom window. The trip to the creek was something they had done several times before and they had not been caught.

Duck looked around at the bathroom floor. The floor was not only wet from their splashing, but it was covered with toys as well. The little bears were sure to be in big trouble if Mamma saw the mess the bathroom was in and found out they had gone to the creek, too. Duck sat quietly as he did not want to explain to Papa Bear where they were if Papa Bear would find them gone.

Kerry hurried through the field to the creek and jumped in while Bandy and Bo took their time and played with their dog, Trey. They picked up sticks and threw them for Trey to "fetch." They were laughing, talking and playing and were not paying attention to how fast the darkness was falling over them.

The little bears finally reached the creek and joined their brother in the water. They were having a great time when Bandy yelled, "Here comes a policeman."

Everyone left the water and dropped behind a fallen log to hide. They laid down flat on the ground and in the growing darkness it was hard to tell them from the log they were hiding behind.

Bo whispered, "I have to sneeze."

Kerry said, "If you do and Uncle Sam catches us, I won't let you come with us again."

As the patrol car came into sight Bo raised up to cover his mouth with his hand so he wouldn't make any noise if he sneezed and he saw a snake lying very close to Bandy. He yelled, "There's a snake right beside you, Bandy. Don't move an inch or it will bite you.

Bo ran after the patrol car yelling and waving his arms. "Uncle Sam, Uncle Sam, stop, please. There's a snake by Bandy and he could bite him. Please, please hurry."

Uncle Sam stopped the patrol car and jumped out. He ran to the back of the car and got a tire iron from the trunk and went to the creek and killed the snake.

"Do your parents know where you are?"

With a sheepish grin, Kerry replied, "No, they do not know but please don't tell them and we promise never to do this again. Bandy could have been killed if that snake had bitten him. Our parents are right we should never go to the creek alone."

The little bears hurried up the path to the house and crawled back through the bathroom window. They were all innocently taking a bath when Daddy Bear knocked on the door.

"Are you little bears through taking your bath? Uncle Sam is here. He was just wondering how you little bears were doing."

"We are taking our bath just like you told us, Daddy Bear," they said.

Uncle Sam just smiled and winked at them as he left.

"That was a very close call," said Kerry. "I will not disobey our parents again and go to the little creek. I don't want to run into any more old snakes in the dark. Mama Bear is right we need someone with us when we go to the creek."

The little bears finished cleaning up the bathroom and went into the dining room to eat their evening meal. They were thankful that none of them had been hurt and they were all home safe and sound.

Duck smiled happily, "Boy, I hope they learned their lesson and won't do that again. At least now, I don't have to explain to Papa Bear why the little bears were not in the bathtub, but I didn't get to go swimming anywhere even in the bathtub."

# A Short Mystery

## Jan Koelsch

Giovanni looked at his watch. 6:45 a.m. Another day was dawning in Venice with the sun providing warmth and brightness. As a security officer at the hotel for ten years, he enjoyed the extra income in addition to his retirement benefits. Most nights were peaceful.  The day would be a great one for the tourists riding in the gondola. His office provided a great space to watch for any unusual activities on the row of security cameras.

"Better get my log up-to-date," he mumbled. Hotel management wanted to know every detail of every hour. It required some creativity to state "no problems" or "refreshingly boring" in a professional way. A phone ringing disrupted the closing process. He noticed the caller ID said it was from Room 666. The front desk person must be occupied with another guest.

"Security. This is Giovanni. How may I help you?"

A man's frantic, deafening voice said, "Sir, Sir, come quickly. There is this strange wailing sound coming from the room next to mine."

The time was 6:55 am. Not one to shirk his duties, Giovanni instructed the man to calm down and he would be there stat.

The hotel guest repeated his plea. "Please hurry. It sounds like someone is being killed."

"Wouldn't you know! Tony is late again. Management will have to speak to him," grumbled Giovanni. They had employed Tony as security for not quite six months. Being on time was not his best strength. Many of the staff had wondered what Tony's strengths were.

Giovanni jotted down the room number 666 on a sticky note. The office door locked behind him as he bounded up the stairs two at a time. "Geez! I should have taken the elevator. What was I thinking!"

Time was of the essence. Many scenarios raced through his mind. A wailing noise could be a woman or a child or even a man. Room

666 always had abnormal activities and sounds reported. No amount of investigating could discover the reasons for paranormal events.

At the top of the stairs, he stopped to catch his breath as he gasped for air. With heart racing and the taser clenched in his hand, he made his way to Room 666. He heard a sharp, high-pitched wailing noise. He rapped sharply on the door as he shouted, "Security" in his gruffiest voice.

No answer but the wailing continued. He pounded on the door the second time. "Security! Open the door!"

Just as he was ready to kick the door open, it opened a slight bit. There in front of him sat a young girl with messy hair and wrinkled pajamas in a wheelchair. She appeared to be about nine or ten years old. Her face was tear stained. Behind her was the wailing noise and the sound of things being hurled against the walls.

"Please, Sir, please can you help me?" the child sobbed. "Please help me!"

"Are you okay?" Giovanni edged his way into the room. "Are you here alone, child? Let's stop a minute and take a deep breath." He patted her hand as her sobs became sniffles. He noticed how petite she was. "Little one, what is that noise?"

"Petey, my service monkey. He has locked himself in the bathroom. I don't know what to do!" The child started weeping. "Petey is a very nice monkey. He really is. It's just sometimes he gets cranky and wants his way. You know, kind of like me. If he doesn't get what he wants, he throws a fit. Trouble is, I don't know what he wants."

"It will be okay. What is your name, little one?"

"Maria," she said as she wiped her nose on her pajama sleeve.

"Okay, Maria. Let's see if we can get Petey calmed down."

Giovanni strode over to the bathroom door. It was locked. He banged on the door as he said in his booming voice, "Petey! Petey! You stop right now. You are scaring Maria!"

The wailing stopped as did things hitting the walls and door. "Petey, you must open the door. You are scaring Maria. Do it right now."

Petey took his time opening the door. The small, wiry monkey was perching in the vanity's corner. In one of his paw-like hands was a tube of uncapped toothpaste. The toothpaste was smeared end to end on the mirror. It plastered his fur as well. He looked like a small version of a white Yeti. The bathroom looked like a war zone.

Maria peered around Giovanni and gasped. "Petey, what have you done! We will be in so much trouble when Mama and Daddy come back. You naughty, naughty boy! What am I going to do with you?" She began to sob once again.

Before Giovanni could turn to comfort Maria, Petey flew past them and landed on the bed. "Come here, Petey. Now! If I could stomp my feet, I would," declared Maria, her tears glistening in her eyes.

Slowly with his head down, Petey went over to Maria and climbed on her lap. Giovanni thought, "Could this be the same ball of fur that terrorized a little girl a few minutes earlier?" He shook his head in disbelief.

He turned to Maria. Petey's head was nuzzled against her neck. She stroked his head and back with a loving touch, as if nothing had ever happened.

"Maria, I'll call housekeeping. You will have to put Petey in his crate. How long before your parents come back?"

"They've been gone about an hour. Well, maybe a little longer. Petey has not thrown such a fit before. He usually tries to make me happy. I even tried giving him some peanut butter. That didn't work. Nothing worked until he heard your voice that sounds a lot like Daddy's."

"Do you want me to stay with you?"

"Nah, but thank you. Petey will take care of me."

Two people rushed into the room. The woman ran over to Maria and Petey. She gave them both a hug. The man came to stand by Giovanni, peering into the bathroom, scratching his head.

Giovanni put his hand on the man's shoulder. He thought about telling the man the details of the past two hours. The man already had his hands full. He still had to settle with the hotel yet. Some things are better left unsaid. "I'll just chalk it up to Room 666."

The man known as Daddy looked at his daughter. "Oh, boy! What a mess! Maria, we will have a lot to talk about later. You have some explaining to do."

Maria looked down at her lap where Petey lay sleeping. "Okay, Daddy," she said sheepishly.

Giovanni excused himself and said goodbye. He had his log and damage/incident report to fill out. Describing his extended shift would not need any creative phrases. In fact, he thought he would just say in the log, "A short mystery solved. Wailing sound discovered. Damage/incident reports attached."

Now for the mystery of Tony.

# A Tale of Two Princesses:
# A Lesson Learned

## T. J. Logue

Even the best of fairies and pixies have their bad days and Princess Abigail and Princess Emmaline had been having quite a few lately. Now normally these fairies were the loveliest of all, both inside and out but as with all of us, they had forgotten what was most important. The King and Queen taught the princesses to always treat others and themselves with respect and kindness. And, if they couldn't think of anything pleasant to say, then they should just stay quiet.

Although the fairies were twins and were usually happy to be identical and even enjoyed playing a prank or two on their friends by switching places, the time had come for them to become their own person. They each wanted to be known for their own unique qualities.

Everyone knew Princess Emma could make flowers grow and be beautiful, but not everyone knew she had a wonderful sense of fun and adventure. She loved to play pirates in the castle and pretend to slay dragons in the tower. She also enjoyed playing dress up and putting on makeup. Princess Emma hid these things from her friends because she feared they would think she was "different," and she wanted to fit in.

The same was true of Princess Abby. Everyone knew the princess could paint beautiful rainbows in the sky, but few knew that she was a wonderful artist and talented writer. Princess Abby was more serious and shyer than her sister and worried her friends wouldn't understand her need to be alone sometimes so she could draw and think of stories she would like to write.

As the girls struggled to find their own identities, they forgot how to treat each other and fought a lot. About everything—toys, clothes, snacks, anything and everything! Even their friends were fed up with their constant bickering. Finally, the King and Queen had enough and came up with a plan to teach their daughters how to treat each other and understand that it is okay to be different.

The King and Queen knew teaching tolerance was difficult, so they asked a friend to help. A long time ago, they met a man who lost his wife and son in an accident. He became bitter and lonely. He chose to live in a small cottage on the edge of the forest where he could live out his life away from others. He spent his days being angry and sad. He missed his family so much.

One day a little boy knocked on the old man's door. The boy had been gathering wood in the forest when it began to get dark and he lost his way. He was very frightened and asked the old man to help him find his parents. At first, the old man refused to help him, but then he began to think about his son and how he would hope someone would have helped him if he were lost. The old man decided to find the boy and help him get home. He grabbed his lantern and began searching. He knew the forest well since he had lived there for some time. It didn't take him long to find the boy. He took him back to his cottage, gave him something to eat and a warm place to sleep promising they would begin searching for his parents at first light.

Early the next morning, the old man and boy began the long walk into town. The old man frequently asked the boy if anything looked familiar. Suddenly the boy began to get excited and pointed to a small brook. He thought if they followed the path by the book it would lead them to his house. They walked and walked. The boy became more excited with each step.

At last they rounded a bend in the path and the boy began to run. They had found his house! His parents ran to hug him and told him they had searched for him all night. After explaining he got lost in the forest, he turned to thank the old man, but he was nowhere to be seen. The old man had quietly slipped back in the forest not wanting to interrupt the reunion between the boy and his parents.

On the long walk back to his cottage the old man thought about the boy and his family. He began to realize that though he had lost his own family; he did not need to be bitter and angry anymore. The old man decided to change his life. He thought and thought about what he could do to help others. Finally, he had it! While he and the boy were walking, he noticed that many of the children they passed had no shoes on their feet. The boy explained that they could not afford to buy shoes.

The old man had supported his family by being a cobbler and selling the shoes he made. He decided to make shoes for the children. There was only one problem. He couldn't decide how to get the shoes to the children without them knowing where they came from. That is how the King and Queen came to know the old man. He approached them and asked if the fairies and pixies of the kingdom could help deliver shoes to the needy children. The King and Queen thought it was a wonderful idea!

Soon it was proclaimed throughout the kingdom that when young fairies and pixies reached an age when their parents thought they would understand, they were told about the needy children and sent to visit the old man in the forest where he taught them how to leave shoes on the doorsteps of the children's homes and silently slip back into the forest.

The King and Queen knew the time had come for their young princesses to meet the old man. Even though Princess Abby and Princess Emma were only seven years old, the King and Queen felt they were ready. The princesses were told they would meet a friend of the family. The fairies were very curious because they though they knew everyone in Fairyland. The fairies fell asleep in the Royal Carriage on the ride to the old man's cottage. When they awoke, it surprised them to find themselves deep in the forest. The curious fairies went into the cottage and discovered some of their friends were also there. There was much excitement as the old man explained what they were about to do. But first, he needed the fairies and pixies to understand why it was important to do nice things for others without bragging about it and to be tolerant of others. Princess Abby and Princess Emma thought about what the old man said and began to feel sad about the way they had been treating each other and their friends. They made a pact right then and there to always try to be kind and helpful.

Soon it was time to go to the children's homes. Each fairy and pixie had a pair of shoes to deliver, a lantern and a map to show them where to go. The princesses flew silently side by side, each thinking about how happy the children would be when they found the shoes. What a wonderful surprise!

The sisters talked and talked during the carriage ride back to the castle. They had finally understood what their parents had been trying to tell them. The princesses would not wait to get home and tell their parents everything they had learned. Of course, the King and Queen already knew but listened patiently as their excited daughters told them all about their journey, the old man and everything they learned. The King and Queen just nodded and smiled because they knew their daughters were forever changed.

As for the old man, he smiles a lot now and knows that his wife and son would be very proud of him.

# Valley

## Mary McKay

Valley stretched his neck and lifted his nose into the crisp, humid air of the waning daylight. One large snowflake after another began to fall into the twilight stillness. Snowflakes, almost as big as his paws. It was late November in Maize, Kansas and anything was possible with the weather this time of the year. No need to become distressed at this phenomenon, however, he knew that the pressure in his ears and the smells in the air were a warning that things could get very unpleasant, very fast.

This wasn't his first snowstorm and border collies were dressed for just this kind of weather. His ancestors were from the highlands of Scotland, where the very thought of harsh winters was as common as the beautiful purple heather, and of no serious consequence.

As the pressure in his ears intensified the volume of the snowfall seemed to increase. The wind also began to blow with alarming speed and instead of lovely, lacy snowflakes, the white fury that pushed him, and a copious number of tumbleweeds, into the low spreading branches of a very large evergreen tree. It was one of many on the south side of a considerable length of trees in one of the many shelter belts that controlled the drifting of snow along the highways of Kansas. Usually running east to west, they were a perfect natural snow fence.

The variety of trees in the shelter belts were pretty consistent. The lower, more compact evergreens were best planted along the south side of the belt. Next might be a mixture of Russian Olive trees hardy in the climate and then the taller Oaks, Elms and Cottonwood trees. It was thought, at least hoped, that these shelter belts would provide a windbreak to the prairie winds and hold the soil in place to guard against topsoil erosion. The prevailing winds were from the southwest during the summer months but could switch rapidly to the north when a winter storm arrived.

To be most effective as snow fences, the shelter belts had to be planted back far enough from the highway, or road, to allow for the monstrous drifts of snow to accumulate along the south side of the trees. The tumbleweeds also found themselves packed into the low-hanging branches.

The variety of wildlife that found a safe harbor in these man-made natural wonders was incredible. Birds and squirrels made abundant nests in the branches of the taller trees and every delightful creature from rabbits, foxes, porcupines, and hedgehogs, made their dwellings in the rich tundra of rotting leaves, broken branches, and crumbling tumbleweeds beneath it all.

Valley decided to stay put and take up residence in an abandoned coyote den that had caved in except for a nice round crater that fit him just fine.

Darkness finally descended on the shelter belt and although the snow had turned to sleet and was pelting down on the nice layer of snow on the top of the drifts, it was a good night for sleeping in the shelter and was enjoyed by all the critters.

Valley was dreaming in his sleep about the many escapades he had enjoyed with his boy. Funny how many things a boy could think up for adventure. There was the old barn in the field west of their place—that was always a great place for the boy to take him for some target practice with the BB gun. It was much easier on the ears than the cap guns that he belted around his waist before.

Humans seldom realized how very keen a dog's hearing was. He could hear his boy getting ready to leave his classroom at the end of the school day. He would stand, swinging his feathery tail with joy, as the boy came out the door of the school. Everyone knew who Valley was and many of the boys and girls took the time to pat his head and give him a hug as they left school.

A bright, sunshiny morning was announced by the chirping of birds and the rustling of underbrush. Valley woke from his warm nest and found himself enclosed in a cocoon of tumbleweeds, frosted with a layer of snow and encrusted with a layer of sleet on top. After some determined maneuvering he could crawl out of his wonderful night's sleep to witness a world of enormous white snow drifts with beautiful violet shadows of sleet in the deep crevices between them. Valley high-tailed it home; he'd be there before his boy was up.

# INSPIRATIONAL
# AND
# SPIRITUAL

# Forgotten

## Vickie Wright

One day as I was walking along,
An old woman, I met singing a song.
A story this woman told to me,
How, many times, God she did see.
Insisted she, that they had talked,
And together down the beach did walk.

But I questioned if this were true,
So I asked, if something she would do.
I said that my belief she would win,
If she would ask of my greatest sin.
To this she did agree,
And we parted, the woman and me.

Some time later by chance we did meet,
And I asked if to God she did speak.
She said indeed they had talked,
And together had walked.
And that upon their last date,
Inquired of all my sins, the most great.

My ears I could not believe,
As these words she said to me.
"Though hard He tried to recall,
He could not remember one at all.
As far as the east is from the west they were flung,"
And so, in shame my head I hung.

# No Goodbyes

### Jean Welle

The echo of voices still lingers:
    The laughter, the singing, the sighs.
The freeze-frames appear when they choose to;
    Sweet memories that fade as time flies.
I laugh, then I cry, my heart aching –
    Reminded again: no goodbyes.

"Jesus, step into my valley.
    "I need You," my anxious heart cries.
With tender compassion He holds me,
    Adjusting my pain down to size.
Jesus, who understands suffering,
    Speaks peace, and my spirit revives.

In love He speaks truth to my being
    And lifts my face up to the skies.
"Your loved one has entered My rest now.
    Be faithful. Don't listen to lies.
One day you will join us in Heaven;
    Forever, My child … no goodbyes."

# Glory

## C.A. Lemont

Starting right now, not tomorrow—
I will lead and not follow.
I will be as I was meant to be.
You be you, and I'll be me.

How could life be any fun?
Were we no different from anyone?
We all have a special little glow.
It's individuality, don't you know?

Don't try to remake me or dampen my glow.
Seems someone tried that, not long ago.

So starting right now, not tomorrow;
I will lead and not follow.
I will be as I was meant to be.
You be you, and I'll be me.

Do that and the glory you will find;
God made each of us one of a kind.
Be special, be different, why should I mind?
Just stand in your own glory, not in mine.

I searched the darkness and found the key.
Unlocked the secrets that were hidden from me.
Each of us must search alone...
To find the glory we can call our own.

# Where is the Beginning of Time?

Sherry A. Phillips

Time in a bottle, time runs out, where does time go? From whence did time come?

A minute is sixty seconds, 365 days a year, ten long or short years make a decade.

Why?

We sleep a fourth of it away; we waste it looking for more time.

Time needs to be saved, not spent. Lock in a moment of time.

Remove me, Lord, from the run-away train of time. God, did you pause in time before declaring the Creation good? Let us also pause to breathe deep.

Contemplate the sky that stays the same through eons.

Sit, absorb time, and slough off the frantic, hectic, ear-splitting, screaming passage of time.

Stop and smell the roses is not good enough.

I tried to stop time when Roy died—no; I knew time had stopped. Everything could not, surely would not, go forward. But it was ugly to feel and look at—like a blurry photo. When the Bermuda grass greened, and the elderberry bloomed, I knew time had not stopped.

The Creator knew time should begin and keep going. Our choice, the Lord said, was to do something with the time we have.

Now I watch as children take time to play. I listen as time rustles the leaves and watch the night sky awake the stars to pay homage to the Creator of time. I taste the seasons of change and look towards the end of my time.

## "The 20 Years of the Living Nativity": The West Side Story – Church of God, That is!

Ptrice Collins

For us, it all began Christmas 1965 when a friend invited us to see a beautiful Christmas pageant that their church put on each Christmas. Started by Pastor E. B. Jones and wife, Marion, back in 1961, it was called "The Christ's Living Nativity," because it is live and moving—not just a manger scene. The first night we viewed it, they invited us inside to meet some of the people behind the scenes. My husband and our daughters, age 2 ½ and 5 were invited to be in the pageant the following night.

At that time, we were going to another church, but these people were so different. They were friendly, and enthusiastic about telling the story how Christ was born, even though it was freezing cold outside in the church parking lot where the production was given. To us it had always been just a story that the pastor read to us each Christmas. Now, suddenly it was real!

We started attending West Side Church in May. By September, the Church was hard at work on the next production. We were excited and couldn't believe so much work was involved in putting on a six-day pageant (now five days). Costumes had to be made, repaired, or ironed, makeup and beard supplies ordered, permits obtained, advertising sought, flyers made up and distributed, buildings erected—hundreds of things had to be done in order to be ready by December 19th.

My husband and I were asked if we would like to be Mary and Joseph one of the nights that first year. That night, as Gabriel was telling me, Mary, that I would become pregnant and bear the Savior of the world, Mary raises her hands toward the sky and says, "My soul doth magnify the Lord my God," and as I looked up into the dark sky, it was starting to snow and with that pure clean miracle of God floating down to clean and cover the dirty earth, I felt as if I was completely engulfed in the beautiful cleansing power of God. If

I felt all of this, what must the real Mary have felt? There really are no words that I can use that would adequately describe my feelings. When you're in the Nativity, you actually feel like you are there. You are a part of the miracle.

We have added a few more scenes to go with the story, but we have always strived to keep it strictly Biblical and close to the original production that Pastor Jones started. The words on the tape are taken from scriptural accounts of the birth of Jesus starting with the prophet foretelling the birth of a Savior; Gabriel telling Mary that she would give birth to the Savior of the world; Mary and Joseph being shown to the stable by the innkeeper; Jesus' birth; the angels appearing to the shepherds; the shepherds coming to the manger; the kings appearing before Herod, and journeying to the home of Mary, Joseph and baby Jesus; then on to the scene with Rachel and a couple of women appearing before Herod pleading for the lives of their infants; ending with the boy Jesus working with Joseph in their carpenter shop.

Each night the cast changes. Mary and Joseph are portrayed by a married couple. Everyone in the performance reports at 5:00 for makeup and costuming. We are having a beard growing contest this year to encourage men to grow their own beard for the production. We feed the entire cast and workers each evening; stopping for devotions at 6:45 before the first of five, twenty-minute performances start at 7:00. The pageant starts on December 19th and ends on Christmas Eve, and proceeds in all kinds of weather, except rain since our velvet and fur costumes would be ruined by rain.

It has been a marvelous gift to the people of Wichita for the past nineteen years. Make special plans to be with us this year.

(This article was first published in the Kansas State Church of God Bulletin, November-December 1981.)

# Dear Child

## Donita M. Davis

That precocious little black girl, so chatty and sweet,
Plopped herself beside me on the small loveseat
In the waiting room of the big hospital.
For a five-year-old, it had been pretty dull.

I asked her Dad, "May I show her a book?
It's about God. Can I give her a look?"
He answered, "Yes," and gave a subtle nod.
I showed her pictures that told about God.

And turning the pages of the book, while I read,
She smoothed my arm, "Your skin is soft," she said.
"I guess so." (Touching hers) "Yours is firm"
On with the story. She was quick to learn.

"Did you ever disobey Mom?" Yes, she had.
"Jesus died on the cross to take away our bad.
Three days later, there was a big surprise.
A humongous miracle happened! Jesus came alive!"

"When you believe in Jesus, your sins go away.
And you'll get to go to heaven some day."
"I believe," was her response to what she did know.
Dear child. Simple faith in Jesus saves your soul.

# Look Up

## C. Holden

When a task is upon us and we are not sure what to do
just trust in yourself and do the best you can.
Trust in the Lord and He will see you through.
We can always look to Him for guidance
because your burden is less than others.
And always have a smile on your face.
So, look up and say a little prayer,
and He will always be there.

# Christ Child Visit

## Ptrice Collins

Years ago, I read a story about the meaning of Christmas in different lands. While I was studying about Advent customs, how and where they got started, I came across several stories or legends about why we put candles in our windows at Christmas time.

The reason for this custom is to tell the Christ Child that he is welcome there.

A few years ago, I heard Reba McIntyre tell this favorite story of mine on her Christmas special just a few weeks before Christmas.

The legend goes something like this: A few nights before Christmas a lonely old man was praying to his Heavenly Father and was telling Him how lonesome he was and what a lonely Christmas it would be. God spoke to him and told him that He would visit him on Christmas Day. He was so overjoyed that he was nearly beside himself. He went scurrying about, cleaning, fixing food, etc. He made sure that he put his candle in the window to let the Christ Child know that He was welcome there.

Christmas morning, he awakened very early for he sure didn't want to be sleeping when Christ came to visit. Not long after the sun burst forth over the newly fallen snow, there came a knock at his door. He thought, this must be the Christ Child. But when he opened the door, it was only a hungry old man. He brought him inside and warmed him and fed him. Soon he was on his way.

The old gentleman felt good but was disappointed that it hadn't been the Christ child. About lunch time there was another knock at his door. He rushed to open it hoping that surely this time it would be the expected visit. Again, it wasn't. This time it was just a lonely cold old woman. Being the kind person that he was, he invited her inside to get warm. Along with some food, he gave her some warm mittens and a scarf and soon she too was on her way.

It was now getting late in the afternoon and still the Christ Child hadn't come. There came another knock at his door. Surely, as late as it was, this would be the Christ Child. Again, he was disappointed when he opened the door to a lost child. The kind old man couldn't turn him away. He calmed the child and dried away his tears, brought him some cookies and milk. Then he and the child set off to find his home.

By the time the old gentleman got home it was growing dark and surely the Christ Child wouldn't come this late.

The old man was so disappointed when he sat down to eat his dinner. He thought he must have missed Christ's visit while taking the little child home. In his disappointment God again interrupted his thoughts and said: Oh, don't be upset for I visited you today, not once, but three times and each time you invited me in and took care of my needs.

As I sat there wiping away my tears after Reba had finished, I said to God, "Boy, it would sure be wonderful if you still did that today."

Almost like He was sitting beside me a voice welled up inside me and said, "I Do! You'll see, all you have to do is really and truly invite me."

"Wow!" Now I got excited! We were having a particularly rough Christmas that year. Our finances were rotten and two of our children had moved out of state and wouldn't be home.

I always had put the electric candles in our windows and that year was no exception.

Christmas dawned bright as usual and I was starting to prepare the turkey, not even remembering about the little talk God and I had had. When my phone rang, it was a friend of mine. A few weeks before they had lost their brand-new grandbaby. In all their rushing to go out of town to visit their son who had lost their child, she had forgotten to order the wreath that they had wanted to take to the baby's grave.

She hated to ask, especially on Christmas morning, but would I by chance have any kind of little wreath that they could use. They were leaving in about an hour. (I'd been a florist and craft designer for years.) I replied, "Sure! Just give me a bit to think about it and I'll have something for you."

As I hung up I almost hollered, "HELP ME, GOD!"

I said some real fast prayers and as I started rushing around the workroom, I felt God impressing me about different items.... First, an angel, but how and where? God showed me. Then as I was about to finish, God impressed upon me that I should add a small plastic nativity creche on the skirt of the angel. Even though God, I felt, had directed me in all this, this really puzzled me. I didn't ask any questions just did it, since I was sure that this was My Christ Child visit that I had asked for.

When Jeane came a few minutes later, tears welled up in her eyes as she said it was just Perfect! She had wanted the wreath to have two things on it, but with such short notice she'd been afraid to ask for an angel and a creche!

As she started to leave, she wanted to pay me. No way! God had given more pay for that visit than anyone could ever pay. This was the best Christmas ever!

# Precious Few

## C. A. Lemont

Hundreds, maybe thousands of people you know;
    Only a few will touch the soul.

One may appear with a light dancing in their eyes;
    The warmth, the glow, catching you by surprise.

One may flash like lightning in the sky;
    The soul thunders back, assured of its reply.

One may reach out in an instant connection;
    The look in the eyes, a true reflection.

A spirit so essential, it beams from the face;
    As if God had given them a special grace.

Precious few mortals have the spirit you display.
    I'm eternally grateful you came my way.

# Learning to Tithe

## Jean Welle

Why do I tithe, the question was asked;
      And why give an offering when the plate is passed?
The answer is simple. It's so plain to see:
      I credit my folks who tithed and taught me.

"Here's your allowance," my daddy would say.
      "A nickel and five pennies – it's easier that way.

You see, Jesus would like a tenth of your pay.
      A penny is how much you'll give Him today."

A few years later my allowance had grown
      To twenty-five cents…quite a lot, but I moaned:
"Two and a half cents? Dad, now what do I do?
      Two cents, I win. Three cents, I lose!"

"That is a dilemma," Dad said in deep thought.
      "You'll have to ask Jesus when put on the spot."
That made it easy, if He was like Dad;
      I'd give what He asked for or else I'd be had!

At first it was hard to give just a bit more,
> But Daddy was pleased. How much more so, the Lord?
All through the years those impressions on giving
> Have kept me in focus and enhanced all my living.

Oh, there have been times when my earnings were sparse,
> And the disciplines of spending were cruel and harsh.
But I've always had shelter. I've not missed a meal.
> Jesus does know what's best, and I delight in His will.

# One January Morn

## Martha Williams Prentice

One January morn
 a girl child was born,
  with golden hair
   and eyes to be hazel.

Hooded eyes
 set wide and clear,
  smiling eyes
   from the very beginning.

Dimpled cheeks
 soft and full,
  and lips so expressive
   as if eager to speak.

Blessed child
 this day appointed;
  chosen child
   by grace anointed.

With searching mind,
 knowing soul,
  musician's spirit,
   and poet's heart ...
    waiting.

# Simple Thanks-Giving

## Rochelle Boster

Recognize your talents,
    Gift what you do best!

Multiply your time,
    Share yourself with others!

Find strengths in all people,
    Bless everyone for something!

Be in the moment, listen,
    Respond as if you heard!

Say thank you,
    At very least, Smile!

# Sisters

## Donita M. Davis

I was surprised when I read that Mary had a sister. (Standing by the cross of Jesus were his mother, and his mother's sister...John 19:25)

They were surely together for the six long hours while Jesus hung on the cross. They saw every tortured movement he made and heard every word he spoke. The last three hours were in brooding darkness, emphasizing the tragedy. (Luke 23:44)

Suddenly, Jesus cried out in a loud voice, "Father, into your hands I place my spirit." —startling the mother and aunt. When his head bowed in death, they cried grievously, their tears being put into God's bottle. (Psalm 56:8)

My imagination had a good time thinking what the sisters might have said after an angel talked to Mary.

"Salome, I talked to an angel today," Mary said excitedly.

"Did you say an angel? A real angel?" her sister asked.

"Yes. He said, 'Peace be with you! The Lord is with you and has greatly blessed you.'"

"OK," Salome said slowly. "What did he mean, 'has greatly blessed you'?"

"Well," Mary said, "he told me I would conceive and give birth to a son and to name him Jesus."

Salome's eyes opened wide. "Mary, you can't do that! You are a virgin!"

"That's what I told the angel. But he said this would be God's holy child and he would be called the Son of God."

Salome was mulling this over in her mind, trying to pull forward something she knew and had learned in the past when suddenly she grabbed Mary's hands and was executing little jumps as she spoke.

"Mary! Could you be the virgin—THE VIRGIN—our father told us about after Synagogue one Saturday, that Isaiah talked about? You know, 'The virgin shall conceive and bear a son and you shall call his name Immanuel.' ('God with us' – Isaiah 7:14) Yes! It is you! YOU are THE VIRGIN. You are to bear God's child who will be 'God with us' to save us."

Mary replied, "Oh Salome, my heart and my spirit are running over with praise to the Lord. I feel so full of joy."

Sure enough. Mary's baby was truly 'God with us' who grew up to be the Savior of the world to those who believed in Him.

# Spider and Crow

## Jean Welle

There once was a spider who thought it would be
    Much better if she were a crow,
Flying with hundreds up high in the sky
    Than to sit all alone down below.
She thought of the gourmet of foods she'd consume
    With options of fruit, grain, or meat,
Instead of laboriously spinning a web
    And wait for a snag:  twig or treat.

"You are the one to be envied," said crow.
    "You thrive in schools, homes, and hotels.
You're able to hide in dark corners or cracks,
    Under tables or vacant seashells.
You may not fly but you glide through the air
    On the tail of a silky thread,
And with eight spindly legs you are able to spin
    Elaborate weaves in your web."

"It's true, what you say," said the spider to crow.
    "I've no reason to whine or complain.
Our Master Creator has purpose for both;
To question His judgement's quite lame."

"I beg your forgiveness," she prayed with remorse.
    "I should be content with my lot.
I truly am blessed and uniquely designed;
    I praise You for what I am not."

# See the Child

## Martha Williams Prentice

(A poem written when I was seventeen.
Twenty-five years later I wrote a melody,
and it became a lullaby.)


See the child who runs and plays,
     His head is full of laughter;
See the child who sits and weeps,
     His heart is full of sorrow.

See the child who kneels and prays,
     He whispers "God, I love you;"
See the child who nods and sleeps,
     He dreams he swings on stars.

# On the Night Christ Was Born, What If...

### Donita M. Davis

Dad (the farm boy) was a shepherd back then?
And actually heard the angel say, "Ben,
Go find your promised Savior today,
Tucked in a manger filled with fresh hay."

Oh, how quickly he would have run
To see the newborn.... God's only Son,
And stuck out a finger, for Him to grab in His hand,
And said with a smile, "You're a strong little man."

As tiny fingers on his own were entwined,
Dad's tender feeling would be one of a kind.
He'd have asked Mary, on bended knees,
"May I hold your little baby, please?"

Gently cradling Him, as tears filled his eyes,
He would have been holding God, baby size.
And prayed, with head bowed to kiss Jesus' face,
"Sweet Lord, make my heart your dwelling place."

# Hearing What I Had, Celebrating What I've Lost

Sherry A. Phillips

*Dedicated to those with hearing loss*

River rapids gush a cacophony crash, blast, roar through the rocky channel and foment foamy broth with booming splash into and around the band of twelve golden trumpets conducted along the ragged route waterway to a soundless, black placid sea.

## Symphonic Sound

I have a humming in my ears. Doctors call it tinnitus. Webster's definition is, "a tinkle." To me it's maddening. Way more than a damn nuisance. There is no cure. Some medications cause it but mine may be related to an inherited middle ear problem called Otosclerosis—the reason for my mother's hearing loss. Lower ranges and this high-pitched ringing I hear but sounds just above mid-range get lost in the air space between source and receiver or drowned out by tinnitus.

I look at the items placed on the table by our writing instructor. I hear their music. Bow drawn to and fro across violin strings trigger a memory of hoedown, country dance, symphony and chamber string quartet.

There is no need to hold a Conch shell near to ear. The quiet roar of the sea pulled to shore by moon with the rising tide. Rhythmic current and drum crescendos are captured by the ear of marine gastropod mollusk once heard never forgotten.

Miniature hummingbirds so small their sound mostly imagined is a contrast to the beep-beep of the cartoon road runner remembered from early television. But it is the summer sound of male cicada mating chirps that resemble my interminable tinnitus—loud but thankfully not so loud as to drown out the indelible.

93

# The Benefits of Hearing Loss

### Sherry A. Phillips

For days following an outdoors Rolling Stones concert at Cessna Stadium attendees continued to complain of problems hearing. Audiologists say the hearing loss will be permanent. The average ticket price was $160. And the 33,000 Stones' lovers paid thousands of extra dollars for hats and other pricey souvenirs. The Rolling Stones enjoy a $156 million annual salary.

Lawn mowers, power tools and earphones are no longer the major causes of hearing difficulties in a new generation who, specialists predict, will be suffering some deafness before they reach middle age. For more, the hearing loss is preventable. Hearing aids are expensive and need to be replaced every five to eight years.

My own hearing problems began before I was born. I have inherited the otosclerosis that caused my mother's deafness.

As a kid, I learned to enunciate and speak louder so Mom could hear me. She taught me to look at her when I spoke so she could read my lips. In school I was asked to read aloud because my voice carried. And as I began to lead, teach and preach in church the little old folks who always sat in the back pews would smile, shake my hand and say, "I could hear every word you said."

Now it is my turn to say, "Huh"?

The ear doctor says surgery may be possible in the future but hearing aids might not help very much now. He gave me a list of things to do that would help:

- If I have a choice, sit with a wall at my back so sounds will bounce.
- Tell my family to make eye contact when they speak.
- Teach the grandkids to keep their hands away from their face when they talk.
- Don't be afraid to ask people to speak up or say again the important thing you know you missed.
- And repeat a name or thought to be sure I've heard correctly.

Last year I became philosophical about my hearing loss to take advantage of what I now feel are its benefits.

When car stereos blare beside me at red lights, I don't get irritated, scowl and mutter, "Turn that blasted thing down." I don't use the mute button on the remote for commercials anymore. A train whistle whooo-whoooing at 4 a.m. no longer wakes me up. I can sleep through hailstorms and thunder. It's easier to ignore the whinny wants of children in grocery stores and restaurants.

At lectures, when keynotes look down to read speeches and mumble or turn and speak without the microphone, I can check my to-do list or finish a crossword puzzle. I may concentrate on my breathing, pray, even meditate. I try to guess the meaning of the body language of others in the room. Restless leg syndrome? Too much coffee? Bored? Maybe their hearing aid batteries are dead.

And I have learned to nod and smile even when I can't figure out if you've just said deed, weed, read, plead, or greed. But would you, please, say your name again?

# Dreamers

## C.A. Lemont

For quite some time;
I've had a tribute to John in mind.
No, John, you weren't the only one.
You another dreamer, who fell to the gun.
Those with vision and insight for a better tomorrow;
      Their lives end tragically, and the world is in sorrow.
The dragon needs to be slain.
Violence brings us nothing but pain.
There are lessons to learn and wisdom to gain.
Wisdom's found in the heart, not in the brain.
      Is there nowhere, a magic dreamer?
      One who could lead all the believers?
      One who could stop the violence and bring peace to man.
      Without having to die at the non-believers' hand.
Why take from us those who know?
Why take the light and leave the shadow?
Is that the price of universal love?
What could mankind be thinking of?
      Bring us the light. Bring us the day.
      Bring us the time to change our ways.
      Open your hearts to see beyond today.
      Ask a dream to point the way.

# Herschel's Story – Part 1

Talking Stones and Changing Lives

E. L. Morrow

One day the stones spoke, whips became silent, and palms paved the king's highway. I know. I was there. My name is Herschel; let me tell you my story.

I grew up poor, in a poor and forgotten corner of a Roman province called Galilee. My father could only find work as a sheepherder. When mother died during childbirth, he swore he would never let me go hungry. He kept his promise. Sometimes we neared starvation, but our neighbors experienced the same shortages.

A sheepherder does not own the sheep. If a sheep dies or is killed by a wild animal, they deduct its value for the tenders pay. These sheep belong to a well-to-do man two villages over. They pay the herder a portion of the wool after shearing each year.

Some at the synagogue teach that God shows more favor to the rich. My father would never disagree with the leaders in public. But in private, he told me, "God must really love the poor people, otherwise why would there be so many of us."

Each year father looked longingly toward Jerusalem as the day of Passover approached. I would always ask, "Are we going to eat the Passover in Jerusalem this year, Father?" And each year he would answer, "O how I long to eat the Passover in the city of our Lord. But it is not meant to be this year, my son. Next year, the Lord willing, we will eat the Passover meal in Jerusalem."

But alas Father took ill, this past winter. His dying request was "this year, Son, make the pilgrimage to Jerusalem for the Passover. When you are there say a prayer for me. Pray that our people will soon see the day of the Lord. Pray that the chosen one will rise up and give glory to our God, restoring Israel to its place as a faithful nation, a light to all people."

The road from Judea has been long. I do not know whether it is the heat and dust, or all the memories of Father that weigh so heavily on my mind and spirit as I travel. Though I am a man in my own right, I make this trip as a final act of honor to my father. Perhaps that's the reason, I hear his words speaking to me like a child. He reminds me of the stories of faith. "That is what makes us different, my son, it is our faith in God, the Creator, and protector of our people." He told him repeatedly, "One day we will go to Jerusalem and see the Temple, sacrifice to the Lord, and eat the Passover in the holy city." I hear my father teaching me about the exodus, the hardship in the wilderness. He speaks of the promised land, the rise of King David, and the divisions. Concluding with the prophet's words about a time of salvation which would be ushered in by the Messiah, the chosen one.

As I travel, I remember Father would always end his lessons by saying, "… and you, my son, will see the Messiah, in your lifetime you will praise and honor the Lord's anointed." When I objected, saying God has had centuries to bring the Messiah, why would he come now, just to please an old man? Father would always say, "… Mark my word: God will show you the salvation of our people." Strange how those words keep coming back to me.

After several days of travel, as I neared the city, the crowd thickened. Others joined from nearer villages. Conditions are hard on the road, but to celebrate the Passover in Jerusalem, it will be a joyous day. A day to fulfill my father's wish. As we neared the city, some people in the crowd up ahead began shouting and singing. What were they saying? I couldn't quite make it out. Sounded like Hosanna. Hosanna? That means God is being praised, and a king is being welcomed.

It confused me. Our king is Herod, and no one would praise him. Only the Romans have real power, and they used it to keep us down, and Herod is just a tool of their vice.

Then someone in the crowd passed the word back, "… they say Jesus is up there." Jesus, it's a common name, which Jesus? "Jesus of Nazareth" he is getting ready to mount a donkey and ride into the city as the Lord's anointed.

I asked the informer to tell me about this Jesus. I wondered if he's the one my father heard about at the market a year ago. One who proclaimed the Kingdom of God will come like a thief in the night. This Jesus proclaimed God's favor on the common people and spoke against the rich and the scribes. He spoke about happiness coming to those who mourn, for they would be comforted, also to the peacemakers because they would inherit the earth. Oh, and he also said, blessed are those who seek righteousness, for they will be satisfied.

But it couldn't be the same man. We later heard that he went off into Samaria, and no true Israelite would associate with the likes of them. Someone said he told a story where a Samaritan was the righteous one who rendered aid to a wounded traveler. No, it couldn't be the same man.

The informer told me he had seen Jesus heal a blind man and met leapers who said Jesus cleansed them. And now he's mounting a donkey to ride into the city as king.

I said, "Won't the Romans do something about that?"

My new friend said, "Let um try, the angels of God will defend him."

Then I heard my father's words, "You, will see the messiah, ... you will praise and honor the Lord's anointed."

I realized this is the beginning of something spectacular. Father's dream for me turns out not to be just the rumblings of an old man. It's real, and this Jesus I heard about could he be the Lord's Messiah? All of a sudden, I found myself no longer tired. New energy surged through my veins as I made way toward the center of the activity. I hoped I might get just a glimpse of Jesus, and the soldiers who would escort him. The crowd was thick, but I saw no uniforms, no guards, no shields, or swords. Only palms spread out before him...like a royal carpet. I soon found himself near the front of the crowd being pushed ahead of the others. I had taken up the shouts of Hosanna.

Then, without warning, I looked up and found myself at the entrance to the Temple. The structure is magnificent. This is the place where our ancestors worshiped God. David and Solomon stood on this very ground. Kings and prophets, and conquering armies all came here to ask God's blessing on their efforts. And behind those doors are the learned scribes and officials who preserve and teach righteousness, even when a brutal conqueror occupies us.

Officials of the Temple soon began to gather around. I thought they're preparing to make an official welcome of Jesus and this large company of the faithful to the Temple.

I felt like I must be in the wrong place. I'm not an official of either group. I hadn't yet seen Jesus, and the Temple officials appeared so regal and dignified, I'm not worthy to be on the same ground with them. They didn't notice me. The crowd surrounding Jesus engulfed me as well.

Jesus and the donkey arrived at the gate to the Temple. The shouts of Hosanna continued, but the Temple officials did not join in. In fact, they appeared displeased or angry. One of them spoke to Jesus, "Silence this rabble. If you don't, there will be a riot."

Another said, "The Romans. If they hear of this, they will cancel our Passover celebration."

I was only a few feet from Jesus when he answered: "If these were quiet, the very stones themselves would cry out."

The people shouted, it was like the stones on the ground, and the Temple walls joined as well. It seemed that loud. I looked around, and the Pharisees had retreated. I understood what Jesus meant—the people have waited so long for God's salvation. No one can silence the mass. This is our day. This is God's day.

Next a strange thing happened. The Temple had been the destination, but no one, including me, quite knew what to do next? Where should I go? The people arrived in the city with a great victory. But most were not ready to enter the Temple. They had to find lodging, to plan for their Passover meal in a few days, and maybe meet up with others who traveled together.

While I wondered where I should go, I noticed Jesus had gotten off the donkey and slipped away from the crowd. Even those who looked like his disciples didn't seem to notice. He entered the Temple. I followed him with a few others. I've never been in the house of our Lord before. I heard stories of its beauty and glory. I have heard about the grand acts of sacrifice, beautiful rituals, worship, and the singing of the Psalms of praise taking place in the Temple.

I stepped through the gates expecting to be overcome with a sense of reverence and awe as I drew near to the seat of our Lord … but I felt … no, I smelled, animals: birds, sheep, and goats. And I heard, voices, loud voices, filling the air not with music but calls, like a marketplace. "Sacrifice. Sacrifice. Get your sacrifice here, the best doves in the Province."

Others were haggling over the price of a ram, and I saw money changers tables. "Got to change your money. Can't spend Roman money in here."

I was disappointed. Then I saw Jesus; he must have had the same feeling. No, it angered him. He was using a whip to drive out those who were selling, not the animals, but the people. I heard him say, "This is not a house of prayer. You have made it a den of robbers."

Jesus came toward me, with the whip raised over his head, and our eyes met. I saw the rage in his eyes, and my eyes filled with tears, I felt his anger at the desecration of this holy place. At once he sensed I was not one of those there to buy or sell. I fell to my knees, and a strange quiet came over me as others fled from the whip. There on my knees, I remembered my father's request that I pray the prayer he would have offered if he had been there.

Palms, and Stones and Whips. I will never see a palm or a stone, or a whip without remembering what Jesus did as God's messenger that day. And perhaps now you won't either.

# Herschel's Story - Part II:

Sharing a Meal and Opening our Eyes

E. L. Morrow

Jesus turned over the money-changer tables and drove out those who bought and sold. I was there. Witnessing the entry into the city and the cleansing of the Temple should be enough for one lifetime. When adding what happened next, I realize I am a most fortunate man. My name is Herschel, and I hope you feel my joy as I tell you the rest of my story.

The week began with a spiritual high. Faith has always been important to me. But never had I felt God so close. I even felt God might have some small part for me to play in his plan. My father must have known something special would happen this year at the Passover. Why else would he have been so insistent I come this year to Jerusalem? At first, I was unsure about being in the Holy city with all the pilgrims, the Temple, or the upcoming Passover. But one thing I know, it all started when I met Jesus. From that moment, I've felt a guiding hand.

In the days before Passover, I came back to the Temple every day. I found Jesus there too. Jesus taught, and the people listened. I also listened and learned. What Jesus said made sense. He talked about so many things, and he explained the great mysteries of God's love to us all. I met others who followed Jesus. They believed he is the teacher sent from God to restore Israel.

I met a man named Cleopas who lived in the city of Emmaus, about a day's journey from Jerusalem. Cleopas knew many followers from Jesus' previous trips to Jerusalem. I found much of what Jesus said clear and understandable. But I couldn't always anticipate what Jesus wanted us to do.

I asked Cleopas for help to understand how to respond to the teacher's messages. He told me of an incident that happened while on the way to Jerusalem to observe the Passover. A band of lepers met Jesus' group. They cried out for Jesus to have mercy on them. Jesus told them to go and show themselves to the priests.

"Wow, you mean Jesus healed them?" I asked.

My friend said there could be no other reason. The law requires when a leper is cleansed, a priest can allow them back into the community. They no longer must live in little bands outside the cities as beggars or robbers.

"Were they all cured at once?"

Cleopas answered, "Apparently but only one returned to Jesus to give thanks; now get this, Jesus praised the one for returning even though he was a Samaritan. He also criticized the others for not returning to give praise."

"But that's my point," I said. "Jesus told them to go to the priests, and then he criticized them for doing what they had been told."

Cleopas said, "Oh, don't you get it? I think Jesus wants us to think for ourselves, not just follow the rules. The law tells a cured leper to present himself to the priest who will then let him back into the community for worship. But if you were miraculously healed, doesn't it make sense to praise God and give thanks to the one who made it possible? If your body has been a slave to a disease and you are suddenly free—healed, what is the first thing you should do with your new freedom?"

I thought I was beginning to understand. Jesus is a different kind of teacher. It's not only about the rules but also about why God made that law anyhow.

Each day I heard Jesus teaching in the Temple. He did not teach like the scribes or Pharisees, but he speaks as one who knew what he was talking about. Jesus spoke with authority. The authority to declare what God desired. He spoke like he knew God's will, and it seemed so right.

The people especially liked it when the lawyers and Pharisees would try to trick Jesus. Like the time they asked about paying taxes to Rome. They asked Jesus, "Is it lawful, for a Jew to pay taxes to the Emperor?"

It was a tense moment—no one likes paying taxes to Rome, and if he said pay them, many followers would turn away. Yet if he told us not to pay taxes …. Well, some loyal to Rome stood nearby. They could have arrested him for treason.

But Jesus stayed calm. He requested someone to show him a coin and then asked, "Whose picture is on it?"

"Why the Emperor's picture, of course."

And Jesus said, "Then give to the Emperor the things that are his and to God the things belonging to God." I think he told us, our lives and souls belong to God, don't worry about a few coins belonging to someone else. Jesus always made the subject larger than the question being asked.

Jesus taught about the right relationship of people to God. He described the nature of God's concern for all nations, not just the people of Israel. He praised a poor widow for quietly giving all she had, while the rich made a big show out of what they gave. The rich still had plenty left for themselves. Jesus warned us to be on guard because the day could come quickly and catch us unprepared. We all expected Jesus to declare himself as the proper king—the true messiah he had told us about.

The day came for the Passover celebration. Everything got confusing. We all hoped Jesus would make an announcement right after the Passover. Like so many others, I made plans to stay the next day, just to be on hand for the great day. We heard Jesus would celebrate the Passover with the twelve, but no one knew where.

I joined some of my new friends at the inn for the observance. It was everything Father had taught me to expect. The recounting of the history of our people, eating the egg, bread, and lamb. Tasting the bitter herbs, saltwater and finally the wine cup of joy. I felt filled and renewed.

Later we sang some Psalms. As we rested, one acquaintance from earlier in the week came to tell us the guards of the high priest had arrested Jesus. If that wasn't bad enough, they said one of the twelve had betrayed him. Some of us couldn't believe it.

But it was true. We went to the high priest's home where Jesus was being questioned. To everyone's surprise, he refused to say anything.

Some of us thought it would outrage the crowd at what was happening, but there seemed to be agitators planted in the group. They went around picking out people dressed like Galileans and accused them of being "one of his followers." We all slipped back into the shadows. Now, I am ashamed of myself for being so afraid.

It was hard to understand what had happened. Had everyone forgotten what Jesus did? I wondered where were the people he healed? What happened to the rest of the twelve? Had they been arrested also? I remembered Jesus saying something about evil people liking the dark so they can hide their deeds. It was night and dark, and this was certainly evil. I did not follow when they sent him to Pilot, and I heard later they took him to Herod's palace.

I went back to be with my new friends. I wanted their companionship. I hoped they would reassure me that it would all be all right. But no one talked much. We seemed to be in shock. Someone said, maybe it's a different Jesus—but we knew it couldn't be. They charged him with treason against Rome. How could they say those things, after what he said about giving Creaser's coin to Caesar? But the truth no longer mattered.

We heard they had condemned Jesus to die on a cross. It happened right away. There's a hill called "the place of the skull" outside of the city. The Romans use it for crucifixions. Everybody avoids the place. For the Jews, being there defiles you, meaning you cannot go into the Temple until you have made special sacrifices.

That's where they took Jesus to be killed on a cross. He had to drag part of his cross. Some of us ventured to the path leading up the hill. I saw when the cross was raised putting him between two others who were already there … thieves, I think. I couldn't take any more. I found a corner in the shadows and just crumpled up like discarded parchment. I thought about heading for home, but I didn't have the strength to move. Besides the Sabbath begins in a few hours. I couldn't get far before I would've had to stop. Travel is forbidden on the Sabbath.

Jerusalem was such a beautiful place when we entered just five days before. But now it seemed hostile, angry, and depressing. I decided to stay through the Sabbath and get an early start on the first day. I ended up in a group including my friend Cleopas. We couldn't believe God would let all this happen. There had been a storm in the midst of the afternoon, the same time Jesus died. One who had been to the Temple said the wind ripped the curtain separating the Holy of Holies from the people.

Cleopas invited me to come home with him and stay awhile. I couldn't face the long trip back, and the sadness of telling my friends I had found the messiah, but they killed him. How could I explain the part our own leaders played in his death?

When sunup came on Sunday, we were saying goodbye, and getting ready for the journey, when the word came—unbelievable as it sounded. The women who went to anoint Jesus' body for burial found the tomb empty. We did not know what to believe. The women could have been mistaken. Maybe they went to the wrong tomb.

As Cleopas and I walked toward Emmaus, we talked. Cleopas had seen and heard about Jesus for years. We tried to figure out what God might be doing. It amazed me to hear, he still had hope. Perhaps things were better than I feared. He said it helped him think to talk about it. I was glad to learn and hear the teachings he knew. But then we were joined by a stranger who asked what we were talking about? We couldn't believe he didn't know what had happened.

We soon found the stranger was teaching us. He explained the words of the prophets and Jesus' teaching. He understood even more than Cleopas.

We got to Emmaus. My host invited our traveling companion to stay. Then it happened. Sitting at the table for a simple meal, he took bread and gave thanks and broke it, and said, "this is my body" and we knew. We had been walking with the risen savior for hours, and now we knew.

You know the rest of the story. We couldn't keep the news even till morning. We went back to Jerusalem the same night, and we found some believers. Jesus had appeared to Peter and others.

Even now, it amazes me. Jesus, on the day of his resurrection, stopped to teach a couple of seekers. Neither of us were rich or powerful people; we were not one of the Apostles; we had not been with Jesus throughout his travels. But he stopped to explain and opened our eyes to the scriptures and prophet's messages. Then in the simple act of sitting down for a meal, he opened our eyes to his presence.

Now every time I sit down to a meal, with a friend, or stranger, I remember. I remember the power of sharing around a table of food. There everyone receives nourishment. We all receive gifts from God's bounty. I also remember the time a simple meal opened my eyes.

# I, James

## Donita M. Davis

I, James, sat on the ground. My whole body was shaking.

"Let it not be true!" I thought, as my heart was aching.

Covering my face with my hands, I sobbed in agony.

My brother, who never did anything wrong, should have been set free.


But His beaten body was nailed to a cross, and He was slowly dying.

This had to be a horrific mistake. Our family couldn't stop crying.

As our Mother stood watching, 'twas like a sword was piercing her soul.

At age thirty-three, Jesus' destiny had reached the ultimate goal.


The girls in our family believed and put their faith in Him.

We four boys did not believe. Our spiritual outlook was dim.

But love him? Yes, we did! T'was scary to hear of death-threat warnings.

When death came so suddenly, our hearts were filled with mourning.


Three days later, Jesus walked out of the tomb, no longer dead.

"Destroy this temple, and I will raise it again in three days," Jesus said.

For forty days longer, He traversed the earth. As alive as could be!

He appeared to five hundred people. And He also appeared unto me.

Yes, me! James! Who finally understood what was obviously true:

Jesus is God, The Saviour of the World, the Messiah whose time was due.

I fell on my knees and cried, "Jesus, forgive my sins, set me free.

I'll trust in you my whole life through. May others see You in me."

I ran to tell my brothers; Joseph Jr., Simon, and Jude.

While talking, I knew their hearts had been opened and they understood.

Now I am a preacher, proclaiming Jesus and His great love,

That others who believe in Him may enter heaven above.

If Jesus is knocking at your heart's door, be sure to let Him in.

Believe He shed His blood for your sins and your new life will begin.

The Bible says He will never leave you nor forsake you. Never!

And you will receive eternal life forever and ever.

# Evolving into Wholeness:
# My Journey of Compassion

### Dianne Waltner

*"We need not accept the rules that our society or species, family or fate seem to have written for us. We can choose a new way. We have the power to transform a story of sorrow into a story of healing. We can choose life over death. We can let love lead us home."*
- Sy Montgomery

I stopped killing myself on July 18, 2018. That's the day I decided that I was enough. Life was worth living and that I deserved to live. That I loved myself enough to stop slowly poisoning myself with alcohol.

This day was a long time coming.

Growing up fat, I'd struggled with feelings of unworthiness and inadequacy for years. Thoughts of suicide were common. But, thankfully, I had a loving family, and that saved my life.

I grew up on a farm about sixty miles from Wichita, and my Kansas roots run deep. My dad's ancestors were part of a Swiss Volhynian Mennonite group which immigrated from Russia to America in 1874, to avoid persecution. Mennonites were known for their farming ability and so were offered some land for settlement in Kansas by the Atchison Topeka and Santa Fe Railroad. Most settled in the central Kansas region and brought with them the Turkey Hard Red Winter Wheat which helped to make Kansas the wheat state that it is today.

One of my earliest memories as a toddler is of sitting in our bathroom with my grandmother, inhaling steam from the bathtub faucet, desperately trying to breathe. I was soon admitted to the hospital, where I remember sleeping in an oxygen tent and receiving what seemed to be very frequent injections. I don't know the exact length of my hospital stay, or my diagnosis, but Mom told me I came very close to having to have a tracheotomy. Fortunately, I recovered before that became necessary!

Mom used to tell me that, prior to this incident, people would jokingly ask her if she ever fed me—because I was so skinny. But that all changed dramatically.

After the hospitalization (and almost overnight, according to Mom) I put on a lot of weight, to where now people would jokingly say she should STOP feeding me!

I don't believe that we ever understood why that happened—Mom thought maybe all the medications I had received affected my thyroid and had it tested. The tests checked out normally, but by the time I started school, I was very fat.

I attended a small country school. For my first four years of schooling, one teacher taught two grades in one classroom. My class totaled eleven students—eight boys and three girls.

Life as a fat kid is seldom easy, and it wasn't for me. I was often the outcast and had no real friends during those years. Bullying and name calling were common; their favorite name for me was "Hippo." As a result, I spent most of my free time alone.

In high school, I attended Weight Watchers and Overeaters Anonymous, eventually getting down to my goal weight—but I didn't stay there for very long. In my mind's eye, I was still the outcast fat kid. Although I didn't remain at my goal weight for long, I managed to keep most of the weight off for some time. But that didn't stop me from being a target.

After a particularly painful incident in high school, I was once again suicidal.

I actually prayed for death and was disappointed when I woke up every morning. I faced the day with dread. Sometimes the pain and anger were overwhelming. Although I never had access to a gun, I would fantasize about going to school, killing some of the worst offenders, and then killing myself. So, I understand the pain that can cause people to get to that point.

Like most kids, I always had a soft spot for animals, and one of the few comforts I had over those years was the companionship and unconditional acceptance of our farm cats and dogs. Some days I'd get home from school and sit on our front steps, talking to our dog, lamenting about my day.

I also spent a lot of time reading, and two of the books which had a tremendous influence on my life were Man Kind? Our Incredible War on Wildlife by Cleveland Amory and America's Last Wild Horses by Hope Ryden. Man Kind? was a scathing indictment of the hunting and trapping industries and I was shocked at what I was learning, astounded at the cruelty involved in those industries.

In America's Last Wild Horses, the author discussed the plight of these horses, many of which were being captured and sent to slaughter for human consumption.

It horrified me! I expressed my horror and outrage about that to my family (I was around sixteen at the time), to which my dad posed the question, "What's the difference between eating a horse and eating a cow?"

I had to pause for a bit and think about that.

My response was something to the effect that "Horses are pets, and cows are just farm animals, here for us to eat."

Although I tried to convince myself of that, Dad's question haunted me over the years. If I were opposed to the slaughter of horses for food, how could I condone the slaughter of cows, who were also thinking, feeling beings?

Later I learned about other cultures that ate dogs and cats. And, again, I was shocked. But how could I condemn that when I continued to consume cows, pigs, chickens, and turkeys?

I had always assumed that chickens and turkeys were so different from humans, that they were incapable of feeling or thinking the way other animals do. This rationalization was necessary as I spent many years working at Central Kansas Hatchery which my dad owned. Some of that work involved de-toeing, de-snooding, and dubbing (de-combing). Although I never performed them, I also witnessed many de-beakings and de-wingings.

At first this was very difficult and uncomfortable for me, and I had to keep telling myself that birds don't feel pain in the same way we do. I also told myself that this was just an unfortunate but necessary part of life—that we needed to eat animals and animal products to be healthy.

I became desensitized to the mutilations that routinely occurred in the hatchery as standard industry practices and remained in denial for years.

After high school, I attended Bethel College for a couple of years. While there, I made some new friends, including my first boyfriend. Living on campus was exciting, and I felt free, like I could start a new life without all the baggage I'd grown up with. I started smoking and drinking, largely to fit in with new friends, but also to quiet the harsh internal critic and drown out my feelings of inadequacy. Although that critic never stayed away for long, it was a relief to have even a momentary reprieve.

At that point, I wasn't drinking daily, but I did my fair share of binge drinking.

I moved to the "big city" of Wichita in 1979 when I was twenty-one. My boyfriend had also moved to Wichita to attend school so, although we weren't living together then, we spent a lot of time together. Most of that time included beer and often some cheap wine.

After a devastating breakup a few years later, my drinking increased substantially. There were days when I would start drinking after my morning coffee and continue throughout the day, taking periodic naps and never leaving the apartment (I was a student at the time and wasn't working, so I could get by with that for a while.)

I also made a much healthier decision—to adopt a cat to help keep me company.

Although we always had farm cats at home, I discovered that it was a different experience living with an indoor cat 24/7. I really got to know Tash and discovered a beautiful, loving soul. She was three and a half when I adopted her from the Kansas Humane Society. I'll always remember how she loved to drink out of the faucet. Whenever I went into the bathroom, she followed me, jumped in the sink, and licked at the faucet until I turned it on just enough (a trickle) for her to get a drink. She also liked to get in the bathtub and peer out from behind the shower curtain. She would come to greet me when I got home and loved to sit in my lap. She was a wonderful companion who brought me much joy, and I fell in love with her.

In the short five years we were together, she helped open my heart and mind to the realization that animals and humans are so much more alike than different.

Up to this point, I did not understand I could feel such love for a nonhuman being, and I was devastated when she died.

I had a hard time dealing with all those feelings. I continued to self-medicate and turned to alcohol to deal with these painful and unwanted feelings.

After living with several other cats, I became even more convinced that animals were very intelligent, feeling beings, each with their own personality, much like us, and I continued to struggle with the question Dad had asked me years earlier.

In my late twenties, I became involved with a local animal rights group protesting at fur stores and discovered that some members were vegetarians.

Although I had pondered Dad's question for years, I still didn't see the feasibility of giving up meat. But here were some people who had actually done it—and they weren't starving!

They introduced me to two more books which would also prove very influential in my life: Diet for a New America by John Robbins, heir to the Baskin-Robbins fortune, and Animal Liberation by Peter Singer. Both talked about the horrors inflicted on farmed animals.

This group also showed the British movie, The Animal's Film, which presented graphic footage of everything from slaughterhouses to fur farms to research labs to circuses.

Of course, I knew about what happened to chickens and turkeys in the hatchery but wasn't as knowledgeable about the plight of other animals and had never been inside a slaughterhouse.

These books and the film were real eye openers for me. Although I had become desensitized to the hatchery practices, I was much more sensitive to the suffering of the other animals. It was a rather long and painful process for me to re-awaken my compassion for chickens and turkeys.

The pain I felt watching this film and reading these books was almost unbearable. Yet I still had a major mental block regarding poultry: I could watch the videos showing poultry mutilation without being disturbed by it. I was very uncomfortable while watching the videos— not for the reason many people thought, but because it didn't bother me to witness these actions.

I had become so numb for so long that it took a long time for me to allow that "dead" part of me to reawaken. And that reawakening was very uncomfortable. Could it be true that those baby chicks and turkeys could really feel pain? They cried out as though they did. But then they stopped, so I had always reassured myself that it was just a short-lived irritation that quickly subsided.

Yet that didn't feel right. Some of them died. And there was all that blood.

And then I would recall the many times when I would hold them lovingly in my hand, stroking their heads, watching them relax and go to sleep before taking them to be mutilated. If they could be calmed by a child's gentle touch, could they not also be terrified by being grabbed insensitively, not knowing what was coming? And how could they not feel pain when their toes, beaks, or wings were brutally cut off their body with hot blades or wires?

If this was all true, then how could we have allowed ourselves to do all those things? People who worked at the hatchery were good people, and I considered myself a good, kind person too. So how could we get to where this torture and death was considered acceptable?

I kept all those thoughts and feelings to myself. At that time, none of my new veg friends knew what I had done or witnessed at the hatchery. I couldn't talk with them about it, because I was ashamed of what I had been a part of, and I couldn't talk with my old friends about it because they had done the same things and saw nothing wrong with it. I felt as though I were living a double life—a closet vegetarian with old friends and family and closet hatchery worker with my vegetarian friends. Not a comfortable situation, and I was plagued with doubt and full of concerns.

Because of these nagging doubts, I now felt compelled to become vegetarian, although I fought hard to ignore that compulsion. The internal struggle was intense, and I often cried (and/or drank) myself to sleep. Change is so hard, especially when that change involves your self-identity and possible disconnection from those you love. I tried to avoid thinking about it, but my conscience wouldn't let it go.

I was torn: would my family feel rejected by my decision?

I loved my parents dearly and the thought of doing something they might see as rejection tortured me. I knew they were good people— pillars of the community—always ready to lend a helping hand. They were very generous and taught me the importance of giving (of time, talent, and treasure)— to the church; to the community; to society. I feel so blessed to have had such loving parents. Yet I struggled with how to reconcile the knowledge that these good people were inflicting such suffering on innocent beings.

Even worse was another possibility: would they reject me?

Much of my life I'd been an outcast, and all I wanted to do was to "fit in" and be accepted, trying to conform to society's standards. So, the thought of being rejected by some of the few people who had always loved and supported me was terrifying. I still wanted love and acceptance by the family, but no longer wanted association with what had been our livelihood, and the business with which our family had been strongly identified.

The emotional and mental pain was so intense that I once again had frequent thoughts of suicide.

Those early years as a fat, bullied child, had taught me a lot about what it's like to feel alone, helpless, miserable, powerless, and tormented. I was seeing I shared an emotional connection, in a tiny way, with the animals who are exploited and tortured daily their entire lives; who are powerless—on farms, in circus, in research labs, in slaughterhouses.

I often turned to alcohol when I couldn't cope with the pain; the guilt; the shame. I relished the feelings of warmth and relaxation as I took those first sips. As I sunk deeper into oblivion, the critical voices in my head shut up and I blissfully passed out.

It was becoming clearer to me that I could NOT continue living the way I had been. I either needed to change my way of life or end it all.

Ultimately, the pain of remaining the same became greater than the fear of change. At least now I had a few vegetarian friends, so I didn't feel quite so alone.

This was back in the early days of vegetarian options (late 1980s), so it was somewhat of a challenge, but probably the most difficult thing was "coming out" to my family and friends.

It wasn't easy, and it changed some of my relationships. I didn't get invited out to eat as often, and I began to lose connection with some friends.

Some thought that this was just a "phase" and that I'd "come back to my senses" after a while. Little did they know that this would last for the next twenty+ years until I took it one step further and became vegan, shortly after turning fifty.

Several things contributed to my eventual transition to veganism. Over the years, I had become uncomfortable with my consumption of eggs and dairy, knowing how they were produced. I couldn't undo what I'd done at the hatchery; I couldn't "unsee" the horrific videos; I couldn't "unhear" the tortured cries, or "unread" the harrowing descriptions of the slaughterhouse. But I could stop contributing to the animal exploitation.

Once again, I dealt with much internal struggle but finally arrived at the decision that it was less painful to risk the ostracism, ridicule, and exclusion I had always tried so hard to avoid, than it was to keep contributing to the suffering of other beings.

I had eventually concluded that consuming animal products was incompatible with my deepest values of love, compassion, and nonviolence.

But I continued to contribute to my suffering by drinking regularly. By now, alcohol was always in the house, there to help drown out the pain of my past, and I couldn't imagine life without it.

Initially, veganism was a challenge for me —I had always loved cheese and it had been a staple for years. I have to admit, the thought of eliminating it from my diet was scary, and I dreaded the thought of a cheese-free life. But when I considered all the suffering and torture involved, it lost its appeal.

While the most visible part of the vegan way of life is dietary, the term veganism was coined by Donald Watson in 1944, who defined it as "a philosophy and way of living which seeks to exclude—as far as is possible and practicable—all forms of exploitation of, and cruelty to, animals for food, clothing or any other purpose; and by extension, promotes the development and use of animal-free alternatives for the benefit of humans, animals, and the environment. In dietary terms it denotes the practice of dispensing with all products derived wholly or partly from animals."

Becoming vegan also involved changes in my purchasing habits, checking labels to avoid purchasing cleaning products or personal care products that contained animal products or were tested on animals. It was time consuming at first, but well worth the time invested to avoid contributing, inasmuch as possible, to animal cruelty.

Society's indifference to animal suffering is everywhere—it's carried in our unconscious biases and even embedded in our language. These days, I prefer to remind people we can feed two birds with one scone, or that there is more than one way to pet a cat, rather than the more gruesome alternatives in common use.

Although things have certainly changed over the last ten years, vegans are still often misunderstood and intentionally or inadvertently excluded.

Sometimes we're thought of as being difficult, that we care more about animals than people and that we're just trying to push our "agenda" down everyone's throats.

But most of us are vegan because we want to create a kinder, more compassionate and just world for all sentient beings.

We can care about people in addition to caring about animals. Contrary to some people's opinions, our compassion for animals does not preclude compassion for humans. They're not mutually exclusive. Compassion is not (or at least should not be) limited to one race, gender, ethnicity, or species.

Yes, there are some hostile vegans, these are usually people who have been so traumatized by the animal suffering they've witnessed that they lash out against humanity. Even I have had to work through some of that anger towards humans who do terrible things to animals.

But then I remind myself of where I came from and recognize that this is a part of our cultural conditioning, which began around 10,000 years ago. We've been brought up to believe that animals are here for our use, not as beings with their own inherent value and rights to a life free from cruelty, exploitation and fear.

Adopting a vegan lifestyle has been the most profound, transformative, and rewarding change I've made in my life, and my only regret is that I didn't make that change earlier.

Mary Lou Randour in her book, Animal Grace, states, "To absorb the extent and depravity of animal suffering can raise us to a new spiritual level…. Our expanding awareness may lead us to feel that we are experiencing disorganization of the self. Writer Joanna Macy teaches us, however, that what feels like a disintegration of the self in these periods of intense transformation is not the self breaking down, but its defenses. The breakdown of these defenses needs to be welcomed rather than feared, for they have dimmed our awareness and stunted our compassion. Their dissolution can free us spiritually…The structure of the old defensive self must die so that a new, larger, and more encompassing structure can be born."

This was what I feel happened to me. Sometimes I felt as though my world were crashing around me, and all I wanted to do was escape. I was being pushed to evolve, although I just wanted to remain the same and resisted that evolution as long as I could—until it became unbearable.

It had taken a great deal of emotional energy to keep my true feelings from surfacing, and now that I was learning to accept and embrace them, I felt liberated and more at peace with myself. As a result, my spirituality deepened. This was one of the most powerful, positive, and unexpected "side effects" of my lifestyle change.

However, I still struggled with what I had done and with the realization that very good people could do some things which I now considered horrible and unthinkable. So, my drinking continued, helping me to numb the pain of my past.

When I was fifty-eight, I had received some rather disturbing blood work results. My liver enzymes were elevated, and they sent me to a gastroenterologist for further testing. By this time, after about forty years of drinking, I was concerned that it was catching up to me.

The gastroenterologist asked me how much I drank. I wasn't completely honest. I think I said, "maybe one or two glasses of wine per day." Of course, I was talking about the "Big Gulp" size glasses, not the regular wine glasses.

After that conversation, I quit drinking for a short while—maybe ten days (at most). The blood work from the gastroenterologist wasn't concerning enough to call for further testing, so I figured I was off the hook. But I promised myself I'd cut back.

And I did. For a while. But one drink became two became three, etc. Four days without alcohol went to three days to two days to every day. Soon I was back to drinking about a bottle of wine per day, going through a three-liter box every three to four days.

That continued for another couple of years until I came across This Naked Mind: Control Alcohol - Find Freedom, Discover Happiness, & Change Your Life, a book by Annie Grace. She offered a 30-Day Alcohol Experiment, a free online program that encourages participants to question their relationship with alcohol and to go thirty days without drinking. It was rough, especially the first couple of weeks. But, with the help of two excellent coaches (Lorrin Maughan and Sheri Barnes), as well as the support of the online community, I completed the challenge, and continued with it.

I was finally learning to love and accept myself and coming to peace with my past. I was learning to feel my emotions, instead of just numbing them.

Once I awakened and realized how much suffering I could ease by going vegan, I committed to not contribute to animal exploitation. Yes, I still had cravings from time to time, especially for cheese (unsurprising, as there is evidence to suggest that cheese is physically addictive. This is because of casomorphins, a naturally occurring morphine-like compound in cow's milk.) But my motivation was strong enough to overcome those cravings. I just couldn't bear the thought of being responsible for causing the suffering and death of animals any longer. No palate preference could ever justify that.

Developing self-compassion took a little longer and was much more difficult. Dealing with all the guilt, shame, fear, anger, and grief was not easy. But that was what I required for me to reach the decision to stop drinking. After all, I wasn't really hurting anyone but myself. I was living alone (with my cat Mandi), and nobody else was really affected by my drinking. At this point, I seldom drank much in public, preferring to do my drinking at home alone so I could consume as much as I wanted without worrying about what others thought.

I had never missed work because of it (although I did, on a few occasions, work with a massive hangover). I didn't cancel plans once I had committed to them (although I did, on more than one occasion, turn down invitations or remain noncommittal because I preferred to stay at home and drink alone). Most people had no idea how much I was drinking daily—or even that I was a regular drinker; I think I hid it well!

I still feel overwhelmed and powerless when I look at all the suffering and injustices in this world. But I know that things can change. And I feel that it's now my turn to work to rectify the situations that I had been a part of for so long, and to work towards a more humane and more loving world for all of us, human and nonhuman alike. My intention is to help counteract our cultural conditioning, by encouraging people to awaken to the truth of what is happening and to live according to their own values of peace and compassion. As Albert Schweitzer stated, "We must fight against the spirit of unconscious cruelty with which we treat the animals. Animals suffer as much as we do…. It is our duty to make the whole world recognize it."

Until I came to this realization that my life had meaning and was worth living, I saw no reason to quit drinking. When I truly felt that I had a mission and a purpose greater than myself, I cared enough to make the effort.

As I continue to evolve on my journey of sobriety and activism, I am learning to be kinder towards myself. Some days it's easier than others. Like many people, I used to think that self-compassion was just being selfish. But I've learned that, when I'm compassionate towards myself, it is so much easier to be truly compassionate towards others.

Turning sixty was a major milestone for me. I realized that my time is getting shorter, and I still have much more that I hope to accomplish in this life. I want to be a force for change— to bring more love and peace into the world and to live authentically, true to my values. So, with the help of some very dear friends, I picked up the broken fragments of myself and pieced them together with love. No longer did I feel the need to live in shame or to hide anything. Or to be two very different people, living in one body. For the first time in my life, I felt whole.

# LOVE AND ROMANCE

# We Sat in the Cab of His Pick-up Truck

### Martha Williams Prentice

We sat in the cab of his pick-up truck,
  metallic cherry red and chrome,
parked at the corner under a streetlight;
  large drops of rain pattered
against the windshield;
  splashing and splattering,
collecting into streamlets, running, reaching out,
  dividing here, and reconnecting there,
where the two of us looked through
  and beyond to somewhere unseen,
following the forever changing maze.

The side windows were down just enough
  to draw in a clean earthy smell of rain,
that watermelon smell of fresh-mowed grass,
  faint scents of roses drooping on the trellis
arched over a garden gate.
  Then we felt a cool rush of air
brush against our faces,
 focusing our attention on the intimacy,
and painful beauty of that evening in May.

Without words we turned and looked at each other.
   He took my hands in his
in the tender way he always did
   that asked me to move closer.
His arms drew me into him, my hand touching his hair,
   our lips caressing, cheek against cheek.
One whispered, "I'm sorry." The other, "Forgive me."

The radio gave us waves of a lovely melody
   that flowed over us and around us,
moving and mending our fragile hearts
   to love and laugh again.

## It Was the Longest of Days

It was the longest of days …
the sea was almost a sapphire blue,
calm and rolling gently.
Along the edge where sea meets shore,
I walked and watched the waning sun,
remembering the color of your eyes,
and the way they sometimes glisten with desire.

# I'll Hold You Gently

## C. Holden

I'll hold you gently in my mind, and forever in my heart.
Time will pass so slowly when we are apart.
Though the road may be not steady, as we journey along our way.
But my rewards are taken in sunsets, as life before us lay.
We'll get through it all together, as we take it all in stride.
And when life is over,
I'll see you on the other side.

# Our Love Will Last

One thousand violins playing
Ten thousand voices singing
through the universe
Like our love will last
through eternity

# Everlasting Love

## Carleen Dix Westover

The elderly gentleman slips his bent fingers around the small, frail hand of the woman walking next to him. Slowly, carefully they walk along the sidewalk, side by side, hand in hand. Nearing a wooden bench in the park, they stop, the man wipes the worn wood seat with his white handkerchief. He gently helps to lower her down to sit back and rest, her small feet dangle above the grassy ground as age has shortened her stature.

Sitting beside her, his arm around her humped shoulders, he gives her a worried look. She hears his deep sigh and pats his knobby knee with her hand. "I'm fine, sweetheart, just a bit wobbly." A smile covers her wrinkled face as her faded eyes twinkle at him, her still handsome husband of sixty-five years. Each thinking of their time together, wondering where the years have gone. So much has filled their lives with children and grandchildren but now just the two of them.

After twenty minutes of watching children playing and admiring the park flowers he asks, "Ready, my dear?" She nods her head. He wraps his shaky arm around her tiny waist, matching his steps to her small ones, they shuffle down the winding sidewalk.

As the sun shines brightly, he removes his brimmed, ragged hat and places it on her head to give her a cooling shade. "Thank you," she whispers.

Slow but sure they travel down the long sidewalk, leaving the beautiful park, until reaching a small brick house. The humble abode needs the trim painted, a cracked window fixed, and the grass cut. Even with that, the small home is inviting, with multi-colored flowers along the cobbled walk and large trees shading the house. A black and white cat laying along one step, looks up at them, yawns and mews with a quivering sound of an older cat. He stretches out

to reveal his tummy, begging for a rub. Carefully, the old man leans over and rubs the cat, invoking a loud purr.

"That's a good kitty," the small quiet words come from the frail woman.

Cautiously, the man helps his wife up the wooden steps, as he has done many times, especially this last year. Bones and wood creak with each step. Once on the porch, they sit on the swing, padded with cushions, gently swaying. She turns, softly touches his wrinkled cheek, and gives him a quirky smile. She places his old hat back onto his gray head as he holds her hand ever so gently.

She whispers, "You're my best friend."

He winks, "And you're mine, sweetheart.

She lays her head on his thin shoulder with a sigh. Home together, just the two of them, forever.

# When We Were Young

## Martha Williams Prentice

(I thought this was to be a poem when I began writing,
but a persistent melody kept playing along, and so it became a song.)

When we were young, and time was flung, to phantom wind,
Our world was small, and we were all, that mattered then.
The nights were long, desire was strong,
We only heard the Mockingbird sing love's refrain.

When we were young, and songs were sung, to starlit skies,
We spoke our dreams, by flowing streams, of paradise.
Our plans were grand, we took a stand,
We only heard the Mockingbird sing love's refrain.

When we were young, our hearts were hung, in foolish pride,
For all to see, the misery, that life can't hide.
Mistakes were made, regrets were laid,
We only heard the Mockingbird sing love's refrain.

When we were young, and bells were rung, to sound the truth,
With wisdom's light, we fought the night, and unchained youth.
We saw our path, so clear, no wrath.
We only heard the Mockingbird sing love's refrain.
We only heard the Mockingbird sing love's refrain.

# Tied at the Heart

## C.A. Lemont

Took a step back in time the other day ...
I honestly didn't know what to say.
So many years have passed us by ...
To remember all the how's or why's.

Memories bring a smile to my face.
All those times I can still retrace.
Remember the clown face for Halloween?
How many years has that been?

Oh, we shared so many things!
We'd laugh! We'd dance! We'd sing!
Then I went and grew some wings.
And like a kite without a string ...

Drifting, with no one to hold me down.
Out I flew from that little town.
So; here we are a lifetime apart.
Still tied together in our hearts.

# It Was a Dark Wet Tuesday

Martha Williams Prentice

It was a dark wet Tuesday,
about 3:00 in the afternoon.
At a distance, thunder rumbled,
slow, low, and long,
out of black clouds
hovering heavy in the north.

My mind wandered back to that evening
you and I walked along the Seine at dusk,
where glowing streaks of pink and orange,
reflected on the water, were pulled by the current,
like molten metals atop the surface of the river,
stretched, thinned,
and curved, around the bend …
out of sight, but always remembered.

# End of the Rainbow

## C. Holden

When I leave this earth
I'll not be far from you
I'll be like a faint light in the dark
Or a fleeting shadow or a slight breeze on your cheek
I'll wait for you on that great cloud in the sky
And when you join me
We will go and find the streets paved with gold
At the end of the rainbow.

# The Rose in the Garden

There is a rose in the garden, it's blooming just for you
The sunlight in the morning sparkling on the dew
Like the diamonds in your eyes and the warmth in your heart
Like the rose in the garden, we will never ever part

Now the rose in the garden will fade away someday
But bloom again with glorious beauty another day
With the warmth of the sun and a true heart
Like the rose in the garden, we will never ever part

# First Love

## Carleen Dix Westover

Jennifer smiled with anticipation; all her plans were falling in place for the big event. A perfect sunny day for her family and friends as they gathered to celebrate her wedding. It would soon be time to board the old-fashioned train car, travel the short distance to the beautiful garden and marry her beloved Tyler. He would be waiting for his princess.

"It's time," her bridesmaid, Teresa, said as her face lit up with a beaming smile.

With careful attention to the long, lacy dress, she helped the bride board the gleaming red train. The inside of the wedding car brought gasps of delight from both as they entered. Lush, royal red lounging seats accented with gold, antique lights hanging from a velvet ceiling and plush carpet to complete the gorgeous picture. Dreams of her Cinderella wedding had come true.

The women sat in complete comfort, deep in their own thoughts. Only a hint of the engine sound penetrated the train car as it moved forward along the track. Scenery of lush trees and rolling grassland passed by the heart-shaped windows. Jennifer felt as if she had waited her whole life for this moment. Thoughts of her first love becoming her final love had butterflies fluttering in her tummy.

In less than ten minutes, the train came to a gentle stop, revealing a breathtaking site before them. A huge castle loomed in the distance, a shimmering sun streaming around it, producing a spectacular sight to behold. Perfection was the magical word for the day.

In her excitement, Jennifer took the steps of the train a bit too quick, catching her high-heel shoe in the iron grate. She heard a crack and knew her silver shoe had broken.

"Oh, no," Jennifer cried out. Teresa helped to gather the plush ballroom dress before it could touch the ground, then assisted her down to the brick platform.

"Now what?" the young bridesmaid questioned with desperation.

"Not to worry, my dear," Jennifer giggled as she placed her other shoe into the grate and broke the heel off. "Matching shoes." She held them up with pride, then slipped them onto her feet. "Let's go," she replied with glee.

As they approached the glorious garden, the scene of white chairs filled with chatting people, stood out in perfect lines on each side of the grassy aisle. Flowers adorned the chairs, making a rainbow of color. A flute began playing as the pretty bridesmaid floated down the green pathway in her light blue dress.

Jennifer slipped her broken shoes off and began her slow walk towards Tyler. Handsome as the day they met, with a touch of maturity he had lacked before. His broad smile and the glint in his dark eyes showed the love he felt for her.

Even more beautiful today than before, he thought. He had waited for this day ever since they had met. It had almost not happened, but today was real, he assured himself. The promise of the future filled him with confidence and happiness.

The preacher began with their story of young love, separation and reunification. He spoke of life interfering with plans yet how time can work it all out for the best. Holding hands, they spoke of their love and hope for the future. After exchanging vows and rings, Reverend Mills announced them husband and wife. The pair shared a loving kiss of the decades amid a smiling and clapping crowd.

Teresa threw her arms around the happy bride and hugged her in excitement. "Oh, Grandma, you finally married your long-lost love in your dream wedding!"

# While Lying in a Summer Meadow

## Martha Williams Prentice

While lying in a summer meadow,
   a bed of lavender and blue,
   my head caressed upon your chest,
   we took the time for food and rest,
   an afternoon in pastel hue.

The golden warmth was spread upon us,
   a glow on arm and legs, on faces,
   to slow the rhythm of breath and heart,
   which beckons tranquil themes of thought,
   remembered scenes of times and places,
   ... while lying in a summer meadow.

# It Must Have Been That Day in August

### Martha Williams Prentice

It must have been that day in August ...
  you walked out of the barn,
  stood in the shade the truck made;
  wiped your brow, your face, the back of your neck,
  slow, and deliberate,
  with a blue-and-white bandana
  always shoved in your right hip pocket;
  a red checked shirt, long sleeves rolled to the elbows,
  snug jeans, worn and clean,
  belt and boots my favorite caramel brown.

You leaned against the truck a moment,
  looked toward the house.
  I was standing by the table on the long back porch,
  pouring iced lemon tea,
  sweetened just the way you liked it.
  You slowly started walking up to the house,
  a subtle eagerness showed in your stride,
  and a flush rushed through me.
  Maxx ran up to beg for attention.
  You let him hear your voice; your face against his face,
  your gentle hands rubbing his back and belly,
  giving him the smell of you that satisfied him.

You walked up the steps, our eyes touched,
  and I fell in love with you again.

# This Late December Morning Is Cold

## Martha Williams Prentice

This late December morning is cold,
with bulging clouds of white and gray;
trees dark, dormant, ashy brown;
decades of winters they've stood like this,
stripped, silent, still;
no wind to push, shove, and bend,
like the fury of yesterday.

Exposed is a squirrel's nest
deep and secure in the highest fork
of the tallest branch of the catalpa tree
on that side of the street.

This scene that's spread before me,
just outside my east windows,
will reappear on a page in my sketch book;
and I'll remember the cardinal
that stopped on top of my balcony rail,
admired his reflection in the windowed wall,
then darted to an arching branch of the pear tree,
and gave a call to summon his mate;
she came to him quickly,
then the two flew, side by side,
over the roof of the church across the street,
past the north side of the bell tower,
and out of sight in a fluttering streak
of scarlet and muted gold.

# There, on the Potting Bench

## Martha Williams Prentice

There, on the potting bench,
laid your hat and garden gloves,
soft and worn to fit your shape.
I sensed your arms around me,
heard your voice against my hair.
Slowly, I turned to the pear trees
that shade the hammock and the swing.
They swung, one, and then the other,
as if from leaf shadows dangling,
and I smelled sandalwood
when your quiet laugh
moved through me.

# The Last Time I Saw You

## Martha Williams Prentice

The last time I saw you
a sudden pain ripped through my heart.
And the last time I heard your voice
I was in a vacuum, the air sucked out of me.

It happened just the way I knew it would,
and now it was killing me,
the blinding flash of truth,
dry consuming heat,
then the gray non-life remains of what had been.

It was done, over, no longer holding me down.
Now your presence didn't fill the room.
The oppression was lifted, I gasped for air.
Why I allowed you to mistreat me—
Why my efforts were never good enough—
It didn't matter, I was free.
Oh, my God, I was free.
I stepped over all of you, and walked on.

# Inspector Noir

## Mary McKay

Having a mirror on the wall next to the front door was a practice in the Arbuthnot house. It had been passed down, without thought, for so many generations that no one knew when or how it had originated. Being a descendant of that illustrious family, Lucille Arbuthnot had hung her mirror to the right of the door at a height that made it possible for her to see the collar of her dress and adjust the angle of her hat.

A lady didn't just plop a hat on her head, any old way, she had to position it and arrange it just so. Lucille had watched her mother inspect her reflection in her mirror and tug and pull the brim until the image of a queen, or an angel, or possibly a coy and simpering tart appeared, as she lifted an eyebrow and pursed her lips in a pouting pose.

Valentine's Day was the perfect occasion for Lucille to wear her new red hat and the thrill of having it project just the right mixture of provocation and innocence was essential tonight. Inspector LaMoyne Noir would call at precisely nine o'clock and she intended to be punctual and perfect. He wouldn't find fault with her.

The small credenza beneath the mirror made life easier for Lucille as she plucked her house key from the sweetly, hand-painted china dish placed in the center of the top and dropped it into her evening bag. Again, the familiar placement of furniture, rugs, and other bits and pieces that make a house a home were inherited from her family history as surely as she inherited her blue eyes and lovely complexion from her genetic pool.

A skittering noise behind her caused her to slowly open the drawer of the credenza and quietly extract the gun kept there. Another family tradition had placed it there for safety and convenience. Who knew who might present at the front entrance.

She quietly turned around and took aim, fired and exclaimed, "Got it!"

After replacing the revolver in the credenza drawer, she calmly walked across the room, picked the small mouse up by the tail and took it to the back door where she tossed it outside into the night.

Washing her hands, she returned to the front of the house to await Inspector Noir. He was always on time and she was looking forward to a pleasant evening of his masculine company. He had features she found most attractive: sturdy build, a chiseled face, a sweet mouth with clean white teeth, even if they were a bit crooked. He wore his hair trimmed short and combed straight forward as if it refused to lay any other way. It made her think of a Grecian Brutus, or a Gladiator. His hair was fine, medium brown and soft and sweet smelling. Everything about Inspector LaMoyne Noir was compelling.

Lucille walked back to the mirror and reflected once more on her own appearance. Was her nose a bit too long? Her eyelashes were straight and not the curving sweep of lashes she had hoped for. What on earth did he see in her? It was distressing to consider all the shortcomings. If only she had been born with a bit of glamour. She had continued to hope that like the Ugly Duckling, she would one day turn into a swan.

A polite knock on the door announced his arrival, and she gave her hat one more pull to hide the high forehead that no amount of powder seemed to dim. She bared her teeth to make sure she wasn't wearing a bit of supper on them and putting her most charming smile on her face, opened the door for Inspector LaMoyne Noir.

"Come into this house," she said.

"Are you ready for me?" he asked.

"Indeed I am."

Inspector Noir entered the quaint little cottage and removing his hat, gave a brief bow in her direction.

"You look delightful," he said. And he meant it. There was something about Lucille that felt safe, warm, and welcoming to him. The smell of a freshly fired revolver reached his nose and it piqued his curiosity. She was a person of substance. Up to anything.

"Thank you, Inspector."

A smile curved the corners of her mouth and he wanted to kiss it and pull her into his arms. It just wouldn't do. He would rumple her hair and wrinkle her dress. I he could just get that hat off her head, he would be satisfied!

"Perhaps we could spend the evening here?" he inquired. There was a mystery here, and he was a curious man, if nothing else.

## Inspector Noir Apologizes

"Forgiveness means abandoning all hope of a better past, and, accepting yourself for better or worse as your lot in life." Inspector Noir could recall his father's words of wisdom as if he had just spoken them.

There was nothing for it but admit that he had made an arse of himself and needed to change his attitudes. He would eat crow and it didn't feel good. He was certain it felt better than contemplating the thought of not seeing Miss Lucille Arbuthnot again. Surely there was a way he could turn the table and repair their friendship.

Inspector Noir knocked on the cottage door and crossed the fingers of his left hand as he held the bouquet of violets behind his back in his right hand. Nothing. He knocked again, this time a little louder. Still nothing.

Frustrated, he decided to do a bit of detective work and using the back of his hand he parted the thick herbaceous bushes to the right of the door and directly beneath the windows. A quick, cautionary peek into the cottage window gave a satisfactory answer to his curiosity. He could see through the cottage interior enough to see the back door standing wide open.

He disentangled himself from the brambles and leaned back far enough to see a nice rose covered trellis leading to the rear garden.

Brushing himself off and sliding the toes of his shoes over the back of each pant leg he opened the gateway of the trellis and followed the stone path to the rear of the house which revealed a tidy kitchen garden with Miss Arbuthnot kneeling amid a nice stand of hollyhocks in the rear corner.

"Hello," he said.

Her lovely blue-eyed gaze darted to him and quickly changed from startled to angry.

"What are you doing here?" she questioned.

"I've come to apologize and beg your forgiveness." He produced the bouquet of violets and thrust them towards her.

"Really? How very nice of you."

He extended his left hand to assist her in standing up.

"I wanted to apologize four doubting your ability to shoot a mouse on the run. It is an accomplishment few of our officers can attain. Even those at the top of their class in school. I have a fault of thinking my knowledge is sufficient to understand the world and human nature. I am determined to change my ways."

"Go ahead and say it," Lucille said in a sarcastic voice. "A young lady shouldn't even be acquainted with a revolver, let alone be proficient in using it."

"I did not say that!"

"You may as well have done," she continued. "Your quick 'lucky shot' implied as much and left me no room for doubt."

Clearly, she was not in a mood to forgive and forget. He didn't really enjoy begging, but he could surely express enough regret that it would convince her. It was important.

"May I ask again for your forgiveness? You see, I realized after my blunder, that I wanted our friendship to continue and in time I have great plans for our future together. My ignorance of women is only part of the problem. You can also blame it on my own inexperience. But I believe I can change and am determined to change. At least I am hoping you will give me that chance.

"Only if I may ask why you are wearing a very large spider web on the back of your jacket?" she inquired.

When LaMoyne looked at her carefully, he could see the laughter in her eyes. They were so blue! Changing his attitude didn't seem so difficult after all.

# Inspector Noir Disappears

Finding a place to hide was imperative. Gossip had it that Inspector LaMoyne Noir was in line for another promotion and he did not want to receive it. His status in the department's hierarchy was ideal for his current goals. Those goals included Miss Lucille Arbuthnot. Working nights was not an option at this time of his life. He could climb the corporate tree later.

He would create a scenario where he was in disguise and rumored to be on a stake-out that made it impossible for anyone to discover his whereabouts. He would literally be invisible. Sherlock Holmes didn't have a thing on him. A nappy wig, a few facial hairs that covered his handsome features and a search through his neighbor, Austin's closet of theatrical costumes, would transform him completely.

Austin's old car would complete the deception. After sitting for years at the curb, the old Buick still ran and other than an occasional backfire it suited LaMoyne's purpose. It was actually liberating to drive a vehicle that had so many dings that a new dent or scrape wouldn't alter its value—it was already a wreck and worthless as anything but scrap metal.

LaMoyne was comfortable with his new persona, except for one important thing. He couldn't show up at Lucille's door looking like a homeless street person. The ability to change from one person to another had become such a pain in the neck that from time to time he found it convenient, and interesting, to stay in his disguise and just observe her comings and goings. It was a rotten thing to do, but hey, if she never knew it wouldn't be a problem—would it?

One day he was so bold as to speak to her in a low, whispering voice, and was delighted to see her curiosity taking him in. It didn't appear that she recognized him, but she seemed to respond to him in a manner that almost made him jealous. Surely, she wasn't attracted to other men?

"May I help you sir?" she asked, from behind the counter of her little bookstore.

"I was looking for a friend's house," he said.

"What is your friends name?"

"Lucille."

"Really!" she replied. "How extraordinary. My name is Lucille. The Undercover Bookstore is my shop."

"Oh, I don't think so," LaMoyne gave her an examining look. "I'm afraid you are much too pretty to be the object of my search," he said. "No mention was made of a beauty."

"My, my!" Lucille said. "I am flattered, I'm sure. Tell me who sent you and for what purpose."

"My father," said LaMoyne. "He said his old war buddy had a daughter that lived in this neighborhood, but he also said his friend wasn't much of a looker, so not to expect much."

"Well, I can clear all this up if you will tell me his friend's name."

"Keith Arbuthnot, was my father's friend's name."

"That was my father, but you are a few years too late. Dad passed away three years ago. Is it possible I could be of help?"

"No, my father simply wanted to renew the acquaintance. However, I would find it all worthwhile if you would share a cup of coffee with me at one of the nearby cafes."

He could see her mind at work trying to decide if she should be polite to the son of one her father's old acquaintances or take up with a stranger. It seemed she was inclined to trust him, even with his outrageous appearance.

"We have a little coffee area here in the shop. If you would care to follow me, I will join you over a cup of coffee and perhaps we can give your father some information on mine."

She headed to the back of the store and a small area dedicated to sitting and enjoying a beverage and dessert. With a few small, round, glass-topped tables and chairs, it was a terrific marketing idea. She poured them each a coffee and placed two nice peanut butter cookies on a napkin and sat down across from LaMoyne.

He sat down and gave a little sigh. It was so nice to sit here and have coffee with her. Now, he feared his disguise might not conceal his affection. Unfortunately, just plain jealousy leaped into the picture and before he could stop himself, he had blurted out, "I love your little bookstore. However, I am more impressed with the owner than with the store. Your sapphire necklace is a perfect accessory for your beautiful blue eyes. Any chance I could take you out to dinner this evening?" All his inhibitions seemed to have fled when he was wearing the disguise.

"I am flattered, but I am also in a very special relationship that I don't care to jeopardize," she said with a finality that felt very comforting.

"Thank you for letting me know," he said. "I am jealous of the lucky fellow that it is fortunate I don't have a rope, or I would be tempted to hang myself. Please, tell me about him."

"That is unnecessary. However, I see a customer that looks like she is ready to pay. Enjoy your coffee and cookie," she said as she stood and walked toward the front of the store.

"Rats!" That was a waste of time, but also made him feel like a real jerk for being such a low life as to hit on her in such an underhanded way. Now, he feared she would recognize him under his disguise and would lose respect for him because of his lack of trust in her. He decided to see if he could just slither out of the store like the snake he felt like and avoid future contact.

"Hey buddy!" LaMoyne heard Lucille yell down the street at him. "You plan to pay for your coffee and cookies?" He darted around the corner and disappeared into the crowd.

"Wait until I tell LaMoyne about this yahoo tonight," Lucille said, with a laugh.

## Inspector Noir Where are You?

I could smell them coming. The pheromones were simply screaming and as soon as they came past the split-leaf philodendron I spotted them without any question. I was hanging out in my hammock and under most circumstances I wouldn't have moved a muscle, but this pair had piqued my interest and being an incurable romantic, I climbed down from my holiday hiatus and crossed the cage to get a better look. I wasn't disappointed.

It was like walking into a cloud of perfume. Think hyacinths and mock-orange bush. Yes, it was that enticing. I could smell a wedding in the near future and didn't expect what happened next. Apparently,

I wasn't the only animal that had sniffed the rarefied air of the Jane Goodall Exhibit at Sedgwick County Zoo. The gorillas were simply making fools of themselves. If they had reached my age, they would have been able to control their hormones a little better.

If I was a writer and had a pencil and paper, I could make a fortune out of the stories my imagination was weaving in my mind. I will do my best to tell you what I saw.

A darned good-looking young man, (I heard her call him LaMoyne) and his pretty sweetheart, (I heard him call her Lucille) were pretending to be looking at the animals. They didn't fool me, I could see the side-ways glances, as they took measure of each other. I would say they were pleased with their evaluations as they both had dilated pupils, a sure sign of pleasure. A piece of paper couldn't have separated them. How lovers can get so close without touching I could never figure out, but it happens.

The young man pointed to that idiot, I call Ralph, as if he was one of the wonders of the world. I can promise you that Ralph is one of the dumbest chimpanzees I have ever had to endure. The lovely lady was shaking her head in disagreement and they discussed the boring topic of Ralph as if he was worthy of mention. My appreciation for the man went up several notches as I saw him place his hand in the middle of her waist and turn her attention to the cage I was in. I could have laughed out loud.

Sly fellow, he didn't remove his hand and I could only suspect that it was burning a hole in her back and giving him a great deal of satisfaction to have been able to manufacture this ruse. The charming pair was examining me like I was a rare fossil or museum piece. I decided to give them something to look at.

I know it was foolish, but I couldn't help myself and looked around my cage for something to use as a prop for my show. The only thing I could see was the rope swing that hung from the attic and I sauntered over to it and grabbed hold and started walking backwards. I thought that would give them the idea that I was going to do something more and I tried my best to think what might make a good impression. Walking backward is a real accomplishment for most animals, especially horses.

Now, I think I should tell you I am not as young as most of the animals at the zoo, but I'm not completely washed up either. My hair is still red and although not as thick and luxurious as it once was, it has a certain charm. At least I sort of vainly think so. Thankfully, it isn't full of ticks and fleas. I took a running jump and swung as high as I could thrust myself into the air. It was exhilarating! They stood still, and their mouths were gaping open.

The young woman seemed impressed and I was so happy that I made a second foray into the air, getting even higher than the first run. Now the young man had his hand up around her shoulder and she had taken her hand and grasped his to show she was happy not only with me, but with him too.

I had done my part and my muscles were feeling strained. I let myself come to a stop and finished my act with a nice flourish. I walked to the window of the cage and looked at them both with sincere affection. They seemed to get the message and she brought her other arm around behind his back and laid her head on his shoulder.

Love is still alive and well and that makes me feel a tremendous satisfaction. I enjoyed several romantic encounters in my youth and my children are all grown and out in the world on their own life journeys. Just seeing evidence of the continuation of love is a good tonic. For now, I am going back to my hammock and give my body a chance to rest up from the exercise.

# A LOVE FOR ALL TIME

### Starla Criser

Her young face eager,
she trails after the boy.
He moans and groans.
She pretends and dreams
of the man he will become.

His youthful face hopeful,
he trails after the girl.
They date and hold hands.
He hopes and dreams
of the woman she will become.

Her mature face thoughtful,
his wrinkled face reflective,
they trail after each other.
They argue and worry
as they struggle and plan.

He sees her health failing,
his heart fills with dread.
They share and remember
the best and worst of times.
Both treasure their life
together ... forever.

# MEMORIES AND MOMENTS

# Mother's Sacrificial Gift

## Jean Welle

The year was 1952. To prepare for the upcoming J. C. Knight Elementary School PTA meeting in Jonesboro, Indiana, my entire fifth grade class had to memorize a song. The boys prepared to sing a song about their pets and we girls memorized a lengthy song about our dolls of which only one stanza remains in my memory: "My dolly has fine dresses." During the last rehearsal, our music teacher asked us girls to bring our favorite dolls to hold on stage while we sang.

I could hardly wait to get home. I bounded off the school bus and raced ahead of my sisters into the house. "Mom!" I hollered. "We need to go to town right away to buy me a new doll for tomorrow night's PTA meeting." She gave me a negative look but said nothing. I persisted. "No, really, Mom! I have to have a new doll tomorrow night because all of us girls have to bring our dolls to hold while we sing."

"We will do no such thing," she said with a set jaw. Seeing my disappointment, she added, "Just what is wrong with your doll, Jeannie?"

I hadn't played with my doll for a year or two except to appease my younger sisters. It took a moment to ponder the unexpected response. "She has nothing to wear," I said woefully, unable to think of anything worse on the spur of the moment.

"Bring me your doll," Mother retorted, not looking up as the sewing machine hummed.

With renewed hope, I leaped up the stairs two steps at a time to fetch my doll. I found her in the toy box without a stitch of clothing on her soft cloth body. Shiny blue marble-like eyes rolled open as I lifted her from the clutter, revealing a few missing eyelashes. An ugly chip on her head flawed her painted black hair—not pretty like the new dolls in the stores who had real hair. Surely Mother would see how embarrassed I would be to hold such a pathetic doll in public.

Mother examined my doll and then said, "She will do just fine." Case closed! That was her final answer.

The next day at school I listened as the girls in my class bragged about their new dolls. When they asked me about mine, I told them I would bring my only doll, and that she would do just fine, desperately trying to convince myself as I spoke. I didn't hustle off the bus that afternoon. Mother had promised that she would try to have my green corduroy jumper finished by the time I got home to wear to the PTA meeting, but I knew how busy she was. Maybe that, too, wasn't happening.

The first thing I saw when I opened the door was my new green corduroy jumper, laid out on the dining room table. I gave Mother my biggest smile and hurried to touch it. As I reached for it, something else caught my eye. Laying on top of my jumper was my doll, wearing a green corduroy coat with matching bonnet and boots. She was beautiful!

My doll was the envy of all my classmates that evening, and I couldn't have been prouder to hold her on stage. Mother's sacrifice on my behalf instilled in me how to brighten another person's day by taking the time to use what I have on hand and the talents I possess. Perhaps that's the reason the only stanza I remember is: "My dolly has fine dresses."

# My Mother

## Mary Brockman

On my journey to get a degree someday, I took an English Literature class this semester. As we studied Chaucer and his Canterbury Tales, we were given the assignment to add a pilgrim to the Canterbury Tales. I struggled to do as Chaucer and write about people I meet in my daily work. I didn't seem to know quite enough about any of them to complete the assignment and I wasn't able to find enough creative ability to make up enough about them either. I went to bed still struggling with the assignment.

The next morning when I got up, I had the idea to use Mother, and I just sat down and wrote. It looked good and I turned it in. It was returned with an A. I asked for help "Polishing" it but the instructor said that he didn't see any way to improve it and was going to submit it for publication in the school paper. Mother is very proud of the paper I wrote about her and so here it is:

I am a schoolteacher, also a reader, a nurse, a widow, a mother.

I have a quiet voice but at times a hint of schoolteacher or mothers voice.

I am dainty and petite, dressed in purple dress with a purple hat and a purple eye to match.

I have a crooked leg and a crooked cane and I fall a lot.

I can tat and crochet and sew, I make my own clothes.

I eat very little meat but lots of salad with dandelion greens and some blossoms for color.

I like to eat ice cream as a special treat.

An apple a day keeps the doctor away and a banana a day for some potassium.

Many years of walking, all of Wichita, back and forth have made my bones strong.

Early retirement years I spent traveling around the word, Russia, Mexico, England and more.

Spare time I go bowling just to keep in shape, we often win first place.

I have a TV to watch when the weather is bad, let Benny Hinn keep me company.

I am surrounded by my magazines and books, collected for my retirement years.

My eyes no longer see well, the books and magazines do me little good.

I have a porch full of cat houses, and a bench to sit upon and tell a tale or two.

I could tell a tale about my cats, they keep me company.

Or maybe a tale from the past, I lived through the depression.

Or maybe a tale about the one room school with all eight grades and a hot lunch program.

Or maybe a tale about being a bride during the war with ration books and a one burner stove.

# I Once Knew A Woman

## Starla Criser

I once knew a woman
not famous by far,
but to those who knew her
brighter than every star.

A light glowed inside her
never dark or grim,
her kindness and caring
unhidden within.

The world was her playground,
her home and her life.
She never gave up,
not in good or in strife.

If someone needed help,
all they need do was ask.
She never said no,
assisting in any task.

She had the warmth of a child,
an angelic soul,
a temper of fire
and a heart of gold.

Her affect on my life
has absolutely no end.
She is my sun and my moon,
my rain and my wind.

In my mind and my heart,
I wish every day
to someday be like her
if only a small way.

I once knew a woman
not like any other,
my heart will always belong
to this woman, my mother.

Written by my daughter, Angela, in 1996.

# Sleep Now, Baby

## Martha Williams Prentice

(This is a lullaby I wrote two months before our first child was born.)

> Go to sleep now, Baby
> Mama's precious joy,
> > Off you go to dreamland,
> > > With your favorite toy, with your favorite toy.

> Go to sleep now, Baby
> Lie so very still,
> > In my arms I'll rock you,
> > > Climb that golden hill, climb that golden hill.

> Go to sleep now, Baby
> Child of blessed grace,
> > Sandman sprinkles star dust,
> > > Gently 'cross your face, gently 'cross your face.

> Go to sleep now, Baby
> Close your sleepy eyes
> > Hear the angels' voices
> > > Sing this lullaby, sing this lullaby

Go to sleep now, Baby
With your dreamy smile
   My heart beats with your heart
      Only for awhile, only for awhile

Go to sleep now, Baby
As I hold you close,
   Little hands so lovely,
      Like a velvet rose, like a velvet rose.

Go to sleep now, Baby
When I lay you down,
   In the glow of moonbeams,
      Shining all around, shining all around.

Go to sleep now, Baby
As you're kissed goodnight,
   In God's tender keeping,
      Till the morning light, till the morning light.

Go to sleep now, Baby
Words can never say,
   Oh, how much I love you,
      Now and for always, now and for always.

# Momma

## C.A. Lemont

Momma, your smile will always be,
The greatest thing on Earth to me.

It warmed my heart and made me grin,
To see that smile when I walked in.

You taught me love was important to share.
You showed me how to truly care.

Momma, if I could hold you right now;
I'd say, "It's okay, we'll get through this somehow."

I promised I would call you every day;
Only the angels could keep me away.

I'll wait for that smile in the heavens above,
And thank our Father for my Mother's Love.

# My Sweet Maxine:
# Goodbye, Mama

## Ann Alvis

*This story is part of one of many stories my mother told me about her childhood days before she passed away.*

It was a cold January day the wind was blowing hard. Maxine heard limbs on the trees snapping off and hitting the ground because of ice accumulation. The snow was getting deeper alongside the house and air crept in through the cracks of the old walls of their house.

She hunkered behind two large wood crates covered with a green wool blanket in the next room. She was trying to hear what the ladies from the children's home said to her mother, who was crying, hanging tightly to her baby sister, Joann.

It wasn't good the way Mama was sobbing so loud. Maxine had seen her tears.

Joann jumped from Mama's lap and raced over to Maxine. She felt safe with her as they hid from the ladies. Orpha, her older sister by two years, made her way there as well. Maxine tried to comfort them, keep them quiet, and shared the blanket with them.

Her sisters squeezed under the blanket holding their ears to keep the noise out. But Maxine wanted to hear what the ladies were telling Mama to make her so upset.

She crawled from behind the crates to a large steel wash tub. It was easier to hear them. It was hard not to cry and she grew angry as she listened. What mean people they were, she thought.

"Mrs. Conners, you need to think about your children. Those little girls can't survive in this harsh cold. There's not enough heat or enough food to feed everyone. They need to go to school. We have no choice. We must take them, and they will be well taken care of, I promise," one lady said.

Maxine's mother, Pearl, sat on the couch. She wiped tears off her dark skin. Her mama was a beautiful woman, a full-blooded

Cherokee Indian. She'd been a princess of her tribe until she married a half-breed and was banned from the tribe forever.

Charles, Maxine's father, wasn't much help with the children, nine girls and one boy. He was always gone on different jobs. He couldn't keep a job to support them all.

Pearl's pride wouldn't let her go back and beg forgiveness from her father the Chief. She would have to leave Charles. She was afraid she would have to leave her children behind also and she was not willing to do that.

Even though her dress was long and torn, Pearl's long flowing black hair and brown eyes, made her beautiful. Today, she looked older because her heart was breaking. She was losing her three youngest daughters.

"I'm doing everything I can. Please, they're babies. You can't take them from me." She clenched her hands. Her body trembled, and it wasn't from the cold.

Maxine stood and placed her hands on her hips, mad as a raging bull ready to charge. Her lips stuck out, nose and eyes squinting. "Leave my mama alone! You mean people. Stop making my mama cry!"

She started to walk closer to the ladies but stopped. Scared she ran back behind the tub.

The ladies were tall and stocky. Their hair up in black bonnets. Their coats were black, and they had black gloves.

"Please, Mama, don't let them take us. Please," Maxine cried as she covered up with the old blanket next to the tub.

Maxine and Orpha had long brown tangled hair. Joann's was black like her mothers. The girls were small. Orpha was ten, Maxine was eight and Joann had just turned six. Joann was the smallest and very fragile. Orpha stayed to herself a lot, but Maxine was a fighter and yet had a kind heart.

One lady handed their mother a piece of paper. She blinked back her tears as she studied it.

"Your girls are going to a children's home where they'll go to school, be warm and fed healthy meals." The lady sat down and put an arm around Pearl. "It's the right thing to do. We both know that, don't we?"

Maxine's mother looked at the lady and shook her arm off. "I have no choice. You're taking them no matter what. One thing your home can't give them, is the love I have for them." She slapped the paper back at the lady.

The lady stood looking at her. "They're good people there and will do their best to make the girls feel loved."

The ladies walked into the room where the girls were. They grabbed Joann and Orpha's arms and led them out to the room where Pearl waited. They began putting coats, hats and boots on them.

Joann cried as she struggled to reach for her mother. Orpha didn't struggle at all.

It confused Maxine why her mother didn't say anything. She just sat there like a doll.

"Say something, Mama. Don't let them take us. Mama, why won't you do anything?"

Maxine watched in horror as the ladies stepped outside with Joann and Orpha. They walked down the broken icy steps to a long black car. After one lady forced the girls into the back seat, she shut the door, then slipped into the driver's seat and started the engine.

Maxine heard the other lady's footsteps on the porch as she returned. With determination, she walked toward Maxine. The lady's a large hand, she lifted her from behind the tub.

Maxine kicked and screamed and tried biting her, only to have a large hand smack her. "You're not going to take me! You're a mean ugly lady!"

She threw herself on the floor squirming around as the lady tried to put on her coat. "I'm not going. Mama, help me please! Don't let them take me. I promise won't eat much. I'll stay under the covers to keep warm. Mama, please," she cried out with tears in her eyes.

She kicked off the boots. One went flying and hit the lady in the head. "You are a mean lady! Go away. Go away. Leave us alone." As she pulled her arm out of her coat, she yelled, "Go away!"

"Maxine, you straighten up right now. I taught you better." Mama grabbed her cheeks. "Stop acting like a wild animal. You must go. I have no choice; I can't stop them. Go with them and don't act like this there or you'll find might get the paddle many times. You will not like it." She looked straight into Maxine's eyes and spoke with authority.

"Remember I love you girls. If there's a way to bring you home, I will find it." She released Maxine as tears flowed down her face. "You watch out for your sisters. Take care of Joann. She'll need you." She gave Maxine a long hug.

Maxine stepped back; tears rolling down her face. She didn't like to cry, this time she couldn't help it. She was saying goodbye to Mama.

The ladies put on Maxine's coat, hat, boots and gloves without her fighting. She always behaved for her mother but wished she could run and hide.

Maxine walked onto the porch. The cold wind felt as if it would freeze her tears. Hearing the front door shut behind her made her heart feel like a knife went through it. She took deep breaths as she walked to the car.

All three sisters sat cuddled together in the backseat. As they drove away from their home, Maxine wiped the tears from her eyes. "Don't worry, I'll take care of you," she told her sisters.

She closed her eyes and whispered, "Goodbye, Mama."

# Babies and Pigeons

## Jerry Boling

During bad weather it was common having babies of all kinds brought in to doctor or just feed and keep warm. I remember baby pigs behind the stove and baby calves too, mooing to be taught how to suckle by dipping our fingers in warm milk and encouraging them to drink or feed by bottle.

We got to baby a lot of things growing up on a farm. Sometimes they would be hurt or too sick and so we learned about death early.

One time we rescued some tiny baby skunks. Daddy said we couldn't keep them, but they were so soft and cuddly we hid them and didn't think the folks knew. (Baby skunks smell good too.) They were doing real good and growing, but one day they were gone. We found out later the neighbor boy had them. Also, we found out eggs were one of skunks' favorite foods. So, we couldn't have kept them, but they were babied for a while.

One year we brought two baby "orphan" pigeons from the barn to feed. We forced their bills open and fed them on watered down milk with a little Karo and soaked bread in it (warmed, of course). It agreed with them and soon they were wanting to eat all the time. They were very awkward looking when young, but they grew up beautiful. One was white and the other dark gray, so we just named them Whity and Blacky.

They became part of the family and they thought of themselves as family. They would go in and out through the kitchen window over the sink. Sometimes they would just soar or just sit outside on the window ledge and coo. If the window was closed and they wanted to come in they would peck on the glass till we opened the window and let them in. They were neat and we all really enjoyed them.

# Deep in the Country

### Jerry Boling

'Neath God's changing sky,
Where nature runs rampant,
Where birds soar and fly—
On a hill there's a home-
A home weathered and worn,
But a sturdy rock home
Where we were all born.
Rows of lilac grow
Down a fence made of rock,
And the mockingbird sings
So sweet on the chimney top.
Trumpet vines ramble
By the front door,
And dream it's the same
As it was years before,
As youngsters we'd play
'Neath shade of locust trees
And wander through wildflowers
Up to our knees
Tho so busy mother was
With the chores of each day,
She always made sure
We had time to play.

And as evening drew nigh
She'd bathe and tuck us in,
Pray that God would guide us
Protect us from sin.
Seems time cannot dim
Those precious memories of yore,
They seem just the same
As they were before.
Where we'd herd cattle—
work—and play in the hay
And chase fireflies
At the end of the day.
Where we swam, fished in the lakes,
And climbed in the trees,
No dreams are cherished
Nor loved more than these.
And they'll grow with the years
And seem oh—so fair,
Our lovely rock home
Our precious mother there.

# Oh No ... Not Again

## Ann Alvis

Being four and a half years old, I know little about the world, only what I see. I wonder why Mom wished I had stayed in bed when the sun came up, not realizing it was only six o clock, way too early for some people. I don't want to go to sleep before the sun goes down even though it was nine and bedtime.

Why did my mother leave for a few days, only to come home with a new baby? How come I was told it was my new brother? Why would I want another brother? Two sisters and a brother were enough.

I wished she would take him back to the store and bring me home a doll. Especially when he cried, or he stunk the whole room up when mother would change him. How could something so small stink so bad?

Peering at him in the small crib Mother had for him, my heart pounded with love. I looked at his small body lying there, not crying, just sleeping. Turning his small head, he grins at me. People say its gas. Mother says the Angels are talking to him. I believe Mother. Gas would make him stink. He always smelled of sweet flowers after Mother gave him a bath.

Watching my mother change him one day, my brother gave me a shower. It was yucky and puki. So, Mother put me in the shower to wash the shower my brother gave me away. I never watched Mother change him again.

Holding my brother for the first time I was a little scared. Mother told me he wouldn't break. I hope not; he looks nothing like the glass doll I have on my bed.

Mother told me we will call him Sonny. Even though his real name was Wilbur, after my father. How does Sonny fit in that? Who knows, grownups are strange at times?

Sonny was eating one day. I don't think he liked it much, kept spitting it back out as Mother pushed it back in. I wouldn't like it either it really looked slimy, and tasting it, I wouldn't eat it either, Sonny.

Little by little Sonny grew each day; his light blonde hair was almost white. Sonny suited him well. His small smiles and laughter made each day sunnier.

I enjoyed playing with him when he started to crawl. Building blocks were his favorite of all toys. Not mine when he tossed them and hit me in the head.

I'd cry after being hit; the blocks didn't feel so good. Sonny would cry when I did, guess I scared him. A big hug from his big sister would always make it better.

It wasn't so bad to have another brother; two brothers, two sisters. It sounded good to me. What more could a little girl ask for? Plenty to play with and being next to the oldest you could play boss and they'd listen.

Leaving for my first day of school, I knew I would miss Sonny and he would miss me. He was always glad when I walked through the door.

I loved being a big sister. Sonny was my baby brother and I loved him very much. It took a little while to get use to him, but now he was perfect to me. No smelly diapers or long nights of crying. It was great until ....

Mother came home with another brother ... Oh no!... Not again!

# My Brother, and Mother and the Possum

### Jerry Boling

One year my brother got a rod and reel. He was real proud of it (because we always fished with long cane poles), but it was so short it wasn't easy fishing off shore with the trees and the wind blowing. So, he got the best idea.

We got in the rowboat and I held onto the rod while he rowed. He was strong and could row fast. It worked, and the fish bit but I was so excited I could hardly stay in the boat, much less reel the fish in (still can't). So, he would have to reel the fish in. It was fun until he got tired. I don't remember how many fish we caught, but what a nice memory.

I'm afraid I was a bit jealous of my brother. He was older than us and got to do so much more than we girls got to do, especially when he got to go hunting and trapping. I could hit the target good when we practiced shooting.

So, one time I took the gun and decided to run his trap line by myself. I did real good until I found a skunk in one of his traps. I liked animals and never aimed at anything alive before. I had the shakes, but I was bound and determined I could do it.

I took careful aim and fired at the area between his eyes. Well, he fell, and I started over to pick him up to take home and show them I could hunt. When he got up and started staggering around, I got panicky and didn't want to shoot again. I came unstrung and ran crying to the house to tell someone and get help. I knew you just don't wound something and leave it. I guess you know they took care of the traps from then on, but they did say I had just creased his skull and dazed him. But I never aimed at anything alive again.

Mother said she had an experience about like that when she was expecting Vernon to be born soon. She heard the chickens make a big racket in the hen house and ran out to see what was wrong. It was a possum and she ran back and got the gun from behind the door.

When she got back, the possum was running away across the plowed ground behind the chicken house. But she shot it and it dropped. The percussion from the shotgun knocked her down and she said it hurt. The possum was dead, or so she thought. She felt pretty proud that she had saved her chickens and eggs and went to get it.

She picked it up by the tail and was carefully picking her way back across the rough plowed ground when the possum started curling up to her hand. She screamed, dropped the possum and ran crying to the house. (Oh, the life of a farm girl.) She never said how long after that before Vernon was born.

# My Heart Goes Flippity Flop

## Nancy Breth

It is August—birthday month for both my son and daughter and also daughter-in-law, Holly. I am on my way back from my annual trip to Corpus Christi to celebrate birthdays with Marty, Holly and grandson, Albert. As I am looking out the window of the plane, Corpus Christi becomes smaller and smaller, while the sweet memories of this four-day visit make my heart grow larger and larger.

My face lights up as I am remembering our trip to Mimi's Restaurant.

On the way to the restaurant I was fussing with my wrinkled clothes and saying, "I should have taken this outfit out of the suitcase sooner and steamed out the wrinkles."

Albert says, "You are wrinkled yourself, Grandma, so what's the big deal?"

What a charmer my dear grandson.

They warned me that Mimi's was an expensive place; but this was my birthday treat and Holly and Marty had been there before and enjoyed the food. So I wanted to give them this special treat, even though I am feeling so not-so-rich in my rumpled clothes.

Before we entered the restaurant, I thought this place must not be too fancy because Marty is wearing an old T-shirt, shorts and flip-flops and Holly and Albert are wearing hats, even after entering the restaurant.

But when I saw the elegant tablecloths, with floral centerpieces and cloth napkins, I got uneasy. And after a waiter pulled out chairs for Holly and me to greet us, gave us menus with names of dishes I couldn't pronounce and no prices, I got really nervous. I was thinking—what are "these people" thinking about "my people"— looking like we are fresh off the beach; and me—what must they think about me, the matriarch of this tribe appearing like she slept in her clothes.

As we looked over the menus, the classical music in the background calmed my fears a bit; but classical and elegant are not the keywords one would use to describe "my people." Soon there was not a chance of getting by without getting stared down by the manners and fashion police.

After his first bite of food, Albert burped out loud. Then Marty told him he should have covered his mouth.

"I couldn't help it, Dad, I didn't know it would happen," Albert protested. Then he flashed this grin; this I-am-so-pure-and-innocent grin. And with the grin, his big dimples grew bigger and my heart went flippity flop; turning over to the open side.

Now, our high-octane energy charged this once hushed and serene atmosphere. The restaurant echoed with our not-serene talking and giggling about burps and farts. At first, I blushed and wanted to hush them all; but when I saw those dimples, I had to let go of Ms. Starched Collar Primly Pressed Perfect me and purr instead.

I was soon taking them all into my heart and forgetting about what I thought we should be doing. Nothing but enjoying the moment mattered after I let go of trying to be perfect; not the stares from the quiet people at the next table, or what the waiter must have thought of me not being able to pronounce the menu item I ordered, or even how wrinkled I was—clothes and body. Just loving them, loving each precious moment and the next that we were together — that was all that filled my heart.

Afterward at their home, Albert and I were playing Ms. Pacman. I barely escaped being eaten up by the ghosts and Albert said, "That was a great move, Grandma."

"I don't know how I did it," I replied.

"They must have known you were old and helped you out," my adorable grandson said.

Yep, this old me gets a lot of help from the young. Help to escape letting my passion for life be eaten up by caution and caring too much what others think and insisting on doing things the proper way.

I count on my children, and my grandchildren to keep reminding me what life is all about and it is not being Ms. Perfect. It is about being "purrfect," just purring along enjoying the moment wherever I am.

Thank you, God, for my beautiful children and grandchildren and help me keep this heart flippity flopped turned over to the open side!

# Call of Nature

## Bonnie Lacey Krenning

Outside the whip-poor-wills are calling me as I dry the dishes. I can't dry the big things, 'cause Mom says I'm too little, just five years old and the pans are too heavy for me.

Mom says I can go outside and play now.

The sun is going down behind the garden fence so I'm going to my favorite place in the evening. I sit down on the green grass and rest against the picket fence that Daddy and the boys made. I listen to the birds sing and watch the clouds as the sun goes to bed. Daddy says the sun goes to bed just like we do.

It sounds like the soft wind is whispering and singing in the trees. Whip-poor-wills and mockingbirds are singing, flying 'round, catching bugs then settling into their nests for the night. Crows are darting 'round and making loud noises. The cows are softly mooing in the pasture while the frogs are croaking, close-by, down by the creek.

The sky is bright blue overhead with lots of fluffy, white clouds floating by and changing shapes. Down low the sun is making bright colors on the clouds. I have only seen pictures of elephants, polar bears and angels. As all the birds are singing, I watch the clouds and see white elephants, polar bears, angels and sometimes peoples' faces. But they soon change into something else as they float across the pretty blue sky.

The sun has almost gone to sleep now, and I can hardly see it. A screech owl screeches and one hoot owl hollers, then another, then another. Soon it sounds like they are talking and answering each other.

Mom is calling me. "Bonnie, it's time to come in now!"

Inside the kitchen door it's kinda dark. Mom says they won't light the coal oil lamps so we can save oil. Besides, everyone is tired. They will get up early in the morning to do the chores and eat breakfast, so

Daddy and the boys can go out and work in the fields before it gets so hot. I go to my bed, take off my dress and climb in.

What's that? The ole speckled rooster is crowing outside my window, telling me it's time to wake up. I musta gone to sleep. I open my eyes and see it's getting light outside. Mom is rattling the iron stove lids and putting wood in the cookstove so she can cook breakfast. I will get up and help her. I'll set the table and help stir the gravy.

Oh, good! I didn't pee the bed like I do sometimes. Now Mom won't call me a pee-tail, but I better get to the outhouse quick. Pulling my dress on over my slip and bloomers I hurry to the door, barefoot. Outside the door my little rooster is crowing, the chickens are clucking, scolding and pecking in the grass for bugs. The little birds are singing in the trees and the sun is shining through the leaves. I know the birds got here from the other side of the house, by flying over, but how did the sun get over here on this side of the house? I must ask Daddy.

Oh! Oh! I better hurry on quick or I won't get to the outhouse in time. Sometimes I see the boys pee behind a tree, but Mom said little girls are not supposed to do that/ The boys would tell on me if I did. If I don't make it to the outhouse will Mom call me a pee tail? Maybe I won't tell her if I don't make it in time and pee my bloomers.

Whew! I made it in time! Now I can hurry to the kitchen and help Mom.

# B.A.B.Y.

## Connie Holt

B is for the many bottles, to be washed and washed.
A is for all the floors, to be crossed and crossed.
B is also for, the burping babies often need.
Y is for the coming years, worrisome indeed!
Together they spell baby, but when all is said and done,
We wouldn't trade them for all the world,
No not a single one!

## Life's Dance

It's funny how a single dance
Can start a life anew.
Your smile, a twirl, now I'm your girl—
No longer sad and blue.

I do not know what God has planned,
For my life or yours.
I only know you patched my soul,
And set me back on course.

# Learning Together

## Jean Welle

As a child, my daughter vented her frustrations by raising her voice. Her angry outbursts pushed me to the limit, and before long we were in a shouting match. It grieved me every time this happened.

I knew Jesus could face an angry mob and remain calm, so I asked Him to help me. He directed my attention to Proverbs 15:1, and I realized that I needed to change my behavior before I could help my little girl.

The next time she raised her voice, I lowered mine. She challenged with more intensity; I responded softly, yet firmly to each subversion. She stopped talking, even though her mouth gaped open. I smiled. She grinned sheepishly, and then answered in her natural tone of voice.

Together we learned the correct way to disagree without being disrespectful. And together we learned that the wisdom of God brings lasting peace when we choose to obey it.

*A soft answer turns away wrath, but a harsh word stirs up anger.*
Proverbs 15:1 (NRSV)

# Days of Gentle Expectations

### Crystal Lynette Ashbrook

Driving through the Missouri hills suddenly threw me back to the innocent, kind days of my youth when my family would visit Aunt Bertha and Uncle D.B. in Hulbert, Oklahoma. I knew the farm folk were quite old; but since they had such young hearts, they never seemed to age.

Aunt Bertha had light, transparent blue, yet bright, laughing eyes that were slightly clouded by cataracts. Her long gray hair was put up into two braids that formed a crown around her head. She made the best breakfasts. I would sit and watch, wide-eyed, while she made biscuits from memory and many years of practice. Measuring spoons were unheard of, because the cupped palm of her hand was the perfect size for teaspoons or tablespoons. Once the mixture was the right consistency, she would pour it out of the bowl and knead the dough with her strong, stout fingers, as she chatted heartily with my mother.

Uncle D.B. was a quiet, almost sad, character. His once 6'1" frame had been beaten down to about 5'9" by the many years of mother earth's gravity beseeching him. When he was young, spry and handsome, he would lug two seventy-five-pound sacks of grain on his shoulders to town every day during harvest, which also helped break him down. He always walked with a cane, taking such small steps that I was certain he would never reach his destination.

I loved talking with him and listening to his stories. One of my favorite old wives' tales he used to tell me was that people with high arches were very intelligent. He would then take off a shoe and sock and show me the biggest arch in a foot that I believe, to this day, I have ever seen. (Of course, I had big arches too!)

He had the cutest, contagious laugh, like short bursts of air being forced through his vocal cords, making a slight, almost wheezing, "hee, hee, hee," combined with such a sparkle in his eyes, that you knew he had tickled himself as well as any listener.

I will never forget the rural dirt road that led up to their home. As we would round that last tree-lined curve to their place, we would all strain to see their farm, which would suddenly materialize over the top of the hill. As soon as I was old enough, I was the self-appointed gate opener to the quarter mile long driveway. It seemed as if we could not get down that drive fast enough.

As we pulled up closer, we would see Aunt Bertha coming out of the kitchen, drying her hands on her apron, to welcome us. Uncle D.B. was usually in the yard, with his black, tail-wagging dog, Buddy, next to his side. Walking through the back porch to the kitchen, we were always greeted by the most wonderful smell of honeysuckle mixed with aromas from fresh-baked cakes and pies.

The house could not hold my two older brothers and me long; there was exploring to be done. The outbuildings always held new adventures, but the woods would draw us to them. We would go down the drive we had just come and turn south right before we reached the road. Along the way, we would stop at the cow patties that were covered with dung beetles. These beetles looked like the June bugs we had at home, except, instead of the drab brown dress, they were bright blue-green and simply shimmered in the light. I could never understand how such a beautiful bug could be attracted to something so disgusting.

Moving on, as we did not stay in one place on that farm very long, the tinkling sound of the creek beckoned us. I loved sitting by the creek—peering into its shallow depths, watching the tiny fish swim in place against the current. Up and off we would go, though, venturing deeper into the woods where the sun could barely get through the ceiling of leaves from the trees, giving us a cool bath of green solitude.

Before long, we would come upon one of my favorite spots. It was a part of the creek where the water ran slightly deeper, and it was absolutely filled with delicate watercress. There was a tree root that draped across the water; forming a miniature waterfall that appeared to have a small, cave-like opening. I always imagined that small, magical elves lived at this special place.

The rumblings in our stomachs were about the only thing that could tear us away from this free searching of nature. Walking up to the lightened house at dusk, we could hear the low utterances of Uncle D.B. talking to my father and see my mom and Aunt Bertha through the kitchen window as they prepared a traditional farm dinner.

We would steal up to the morning glory, honeysuckle-covered porch, which bordered the entire front of the house, to see if we could catch sight of the hummingbirds that would frequent this nectar-filled area. They were such delightful creatures to watch as they chased and played with each other, filling the air with the sound of the beating of their small wings.

After dinner, we would all sit on the front porch and listen to the folks tell stories of years gone by. The night air would be still, yet so clear that you could see, I was sure, all of the stars of the universe. Listening to the talk, together with the soothing sounds of the night, our eyelids could hardly stay open, and we would sometimes find ourselves suddenly tucked into the comfortable featherbeds we were to have for dreaming our happy, carefree dreams during our stay.

# Hobo Mystery

## Connie Holt

I live about six blocks from a railroad track. Sometimes in the stillness late at night, I hear a lonely train whistle. It takes me back to my small hometown and the last house on Oak Street. We lived right across the street from the Rock Island Railroad tracks, about half a mile from the station.

There in the front yard, my seven siblings and I would happily wave to the passengers as the train sped Northeast out of town. It thrilled us when a few of them waved back. Then there were the other class of passengers: hobos, who strolled across the street with some regularity, removing their hats before knocking on our front door.

My mama, Emily, would answer the door smiling, her blue-green eyes shining. They would no sooner get their polite request out, when she promptly asked them to wait at the door. She hurried to the kitchen, busily prepared a fried egg or baloney sandwich with a cold jar of ice water to wash it down. She collected and washed mayonnaise and pickle jars with their lids to give them the ice water to go, so they could jump on the train without spilling it. The sandwich was wrapped in a saved Rainbow Bread wrapper. She was a kind, sweet lady who had been a teenager in the Depression. She never sent a hobo away without something to eat, quoting the Bible verse about "entertaining angels unaware" to us to explain why she did it.

My dad, Ivan, was a sign painter who worked out of our home. He was a kind, quiet man who explained to us that the hobos were mostly men down on their luck, riding the box cars from town to town, looking for work. This was in the late fifties and early sixties.

Over the years I pondered how the hobos knew they could get something to eat and drink at our house and not fear we would call the police on them like one of our neighbors down the street did. Recently I read a magazine article about hobos marking places, houses where they would find kind people to feed them. From the article, I decided our hobos must have marked our house with their code of a simple drawing of a cat, (kind woman), and a circle with an x inside it, (a good place for a handout).

I was so excited and smug in my discovery; I couldn't wait to tell my sister, Carol, my new found knowledge! She listened to me, then said, "No, that's not it." But she knew the answer to the mystery. She once overheard our mama ask one hobo how he knew to come to our house, and he explained, "All up and down the line, Mrs., we pass the word that when you come to this town, go to the last house on Oak Street with the Conner Signs placard hanging on the front porch!"

# The Purple Eye

## Doris Martin

Dear Ones: Relatives and Friends

Three events of this year 1995, the year of my 88th birthday, the 23rd of July have happened as follows;

My only granddaughter, Pattie Brockman, announced her wedding to be in Corpus Christi, Texas, the 25th of March. Our plans were made for Mary, Wayne, Chris and me to drive there in a rented van with Wayne driving. Once on the road, he drove without stopping until we were south of Dallas. It was there we discovered in our haste to get away from Wichita we had left my big suitcase. I did have with me my purple dress and purple hat and good shoes. Mary decided we could shop for anything else I needed the next day. We stopped at a Walmart the next morning and SHOPPED. We stopped to visit Pattie and Troy in San Antonio and to spend the night at a nearby Motel. As we were unloading, I went toward the back of the van to answer a question about what I wanted to take into the motel for the evening. In spite of my cane, my face met with the rock border around the parking lot instead. My glasses were broken, and I was to have a purple eye to match my purple hat and purple dress. The Wedding was in an outdoor gazebo in a Historic garden surrounded by restored Historic homes. The weather was warm, windy and balmy. The wedding was BEAUTIFUL.

The second event was Theodore Martin's estate sale in Anchorage, Alaska, during the month of August. Mary and I flew up there for a week and enjoyed some shopping in the basement but only after I missed the step into the basement room and got my second purple eye for the year, no broken glasses this time and no broken bones, either. The youth group from the Methodist church were in charge of the sale and they did a wonderful job. We had a wonderful visit.

Our return trip from Alaska did not go smoothly. We made it to Salt Lake City but the plane we were to take to Dallas had some problems and they repaired it but not in time for us to make our connection in Dallas. Delta was nice enough to put us in a hotel just five minutes away from the terminal and we spend the night in a very nice hotel without our luggage. We had room service breakfast and then on to Wichita. Home sure looked good!

The third trip was to Dilley, Oregon, to visit Lois Lambert and her family for Thanksgiving. She had a nice dinner at the church with a lot of her children, grandchildren and great-grandchildren in attendance. We had plenty of food and plenty of left overs, plenty of visiting and a VERY GOOD TIME! Theodore had been visiting a cousin in California and stopped in Oregon for several days on his return trip to Alaska, so he was also part of the visiting bunch. Our return trip took us through Las Vegas where I won a few nickels in the slot machines.

I continue to live alone at 1712, with five cats to keep me company. Mary takes me occasionally on a day trip to Wellington where we visit a friend who is recovering from a broken hip. She is also Mary's neighbor. I walk to church once a week and have enjoyed sweeping the leaves in my yard this fall. I enjoyed a visit from Dixie this summer for about a week. She continues to work at the hospital/long term care center in Cody, Wyoming. Mary discourages any long walking trips for me but I do plan to start making some short walking trips this next year and accumulate about one miles a month.

NOTE: As editor of this collection, I chose to include this semi-typical family letter. Many of us our familiar with writing a letter to friends and family at Christmas time to catch up on our lives. And many of us have events happen during the year that don't necessarily go according to plan. Such as the annoying fall and getting a purple eye, or plane problems when flying.

(Mary Brockman's mother)

# Home

## C. A. Lemont

Let's expand on your human emotions.
They're as vast as any ocean.
They're deep and wide, and dark and clear.
And you can't deny, the salt in a tear.

The moon's pull has an effect on the tides.
And yet we dare to act wide-eyed!
We've known this fact for years.
We share emotion; there's salt in our tears.

We share emotions and feelings; we can think and speak.
The dignity of man is all I seek.
Such a wondrous creature as you or I,
Once believed man could never fly.
I believe in man and all that we share.
Look at man, the animals, our planet, our air.

So careless and foolish, it's such a waste.
We've forgotten we share that salty taste.

The existence of man depends on our tears.
We share the world. We share the fears.
There's not one of us who stands all alone.
Not if you believe in what you've always known.
That after all is said and done, we share our home.

# Weeping Willow

## Mary McKay

I can remember the wind sighing through the lime green fronds of the old weeping willow tree as I crawled underneath its canopy. To my ears it was a beautiful sound. The spring leaves were almost big enough to turn a lovely sap green and provide a private place for me to set up my little tea party. It was just across the road from my childhood home in Maize, Kansas.

A dense fog helped to obscure the view from prying eyes and the old chenille bedspread, which I often confiscated from the linen cupboard, was dry and spread out to provide a soft carpet for my make-believe home. Here, I was in control and the confusion of my real home seemed far away. I liked it. The bedspread smelled slightly of mothballs. It had been washed so many times that you could barely see the pink tufts of the rose patterns that were the focal point of the spread.

My father said the septic tank would not like the weeping willow and its roots would cause problems for the lateral field. However, it was such a complement to the entire neighborhood that no one wanted to cut it down. It would have been a sacrilege. To this day, I love to see a weeping willow in early spring.

The dampness of the fog intensified the fragrance of the early spring morning. The hyacinths, tulips and daffodils blended with the grasses, and created a symphony of scents that gladdened the nose, like the soft wind caressed the ears. Spring was here and I was promised a lovely day to be outside. After a long, cold and bitter winter, and a nasty strep throat, I had been confined to the indoors and the racket of my crowded family.

My grandparents were frequent residents in our home and with two brothers and two sisters, Mom and Dad, we were a large and noisy group. I loved the solitude I found outside in the privacy of the curtains of leaves around my nest as it gently brushed the ground with every whisper of a breeze.

In a Kansas springtime, the winds are frequently known to come in every direction, sometimes up and down. During a wind-driven rain it can suck the umbrella up, only to slam it back down as the crosscurrents rip and tear it from left to right. It is an exhilarating and exciting struggle. The weeping willow would dance about like a ship on a storm-tossed sea. The limber branches also made a great whip that whistled in the air after the leaves are stripped from the stem.

The nesting instinct is strong in me and I have been feathering my nest from the earliest time I can recall. Over my long lifetime, I have had close to a dozen different homes and always found a way to make them comfortable and pleasant. My sister, Julie, once said, "No matter where you move, within two weeks it looks like you have lived there forever. I almost never move my furniture about."

I have observed that there are a select group of women, whom I call nesters, that like to make their homes lovely and inviting. I am always surprised at those people who live simply, without ornamentation or decoration. Their homes lack interest and I wonder if the same inhabitants are without color, texture, and depth, in their minds.

Do they lack taste? Is there no enrichment in the world around them or just within their houses? When they come home after a difficult day at work and take off their shoes, does their house welcome them and comfort them? What are the ramifications of this phenomena? How could this theory be tested and what would it indicate?

When company comes, do they offer a cup of tea and cookies, or do they leave their guests standing at the door, without any promise of hospitality?

Can you smell the home-made bread baking? The supper on the stove? Is there any reward for being here?

# Train to Training

Julie Lovelace

Hope began to become a reality when the conductor helped me with the first step onto the train. I looked back only once as I heard the familiar command to stragglers to "boar–r-r-d-d!" There stood my family proudly waving to me as my West Texas dreams of education as a nurse began.

I probably should have taken a picture to commemorate my send-off, but actually I have never forgotten how my family looked that day. My dad was strong and handsome, even with his self-give haircut. Do it yourself projects plus a little overtime helped the tuition money increase. My mom was stylishly elegant, because she fashioned her outfits and all in my sisters' clothing. My two sisters' eyes were brightly shining, knowing their turns for college were just a few years away. Financial and moral support were abundant.

I was comfortably seated in the coach and soon the rhythm of the train making its way down the tracks soothed me. This was not a day for jitters. The steel rails pointed toward Fort Worth Texas, where I would matriculate into TCU. I would study nursing and I would play my flute in the TCU Horned Frog marching band. There were no castles on the beautiful campus, however, dormitory living was the perfect place to make lifelong friends.

Yes, that train transported me, as a childish girl, to the place where life would teach me to care, to lead, to serve, and to grow into maturity.

# Life Launched

## Rochelle Boster

Hanging laundry with Mama in the backyard of the two-story farmhouse, seemed like the most normal thing in the world, at least on most washdays. However, this day with every clothespin I attached to a shirt or pair of jeans more tears filled my eyes and streamed down my cheeks. As Mama and I worked together our conversation was the same topic it had been for weeks now. Tomorrow was my D Day, and I didn't want to face it!

It was 1965, and I was heading off to college at Kansas State University.

My parents had never asked their children if they wanted to go to college, but rather where they were going to college. As the baby of the family, I had watched my brothers and sister go off to school, decide on careers, and start to make their way in the "bigger world."

College was so important to Mama and Daddy. They would make sure that all of their children had the opportunity to experience what they had not. No matter what or how big the financial burden.

As a young child, I felt I had a big part in this grand education plan for my siblings. Each August I would accompany my parents to the Savings and Loan where they borrowed money for tuition and room and board for my brothers and sister. Then each month without fail the three of us made the trek back to the S and L to make the monthly installment payment on the loan. In January of the new year my parents, with me in tow, would start all over again with a new loan.

My turn had come to leave my home and parents. Homesickness had taken hold long before I had even left the farm. I didn't want to leave Mama and Daddy. As long as I was there nothing could happen to them. Life would go on just as it had up to this point. How could I be in control of situations if I wasn't there? Change was for the birds in my way of thinking.

As we hung out the laundry together. I mustered up my courage to express my fears and concerns to Mama. Following up with a tear-filled request to stay home and not go to college right now. Mama stopped hanging laundry with a clothespin in mid pinch. And without taking a breath or hesitation informed me it was my turn to go to college. I would go tomorrow!

Tomorrow came! As we rode three abreast in the pickup truck, the surrounding air was thick with the summer heat and thoughts unspoken. The conversations included reminders of financial responsibility, long rehearsed good choices and behaviors, and assurances that the phone would keep us close with news.

As I sat between my parents in the pickup, I sensed something different in Daddy. He usually was calm, cool and collected. But today he seemed a little anxious, and that was out of character. He seemed to be in a world of his own while driving and keeping up with our conversations. As we approached the turn onto I-70 for Manhattan, Daddy turned left instead of right. I was never one to question my father, but when I saw the mileage sign for Russell, Kansas I knew we had turned the wrong direction. I brought it to his attention. Only after verifying the wrong turn with another mileage sign, he acknowledged we were indeed going the wrong way. It took us a while to find a safe turnaround spot.

This mistake provided a huge release of tension and a great amount of laughter and joking on all of our parts. Whether by accident or design Daddy had turned the ride into the most fun and joyful time we could have ever had!

When we pulled up in front of Moore Hall, my heart plummeted to my stomach and my feet wanted to run. I knew the strength of Mama and Daddy was in me. I had to appear like I was excited. I had to show how much I really wanted to do this. After all, hadn't this been my dream too?

Mama and Daddy helped me carry my things to my assigned dorm room on the sixth floor. My roommate had not checked in yet. We unpacked and put my things away. Mama even helped me make my bed with a brand new bed spread. All of our work was done efficiently and with alacrity.

Then as if I was a hot potato being dropped, Mama and Daddy on cue walked to the door and unceremoniously said they had to go. I was shocked, but I knew they meant it. Begging had never worked on either of them.

I hugged them and kissed them and walked them back to the parking lot. Of course, I hugged and kissed them again.

As I watched them pull out of the parking lot, I realized I was alone for the first time in my life!

My eyes burned and my head ached from tears I wouldn't let flow.

Mama and Daddy had given me the most amazing gifts that day. The freedom to explore my life. The confidence I could do anything I wanted. The directions to a moral compass to always find True North. The greatest gift, their unconditional love!

It was time for me to make my way in the "bigger world."

*From Memories of Mulberry Hill Farm

# The Letter

## Sara Hittle

On June 9, 1997, my mother left this earth. About a year before, she had suffered a stroke that left her partially blind. Her hands were crippled arthritis and had a painful back. It was difficult for to engage in her favorite pastimes, crocheting and drawing. She was tired and weary and ready to move to the next place of her spiritual being.

As I awakened the next morning, my first thoughts were of her. I felt at peace and was comforted, feeling that she was in a happy place, awaiting the resurrection. It was as if she had sent this letter to my sisters and me.

The Letter

Today, I awoke to a new day. I was lifted from the infirmities of life to walk in the freshness of spring. My eyes are once again whole. I can see clearly, and the darkness is gone. I see children laughing and playing as they frolic across the open field of sunflowers, daisies, and other wildflowers. They were playing games in the gentle breezes. The beauty of God's Hand is mirrored in the beautiful lakes and streams. I walk by the brook as it babbles along. The leaves, the flowers, the moss and the mushrooms renew me as I know I am in the presence of God. I can now hear clearly the sweet song of the redbird, uplifting me to new realms of glory. The mockingbird is singing in the radiant chorus of God's beautiful creatures. Even the big, big Kansas blackbird welcomes me as he flaps his wings and greets me with is "Kaw, Kaw, Kaw." This is a new day and I am not tired from my journey. I was carried on the wings of angels, viewing the magnificent sights of God's Creation. Do not grieve for me but be happy, for I have eternity to walk among the flowers and trees, never having to rush to the next appointed place. I can talk to the birds and stroke the soft downy fur of the cats. There are mountains for me to scale and a quiet little place to dwell in my own thoughts. I am in the company of loved ones and the sweet chorus of children. I can talk with Moses and tell him of my grandchildren (how, one of them knew that he, Moses, was my best friend).

As I was moseying down the path through the valley, I felt the presence of My Dear Friend, Jesus. I stopped and had a little talk with Him. It seemed so right, as the precious children came running to Him. What a wonderful sight ... Jesus loving the little children. Their little faces were as sunbeams, as Jess bade them shine. Even with all of the closeness of these friends and loved ones, I anxiously await your coming. Do not hurry on this journey but love one another. You know I will be here, for you when you come. Then, once again, I will have my four little girls with me. There's Aunt Katie, Aunt Lula, Aunt Phoebe and that pesky little brother of daddy, Frank. Mom and Dad are here with me also. I join Grace and Helen and we talk about old times. The reunion has begun. I love you and do not cry, for I am well and happy. This is a beautiful place that God had planned for us all.

Love to my four girls and grandkids,
Mom & Ma-Eva

# One Time Love

## Misty Colbert

I sense you close to me; the covers move.
I feel your body as it slips in next to mine
touching me, holding me.
You place a kiss on my shoulder, my neck, and spine.
I turn. I wake. You're not here. I miss you.

# My First Hand Hold

## Mary McKay

It wasn't a human's hand. I was about twelve years old and still remember it as if it was yesterday. That was over sixty-five years ago. I have a vague memory of holding my mother's hand as a very small child. But the memory of my first hand hold came to me with lightning speed. It was in St. Louis. Perhaps I should start from the beginning of my story.

My sister, Pat, and I were sent to St. Louis, Missouri for a two-week summer vacation at our Aunt Ruth's. I was starting middle school in the fall and Pat was one year ahead of me. She was given full responsibility for both of us. I was given orders to do exactly what she told me to do. That was the way it was always done—she was the boss; I was to obey. By the time we boarded the Missouri Pacific passenger train at Douglas and Water, in Wichita, Kansas, I was sick with fright. I had thrown up that morning and was running a fever by the time my mother ushered us up the steps of the train.

"You'll be okay once you get started. Just do what Pat tells you and you'll be fine." That was the end of my chances to escape the unknown that was looming ahead of me. Once seated, I fell asleep as the train rocked back and forth. The clickety-clack of the wheels on the railroad track sang out a soothing lullaby. When I awoke hours later, I was feeling better and by that time Pat had a sick headache. She instructed me to behave myself and not leave my seat while she took a nap.

Just before the sun went down, we ate the peanut butter sandwiches Mama had prepared for us. The next morning, we were up at dawn to eat breakfast onboard the train. It was a box of cold cereal, served in the box with one side opened to resemble a bowl. They provided a small carton of milk, which proved to be sour. My sister had a sensitive stomach and, being braver than me, asked the porter for new cartons of milk. The second cartons were just as sour as the first. The porter was a very tall and forbidding fellow that I didn't dare speak to. Apparently, Pat decided she would rather go hungry than bother him again. Being ravenously hungry, I ate mine, sour milk and all. Pat did not eat.

The train station in St. Louis was a beautiful and awesome building that had a grand fountain out front. Our much-loved Aunt Ruth and her little daughter, Susie, were there to greet us as we stepped down from the train. We all walked to the car where my Uncle Jack was waiting for us.

Please let me prevaricate a bit here and say that my Uncle Jack was a story unto himself. His name was Goddard Laird Kelly, and he was Lord of his world. I was one of the few people on this Earth he tolerated and that was because we shared the same birthday, December 21st. "We are special people," he told me, from time to time, and I believed him. I have never met another soul in seventy-eight years with that same birthday that made us so special. I am sure there are others, just none that I know.

Back to my story. My dear little Aunt Ruth had planned the vacation with a variety of sights for us to enjoy in St. Louis. The zoo was first on the list. Anheuser Busch had donated the funds to provide the best zoo in the world! Not only were all the animals one could hope to see at a zoo on display, but throughout the day three special acts were performed for the visitors. One was a fun show of elephants, with one sitting on a small stool while his companion put a large white bib on him, slathered shaving foam on his checks, and gave him a shave. They were a delightful entertainment.

Next, was a lion and tiger act. It was similar to the ones we had seen at the circus when it came to town. I was always anxious during those acts for fear someone would get eaten. To heighten my anxiety, occasionally, announcements were made over a PA system to, "Watch your purses, pick-pockets have been reported at the zoo." We were in a big city for sure!

Last, and certainly best, was the chimpanzee act, which resembled nothing I had ever seen. The best part of the act was a group of mother chimpanzees and their small babies that came out onto the stage along with a number of Shetland ponies. The babies had learned to hop up on the backs of the ponies and as the ring master directed, they ran around the ring with real skill. The mothers sat on the sidelines watching with rapt attention.

What fascinated me about the chimpanzee act was the way the mothers clapped and encouraged their babies to perform well. Afterward, the babies ran to their mothers and like all mothers on Earth, they hugged and patted them and were obviously very proud of them. The ring master then took his microphone over to one mother and baby and said, "We have even taught the babies to speak!" Sure enough, he put the microphone up to the mouth of one baby that said, "Mama!" I was surprised to think these wild animals were so human like and shared emotions just like we have.

Later we went to a pavilion, shaded by a giant pine tree. We ate the egg-salad sandwiches that Aunt Ruth had made for our lunch. A fresh peach for each of us was a simple desert. We put our rubbish in the receptacles provided and went back out on the walkway leading to the next exhibits.

I was hoping to see the Clydesdale Horses that were on display. Anheuser Busch had asked my grandfather to move to St. Louis to train their horses and I knew all about them. Grandpa was known to be a great horseman.

As we approached the display, a stab of fear tore, with lightning speed, up my arm to my heart! Someone had grabbed my hand! Terrified, I looked behind me and there on a leash was a chimpanzee! He came up to above my left knee. His hand was just like a human hand, except that it was moist and slimy. He would not let go of me. He had a banana in his other hand, and I could only shake and try not to scream. It was just like holding a human hand, but obviously not human either. The trainer was laughing and so was the small crowd that had stopped to watch the chimp. It was repulsive! I wasn't laughing. I have an aversion to monkeys to this day. I had nightmares from time to time after that, of monkeys grabbing me and tickling me. I always woke up anxious and exhausted.

Epilogue

I suspect many will judge me as a real wimp. My sister frequently called me a scaredy cat or a chicken. Being bigger and braver than

I was, she often frightened me by the activities she bossed me into participating in with her.

The upsides: My sister was a great deterrent to others who might have bullied me. I didn't wet my pants or scream or cry. I may be braver than I think.

That I could write an assignment featuring an orangutan, with such a tone of affection, was a real surprise to me. I am always surprised at what my Muse brings out of me

My brother has owned multiple horses over the years. His daughter, who is drop-dead beautiful, hired out on a ranch while she was in college. Up in the foothills near Tucson, Arizona, her job was to break horses on the ranch. I guess it runs in the family. I have been to St. Louis many times over my lifetime and have never seen those awesome Clydesdale's, except on TV.

The Moral of this Story

My instincts proved to be spot on. Several years ago, a chimpanzee tore the face off of the owner's friend. Jealousy? The woman lived but had to have a face transplant and endure many surgeries. Trust your instincts to the end!

# Church in the Schoolhouse

Bonnie Lacey Krenning

There were no churches in our community close enough to get to by team and wagon. One day I heard the neighbors and kids talking about a preacher coming to have church in the schoolhouse. I wondered what church was and Mom told me it was about Jesus. I heard her singing about God and Jesus most of the time while she was working in the kitchen. I loved to hear her sing but didn't understand what it was all about. I was five years old.

It was a beautiful summer Sunday morning when the preacher was coming. Daddy and the boys hurried and fed the animals and milked the cows. They dressed up in their good overalls, chambray shirts and hand-tied neckties. All the boys and men wore neckties to church. I wore my best dress.

I helped Mom cook her usual big breakfast. After we all ate, Daddy and the boys hooked up the team to the wagon, and my brothers and I climbed in. Daddy sat on the spring seat in front. Mom stayed home with our youngest brother. We headed for the schoolhouse over a mile away.

As we got close, I could hear the piano playing and people singing. I had never heard anything like it. It sounded so pretty. Inside, the room was filled with our school friends and neighbors. Some were standing because the room was so crowded.

When we started singing, I thought one song was the prettiest of all: "Brighten the Corner Where You Are." When I asked Daddy later what the words meant he said, "It tells us to be happy and help each other when they have troubles."

I thought, "That's what Daddy and Mom do for our neighbors." They always seemed happy helping others.

The preacher talked about the Golden Rule: "Do to others what you want them to do to you." He talked loudly. Everyone there seemed happy, clapping their hands and hollering, but I was getting tired. Then we sang again for a long time and I was getting hungry.

When we got home from church, I asked Mom if she knew, "Brighten the Corner Where You Are." She sang the whole song from memory and I soon learned most of it, even though I didn't understand most of the words.

I didn't know at the time that I wouldn't get another chance to go to church for three more years. They never had church in the schoolhouse again while we were living there. The songs, the preacher's words and hearing the Golden Rule, which is Jesus' words, made a lasting impact on my life. Mom and Daddy set the example of caring and how to treat others, even my brothers...

That was the hardest!

# The Gift of Niagara Falls

## Ann Alvis

On my twenty-fifth wedding anniversary, my husband surprised me with a trip to Niagara Falls. The weather was beautiful when we finally arrived. We checked into Days Inn, which was the closest to the falls, close enough we could walk. Settling down for the night, stretching my tired body out on the bed was a big relief after the twenty-hour car ride. It didn't take long to fall asleep, smiling and excited about the next few days at the Falls.

Waking up, we both hurried to dress. We ate at a small family restaurant on the strip. The bacon, eggs, hash browns and pancakes were excellent. After finishing up with breakfast, we held each other's hands as we walked to the falls. Several black squirrels ran across our path and hurried up one of many tall and beautiful trees on the side of the long and wide sidewalk that led to the falls.

As we got closer, we heard the loud roaring as the water went over the side of the falls. Coming upon the falls, I saw one of the world's majestic natural wonders, a beautiful sight.

We walked by the Bridal Veil Falls, the smallest of the three falls. It really looked like a veil. As if nothing around me existed, I got lost in its beauty. The blue skies over Niagara made it more exquisite.

We headed down this long trail which led to a boat called Maiden of the Mist. They handed us raincoats and warned us that we would get wet. The Mist drove right up to the basin of Horseshoe Falls. The ride was awesome. Seeing the falls so close made my heart beat faster as I held on tight to my husband's hand. The water flowing over had colors of light blue mixed with teal green and white. It felt like you were in another world. Sure, enough you got wet. I was so thankful for the raincoat.

The next ride we went to was the exhilarating Whirlpool Jetboat ride. The thrill of riding through the Niagara rapids, made me think it was the greatest ride on earth. The jetboat had three motors designed to take on the roughest, wildest whitewaters in New York.

It performed 360-degree spins and a few other heart-pumping maneuvers. The captain was from the U.S. Coast guard. The ride lasted for almost an hour; it was scary, yet amazing all at once.

We ended the night at the Niagara Falls restaurant, with a wonderful meal of steak, corn on the cob, baked potato and a salad, followed by a cheesecake dessert. The day had been like a dream, one I dreamed about that night while cuddled close to my husband.

The following day we took a tour with a group. We stood on the Canadian side on a bridge that overlooked this enormous whirlpool in the lake. I sure wouldn't want to swim around it; it would swallow anyone who came near it. The whirlpool reminded me of a black hole seen on television, yet it was blue and grey water. We toured the small city in Canada and did a little shopping. There were venues up and down the sidewalks. All the people we met were kind and generous.

We also toured up to Skyline Observation Tower on the Canadian side. Looking down you got a panoramic view of all three falls. Several people admired the falls, while others did a little bird watching. I was pointed out several falcons and bald eagles, which I had never seen before. A couple seagulls had made it to the top sitting and watching us. They waited for someone to throw them a crumb or two. I could have sat up there for hours and looked at all the beauty above and below.

As night approached, we saw the illumination of colors over the falls, and city. A spectacular view from the middle of the bridge between New York and Canada. The fireworks over Niagara Falls was truly a magical experience. We stood there amazed with the colors almost reaching the stars.

As the night ended, my husband surprised me with a dozen red roses and a horse carriage ride through the city. Listening to the trotting of the beautiful white horses, seeing lights of all colors, people holding hands, lots of smiles and laughter was so romantic. I entwined my arm in my husband's arm, looked up at him and smiled with tears in my eyes.

I will always cherish these memories forever. I will cherish my husband's love for me. I will always dream of the amazing trip to Niagara Falls.

# Memories of a Trip

## Jan Koelsch

As I sit in front of my computer and listen to a train in the distance, my memory goes back to 1968. I completed my destination of graduation from high school. The diploma was in my hand. A new adventure was on the horizon for July.

It was the year I was privileged to go to the Baptist World Youth Conference in Berne, Switzerland. A tour would include five-six different countries. For a young girl from Kansas, that was a big adventure. With rolls of film, passport and plane tickets in hand, comfy shoes for walking, and a light, all-weather coat, the group of excited teens and their sponsor boarded the jet. A dream trip and experience were a reality.

Paris, France was the first stop of the whirlwind trip. Home to the beauty and majesty of Notre Dame Cathedral and the Eiffel Tower was our home for two days. The first night we were cautioned not to tour the streets of Paris alone. The water we learned was not like at home so mineral water became an added expense. Celebrating one of our sponsor's birthday gave us a taste of real French wine.

London, England would provide historic reminders of British monarchs as we oohed and ahhed at Buckingham Palace and the Tower of London with those flashy, sparkling crown jewels. Queen Elizabeth was nowhere in sight. The unsmiling guards were everywhere. Shopping and enjoying fish and chips were highlights only imagined at one time, but now a reality.

Amsterdam in the Netherlands gave us a "no touch" look at diamonds, spread before us on a black velvet cloth. This was also the home of Anne Frank who wrote the epic Diary of Anne Frank. It was the journal of a young girl, the same age as me. As we stood in front of her home, we could only imagine what the terror of hiding from Nazi soldiers must have been like for Anne.

Germany hosted us with a splendid view of the Rhine Falls and the Rhine River. One of our sponsors, Pastor Roy, will always remember the Rhine Falls. He slipped on stone steps and injured one of his knees. He learned about emergency medicine in a foreign environment. The rest of our troupe enjoyed the scenic views on a cruise ship while Pastor Roy learned about ka-nees, so said the ER doc. There was the Maus Castle and learning how to identify Catholic and Protestant churches. Going through the Black Forest was entertaining. There are gnomes in that forest. We saw them. People were living in barn-houses. The owners lived upstairs and the animals downstairs. The experience of living in such an environment must have been an overwhelming sensory experience.

We arrived by bus at the Baptist World Youth Conference in Berne, Switzerland the second week. Many miles traveled with many more to go. The big news was we were being housed in bomb shelters. Switzerland was a neutral country surrounded by The Alps. This was supposed to be a country that was impenetrable. My idea of world peace was altered. That view disappeared at the conference. I renewed my faith as I sang with over two hundred young people from around the world. A symphony orchestra of over a hundred youth provided accompaniment for the choir and soloists and attendees. The theme song of the conference was One World, One Lord, One Witness. Billy Graham's arrival on the platform, just a few feet from my seat in the choir can never be adequately described. He was a man of stature, not only in height but spiritual stature. He preached via translator of salvation and peace. The Good News Bible sprang to life with the illustrations of Annie Vallotton. She was a little-known Swiss artist prior to the Good News Bible. We watched with amazement of how her "stick people art" gave parables a new meaning as she told the story. We understood she knew the original storyteller in her life. The conference gave much to young world travelers.

Rome, Italy was the last but not least city on this trip. The fountains, the Spanish Steps, Vatican, and the statues of St. Peters were inspiring. Knowing Leonardo DaVinci had lain on his back to add the classic art to the ceiling in the Sistine Chapel was incomprehensible. There was a new appreciation of holy ground. Seeing the Coliseum where many gladiators and Christians perished gave me wonder if we were not so far from similar times in our country. Viet Nam was on the mind of everyone and on the tips of their tongues. Little did we know there were modern day gladiators being captured and tortured in prisoners of war camps. There were members of my high school graduating class being shot down as they piloted helicopters over the jungles. Some died.

I will never forget the memories of this 1968 trip. My world view was never the same. Arriving in New York City on the day before setting foot on the soil of Kansas was a bittersweet remembrance. Seeing family and friends at the airport felt so comfortable. The journey of a thousand miles had started with one foot getting onto the plane. The message received was the needs of today had changed little since 1968. We still have wars and rumors of war. There are still ideologies that neither improve nor bring peace. The world continues to grow closer to home. Today we need a flute to play "Let There Be Peace on Earth," another favorite tune at the conference. As the chorus of that song says…let it begin with me.

# The House on Terrace Place

## C. Holden

Built in the 20s with beauty and grace,
this house became the home place.
It had many a party and happy times,
entertained many guests with sharp minds.

If those walls could talk, and windows could gawk,
what tales could be told, of birthdays, holiday events and guests
untold.

Fun times are many, though remaining guests are few.
All remembered in walls of this old house, but out of view.

Lots of good times and laughter from this old place,
and good memories with style and grace, from this old house on
Terrace place.

# Nurse Friends: Gypsy Adventure

## Sharon Lee Brown

There are three of us emergency nurse friends who like to share expenses at seminars. Janis is good under pressure. Charly is adventurous and enjoys target shooting. I'm Sue and I can usually hold my own with them.

We had a couple days before the seminar in Chicago. We planned the first day at Navy Pier. It started with a Duck boat tour of Lake Michigan. After that, Janis challenged me to ride the Ferris wheel with her. Charly stayed on the ground and wanted to shop.

She had fun and lost track of time, and we lost track of her. Janis and I started looking for her, but it's a big place. After an hour, we told a security guard we were getting concerned. He agreed to keep an eye open for our friend.

We learned later that by the time Charly got back to the Ferris wheel, we were gone. She looked for us, too.

She got tired and found an interesting shop called "The Gypsies" and wanted to rest. The three gypsies seemed nice and suggested she stay in place to be found. They put a sign up saying "Charly's here."

Dahlia, Dixie, and Dora were young, maybe late twenties. They had long black, curly hair, heavy makeup, gaudy big jewelry, and colorful dresses. Dixie said she read palms in the back of the shop.

Fascinated and a bit blunt and unfiltered, Charly began her twenty questions. "Are you like Irish Travelers?" "No, we are different." "Not you, but do other gypsies steal and pick pockets?" Enough!

They told her they were born and raised in Chicago. Their parents had been traditional gypsies but insisted they fit in. They went to public school and were "normal." Because of tourists, they opened this shop, and had fun with it.

After three hours, a lot more questions, and a palm reading, a security guard saw the sign about Charly. He radioed around until her friends were found.

They escorted Janis and me to the shop. Exhausted and hopeful, not cool at all, we were reunited with our lost friend.

Charly knew better than to let us think she had been having a great time with her "Gypsy friends" while we'd been worried about her. Quietly, she hugged them goodbye.

We all had a hard lesson about staying together. But at least Charly got to have a Gypsy Adventure.

## Nurse Friends: Hostage Adventure

There are three of us emergency nurse friends who like to share expenses at seminars. Charly is a Triage Nurse whose hobby is target shooting. She is cool under pressure and super smart. Janis is sharp and super smart. She took karate for a couple years and has an "I can handle anything attitude." I'm Sue and I think of myself as a good old hands-on nurse, quick thinking and a problem solver.

I had to work a long stretch to get enough time off. Charly and Janis were delegates and had two days of meetings before the seminar in Philadelphia. I went with them looking forward to a couple no stress days. My plan was to make a relaxing and safe adventure getting on and off the trolley myself.

Charly's mother came along. She is a bright, energetic 89-year-old neat lady called "Grams." My friends knew I would not leave the sweet lady alone all day in the hotel room. I was not happy! I had a ton of guilt because I was exhausted and tired of the responsibility taking care of people. She could fall, have a cardiac event or stroke and I would have to jump to handle the situation.

I stuffed my disappointment away and pretended it was fine for her to come along.

I am a bit high maintenance and get up early so I can take my shower, fix my hair and drink my coffee.

In the mostly dark room, Grams sat on the floor by the wall putting on her nylons. Startled, I think I screamed. I woke the others.

She asked if she could fix her hair while I was in the shower. Not attempting to be nice I said, "No." That's how the day started.

Two cups of coffee and a Danish later, we caught the trolley.

We made a few stops, and I had to admit she was nice company. About 2pm we decided to have lunch at the Small Mall in a little café by the entrance visible from the street. I ordered a yummy cheeseburger and fries, my vacation treat. Grams got a baked potato. She said that was her usual. No decision, cheap, and always good.

We were enjoying our food when a loud, scary group of angry people with signs stomped into the mall. They zeroed in on the café. I learned later they were anti meat and very serious. They blocked us in the café and were yelling. My burger lost its flavor. My heart raced in my concern about our safety.

They let us know we were staying with them, calling us hostages. Great! My training in crisis intervention included nothing like this situation.

News cameras and police came. A Negotiator was trying to identify the leader, they all seemed to be very verbal. They wanted attention, and they were getting it. Calm, Grams had a kind of smile on her face. I was not calm and not smiling.

Meanwhile, Charly and Janis arrived back at the room about 5pm. Charly said, "Where is my mother?"

Janis pointed at the TV that we had left on. There we were on the news.

They went to the desk to get help with finding us. The flustered desk clerk called the Manager. She volunteered the Courtesy Car and driver.

When they arrived at the cafe, the police and a crowd were still there. The loud group had been taken into custody and were gone. Grams and I stayed in our seats. My half-eaten cheeseburger and her potato remains were still on the table.

The Courtesy Car took us back to the hotel. It had been an adventure all right. My friends had the audacity to be a bit mad at me, like I had planned it.

We freshened up and headed to the dining room.

Grams asked, "What are we doing tomorrow?"

The next day we took a tour sponsored by the hotel. A quiet, almost boring day.

Grams will be 90 years old next year when we expect to attend the seminar in Dallas. She is excited and planning what to wear.

# All My Childhood Dreams Have Come True

## Bonnie Lacey Krenning

Tired of running and playing in the yard, I was lying in the cool grass on my back, watching the floating clouds and pretty birds in the clear blue sky. The birds were dipping, dashing and floating about in the air. I wished I could fly like a bird in the sky.

Relaxed and half asleep, I heard a loud noise in the sky. I jumped up, so very scared. There was a big bird in the sky making the loud noise. I ran to the house to find Mom who was working in the kitchen, as she always was. When I told her what I saw and heard she said it wasn't a bird, it was an airplane; I had never heard of an airplane. She said they have engines in them like our neighbor's truck and men fly in them.

In the sky the airplane looked littler than I was. I wondered how a man could fly in something so little. Maybe they laid down on the airplane and held onto the wings. I thought, I will fly like a bird in an airplane when I get big. Not now when I'm just five years old.

A few days later Daddy and the boys went fishing. They wouldn't let me go along because they said I was too little and couldn't keep up with them. I think it might have been because I was a girl. So, I decided I'd show them I could go fishing, too, by myself.

I tied a long piece of string to a long straight stick. Then I tied a nail to the other end of the string, using it for a fish hook, just like Daddy did. Sitting on the high side of the front porch floor, I hung my line and hook over the side of the porch and fished. It didn't matter that there was no water. Sitting there I dreamed and thought and planned about what I would do when I get big

I already knew what I wanted. I wanted my own house and my own husband. I wanted just four children, two boys and two girls. I knew that I was plain looking with short, straight, brown hair and suntanned skin, not like some little girls who had blonde, curly hair, blue eyes and pink skin. My husband would be good looking so I could have good looking kids. I had seen some men in the neighborhood that were not good looking, like Daddy. And my husband must own a candy store, so I could have all the candy I wanted and not have to share it with my brothers.

Also, I would be a nurse. An older brother was a Medic in the army. He brought me a book that showed what we look like inside. Not knowing how to read I just looked at the pictures. Fascinated and curious, I asked my brother what girls do where he works. He said they are called nurses and they take care of sick people. I will be a nurse when I grow up.

A few years later, when I was ten, I started hearing grownups talking about the war across the "pond" and I was so scared. I knew Daddy and the boys shot animals for food, but I didn't know men shot each other. Soon, four of my brothers had to go fight in the war.

Daddy said we had to sell the farm so he could work building army bases and ammunition plants for the war. I missed the farm but there was so much to see and learn through the war years. We moved three times before the war was over. We had a car and a radio for the first time and sometimes electricity, running water and a bathroom for the first time in my life. Best of all, when the war was over, all my brothers came home alive. So many others did not.

The summer they ended the war we moved from a small town in Kansas to a small town in Missouri where I started my freshman year of high school. My dream was still to become a nurse, a pilot, a wife and a mother. But I would not get married until I was twenty-five years old.

When I turned sixteen, I had a busy schedule in school and helped Mom a lot at home. I was involved in church, school sports and skating. I wasn't interested in dating although I had many opportunities. My brothers thought I would be an "Old Maid."

One Sunday morning at church my girlfriend told me about some guys she met at the skating rink the night before. They had just come to town. She said they were bridge painters for the state and wanted to meet some girls: I told her I wasn't interested.

That afternoon I was walking several blocks to Easter choir practice at the church. The weather was beautiful, it was March 15th. A Model A Ford drove up the street behind me, then stopped and I turned to see who it was. I saw two guys and my girlfriend in the back seat of the car. The driver opened the passenger door and asked me where I was going. I noticed he was handsome, with bright blue eyes and dimples as he smiled. The driver said his name was Bill.

He asked me where I was going. I told him and he offered to take me the remaining few blocks to church. Since my girlfriend was in the car and it was broad daylight, I took the offer and climbed into the passenger seat. We got to the church early, so we walked to a park close by and took pictures, so we have pictures of the day we met. Before I left for choir practice, Bill asked me to go with him to a movie that night. I told him I was going to church and invited him to go with me. We went to church together. It was our first date and my first date.

We started dating, going skating, bowling, to church and to the movies together. He was so quiet, but so much fun and so nice, not rowdy like my brothers. Also, I had no one pay my way before, that was nice, and he was so handsome. I didn't realize it then, but it was a good start on the dream of a good-looking husband, so we could have good-looking children, because I thought I was plain looking.

A few weeks later, on another beautiful Sunday afternoon, we were riding around in his, new to him, '37 Hudson coupe and an airplane flew across the sky. I mentioned that I wanted to fly in an airplane someday. He said now is as good a day as any. He drove to a small airport about twenty miles away. I could not believe what was happening. I rode in a Ryan open cockpit airplane, flying like a bird. I thought, "One dream come true."

When I finished high school Bill and I, being very much in love by then, were married. I was eighteen years old, not twenty-five. Also, Bill didn't own a candy store, but I did, however, had all the candy I wanted.

Our four good-looking children, two boys and two girls, were all born before I was twenty-five years old. I now have a Masters' Degree in Nursing. I started to nursing school after the four kids were grown. Then, Bill gave me a Cessna 150 airplane for my graduation from nursing school. Neither of us could fly. I now have a pilot's license. By the grace of God and with Bill's help and with a few nightmares thrown in along the way: All My Childhood Dreams Have Come True!

# Day on the Farm

### Jerry Boling

It's morning on the farm
the air is fresh and sweet,
the aroma of hot coffee
and sizzle of breakfast meat.

Throw in some fried potatoes
and biscuits tender brown,
dripping with golden butter
and sweet strawberry jam.

Or maybe apple butter
from the tree in the backyard,
that Grandma "with her secret ingredients"
put up in quarts last fall.

Listen to the sounds
before the morning dawn,
the creaking of the windmill,
frogs down by the pond.

The mooing of the cows
waiting to be fed,
roosters crowing before sunup
making sure we're out of bed.

The mourning dove's soft call
comes over the field,
down by the creek
where it's peaceful and still.

Light up the lantern
for there's stock to be fed,
and cows to be milked
Hey—Get out of bed!

# A Christmas Gift

## Bonnie Lacey Krenning

The summer I was fourteen years old my family moved to Rich Hill, Missouri where I started high school. Daddy worked as a foreman for a construction company in Kansas City. Because of the work being seventy miles away, he could only be home on weekends.

I missed Daddy not being home all the time as he was on the farm. I remember him there reading The Weekly Kansas City Star, farming journals and often the Bible in the evening by lamplight. When he came home on week-ends he and I often spent an evening talking about news, politics, history and the Bible. I would check out books from the school library, read them, then he would take them with him to read during the week. He would bring them back the next weekend when we would discuss them.

When we moved to Rich Hill, I started going to church. In the fall of my sophomore year, I decided one Sunday morning to accept Christ into in my life and to follow him. They baptized me that evening. When I told Mom and Daddy that I had been baptized, Daddy looked thoughtful, then said, "That's good! I just hope you stick with it."

As we often did, Daddy and I spent one Saturday evening discussing the books he had read during the week. Soon our conversation turned to talking about the Bible. I asked Daddy what he believed about going to Heaven. He said, "I'm not sure. How do you believe we get to heaven?"

Fumbling for words and not sure how to answer, I said, "You just have to be saved."

He answered, "I don't know how to be saved."

Still unsure how to express myself I stammered, "You just have to believe that God sent Jesus to save us and then follow Him." The discussion was dropped and soon we were discussing the books he had taken with him the past week.

The following weekend, October 11th, Daddy was on the way back from Kansas City. About ten miles from home, he died in a single car, roll-over accident in which he was driving. He was thrown out of the car. The report said that he died instantly. Daddy's accident, and death, was and is, the greatest tragedy and loss of my entire life.

Mom wanted me to quit school and go to work. I was sixteen and in my junior year of school. I wanted to finish school and I knew Daddy had wanted me to finish school. Mom had a small amount of life insurance and somehow the family managed to get through the winter.

I had met Bill just a few months before the accident. He became my greatest emotional support and offered to marry me. But we would have to live in motels because the Missouri State paint crew he worked with moved often. When I told him I wanted to finish school, he agreed that would be best. Besides, at just sixteen, I knew I wasn't ready for marriage. I made it through the school year, with the help of family, friends and teachers.

The following summer, between my junior and senior year in high school, I went to Kansas City to stay with a relative and got a job with a mail-order company. Bill was working in the area that summer, with the paint crew; the main reason I went there. He and I saw each other at least each weekend and sometimes in between weekends. It was a calming and healing summer.

While I was at Kansas City that summer Mom moved from Rich Hill to El Dorado Springs, Missouri, about forty miles away. She wanted to be close to two of my older brothers, who had married and settled there. They could help Mom and make life much easier for her and the family.

When it was time for school to start, I wanted to finish high school in Rich Hill. Bill made it possible by paying my room and board. I moved in and started to school. He paid five dollars a week, which was a huge amount of money at that time. After a couple of weeks, I realized the cost for him was too much to continue. I started looking for another arrangement.

A wealthy couple in town had identical twin girls about eighteen months old and a new-born baby. I would have my own room and help with the babies and do routine chores. I moved there, but soon it became obvious the situation would not work. The expectations were too much for me to keep up with my schoolwork.

Then I heard about a woman who had a large house and rented rooms to men in the area. There was an extra room for a maid which was vacant. The owner was looking for a maid. She also owned the best restaurant in town and was looking for a waitress. The woman, who would become my boss, said if I wanted them both positions were mine. I surely did! I moved into my room the first part of November.

I did the laundry and cleaning once a week on Saturday. At mealtimes I went to the restaurant when I soon learned the routine of waitressing. My boss, however, allowed me to put school first and I studied in my room, late at night. I managed to finish my senior year at mid-term, in January, on the Honor Roll.

Still very much grieving the loss of Daddy and with the stress and hard work of the past many months wearing on me, I was exhausted most of the time. Ever since he died, I could not get the memory out of my mind of him saying, "I don't know how to be saved," the last time we talked. I often wondered if how I answered was helpful for him.

One Saturday night just before Christmas, after doing laundry, cleaning house and working three meals in the restaurant, I collapsed into bed. Exhausted, I fell into a deep sleep. Soon I was back in the restaurant, behind the counter, wiping the countertops; there didn't seem to be anyone else around. Then I heard someone and looked up. Daddy was sitting on the stool on the other side of the counter, smiling as usual. I was bewildered and amazed, but so thankful and happy.

At first, I was speechless! Then I said, "How did you get here?"

Smiling, he said quietly, "I just thought I'd come down and see you for a while."

I awakened and realizing I had been dreaming, I sat straight up in bed! Peace and joy flooded my being. It had lifted such a weight off my shoulders I felt like I could float.

The dream is as real as anything that has ever happened in my life. I believe God sent me a message through a dream: Daddy is waiting for me in Heaven. God revealed to Daddy how to get to

Heaven and that Daddy believed and accepted God's promise before he died. This I Believe!

What a Wonderful Christmas Gift!

# Christmas Memories

Ann Alvis

Christmas has always been my favorite time of the year. I loved it as a child but more as a mother of five children: four daughters and one son.

The Christmas decorations on houses, streets and in stores, made me excited about the approaching holiday.

Raising my children, we tried to make the holidays as memorable as possible.

The day after Thanksgiving we drove to a Christmas tree farm and looked around to find that perfect emerald green tree. Their father would take his saw and cut it down and tie it on top of the car.

One Christmas the children picked a very large tree. So big we had to bring it in through our large window in the living room because it wouldn't fit in the door. I was reluctant to get it, but the children were set on this particular tree. It took an entire day to decorate it.

We hung tinsel, bulbs and strung on the lights. Their father always put the star on top. This year he had to get a ladder. There was laughter in the air as they turned the lights on for the first time. I got a warm cuddle and a kiss from my husband under the mistletoe. We smiled as we watched the excited faces of our children.

Christmas presents surrounded the tree. The children tried to guess what was in the packages as they sat near the tree and shook them around. It was fun for them, until I caught them and told them, "Keep it up and you might break them."

The children and I made cookies of trees, snowmen, stars and candy canes. Seeing flour in their hair and on their small faces and frosting on their small hands made my heart pound with love. They had so much fun.

On Christmas Eve, the children's father would tell them the Christmas story and about the true meaning why we celebrate the holiday. They held cups of hot chocolate as they listened to his voice, taking it all in. We gave them kisses and hugs before going to bed, knowing they would find it hard to sleep.

Christmas Day was full of laughter as they tore their gifts open. Then we headed to the big family dinner. When we walked through the door, we could smell the turkey cooking with all the fixings. Aunts, uncles, cousins and Grandma and Granddad were there waiting for everyone to arrive.

Women worked in the kitchen; men set tables and chairs up for our big family. If snow was on the ground, the children made snowmen and had snowball fights in the backyard. Some of the adults joined in. On nicer holidays it was a game of football.

At the end of the long day, the children's eyes were closed with smiles on their faces.

My children are now grown with children of their own. They're making memories with their children and remembering their Christmas memories.

My husband and son spend Christmas in heaven.

The family made a tradition of laying wreaths on veteran's graves on the Wreath Across America Day. They lay a wreath on their father's grave as tears fill their eyes and they remember the wonderful memories he gave to them.

We thank each soldier who gave their life and years to make sure we kept our freedom.

Christmas is still exciting. I am older now. I still enjoy the holiday with my family and thank Jesus for the blessings He has given me throughout my years.

# Two Separate Worlds

## Jean Welle

She studied her face in the mirror and wondered why he no longer remembered his little angel. How she longed to hear him call her that once more, or even say she would always be his beautiful princess. She studied his reflection, lanky and good-looking, slumped forward on the edge of the over-stuffed sofa, shuffling the photos she'd laid out on the coffee table for him. He picked one up only to put it back and shuffle some more.

"Dad," she said, returning to sit next to him, "remember when you bought that BB gun for me? Mother thought you had lost your mind." She laughed…alone. "This is another photo taken the same day, Dad," she said, picking it up from the assortment. "You set those bales of hay up against the barn and made that target so I could practice. And I love this one," she continued, picking up another. "Mother captured the thrill we shared when I finally hit the bull's eye."

No response.

The lump in her throat swelled as she fought back the tears. Please, God! Just one more moment with my dad. "Oh, and this one I took of you holding that tiny mouse by the tail that had tormented Mom for weeks. You were always her hero!" She laughed again. Alone.

"That one over there is a once-in-a-lifetime photo, Dad." She pointed and placed her finger on it. "Remember this swarm of honeybees clustered against the lamp post? I remember how shocked I was when you bravely waved your unprotected arm through them without a sting. You explained to me that they were from a hive somewhere and would all die because something had happened to their queen. Their purpose for living was gone." She felt his hand as he reached for the photo. A frown furrowed his brow as he turned to look at her. She held her breath.

"Maggie!" His eyes locked affectionately with hers for a moment, his hand reached to touch her face ever so gently. She hugged him then, resting her head in the crook of his neck as his arms held her close in response. Then they went limp. He returned to the world she could not enter.

"It's okay, Dad," she said, unashamed of the tears that slid down her cheeks as she spoke. "It's Mama I see in the mirror now and I miss her, too." She kissed him on the forehead and patted his arm. He had returned to her world one more time, and she resolved to be with him for the duration.

Maggie would have.

# We Travel On

### Cherise Langenberg

Through laughter and grin,
thickness and thin,
We travel on, ...

Through faith and hope,
with limited scope,
We travel on, ...

Through sunshine and rain,
disagreement and shame,
We travel on, ...

Through girls and boys,
happiness and joys,
We travel on, ...

Through quick and slow,
with little ones and big ones in tow,
We travel on, ...

Through mirth and sorrow,
new mercies tomorrow, ...
We travel on, ...

Through sickness and health,
needs and wealth,
We travel on, ...

Through Jesus' might,
s  eeking eternal delight,
We travel on, ...

Through death and pain,
for Heaven's reign, ...
WE TRAVEL ON!

Celebrating 20 & 30 years of marriage,
written for my beloved, Scott Langenberg
With all my love, Cherise Langenberg
September 23, 2009 and 2019 reprised

# A Good Ghost Story

Mary McKay

When my last castle, which was on the Little Arkansas River was demolished, I finally figured out I would have to move. I thought of staying in my old neighborhood but listened to that little voice inside my head.

Truth is, I hate to move. It is also true that I knew what I should do, go to Scotland. I knew exactly where I needed to go and why. I would like to haunt a handsome highlander and love to hear that beautiful accent. Not only that, but I am drawn like a moth to a flame to a man in a kilt. Most important of all, I wanted to solve a family tree mystery. It would make my mother happy.

Superstitious people are the best kind to live with. They are more in tune with the possibilities of ghosts and more likely to respect them and leave them alone. Nothing makes me happier than to see a rabbit's foot or a saltshaker on the table. I'm always on the lookout for candles that haven't burned, just for good luck. My grandmother always lit them and then blew them out. She said it was bad luck to have a candle that hadn't been tested. Almost as bad as opening an umbrella inside the house.

Being a McKay, I was interested in that family tree the most. The McKays and the Lynchs moved to America and came across the United States in covered wagons. They lived in Chapman, Kansas, where my paternal grandmother, Ellen Josephine Lynch, was born. Eventually, they went to Avery, Lincoln County, Oklahoma, and homesteaded.

The movie, Far and Away, with Tom Cruise and Nicole Kidman, was about as good a portrayal of their lives as I can refer you to. I have the old family Bible of John Joseph Lynch, and it lists the family records, along with several daguerreotypes that portray the family.

According to a small newspaper clipping in the Bible, my great, great grandmother, Eliza McKay, was said to have read more than any other woman in Indian Territory. I often thought it would be wonderful to go to Scotland and see where they came from. Documented in the family Bible, John and Ellen's first daughter, Eliza, died and was buried in Scotland. When they came to America, they had a two-year-old son. The remainder of their eight children were born across the states and in Kansas.

I was so wrapped up in their lives I searched out the very spot on the globe where they came from. As I put my finger on the spot, something in my spirit said, "NO, your ancestors came from the Highlands!" My finger moved involuntarily and pointed to a spot on the globe where I needed to go. The Grampian Mountains in the north of Scotland. I was mystified, but hey, what do I know? Of course, now I know it was the ghost from the Burnett castle in the Highlands. I was younger then and not sure if I believed in ghosts, now I was one.

My mother had spent good money to send me to a class on genealogy and handed me a large box of old papers on her family tree. I was angry at first, but my anger soon turned to awe as I picked through the box of old documents. I sorted them and organized them into notebooks. One for each family surname. My bookcase was almost full of family histories. All my previous efforts had been on my father's family and I decided she was just jealous. I discovered she didn't need to be.

The class was put on by Everton Publishers, a company out of Logan, Utah. They print forms and books for sale to people wanting to trace their family roots. They not only sold forms and books to organize your records in but also taught how to go about searching libraries, courthouses, church records, cemeteries, and other sources for factual information. The church of Latter Day Saints, in Salt Lake City, Utah has one of the largest genealogy libraries in America.

Once Mama gave me her family records, I began to organize them. The Burnett family, that she is descended from, was detailed in a book, called The Burnetts of the South. It listed my Burnett ancestors in North Carolina, back to the American Revolutionary War. Two of the three Burnett brothers, known as "the Virginians," died on October 7, 1780 in the Battle of Kings Mountain. The family were first documented in Ashville, North Carolina.

After many years of research and study, I eventually learned that the Burnetts in America could not trace their family tree back to the castle in the highlands. Now, I felt compelled to go there with the information I had and settle in that castle. The ghost had obviously wanted me to know where to go. If my facts were correct, the only way to prove it was to go there and investigate.

Now, for the mystery that I am hoping can be resolved. In the book, The Burnetts of the South, we were left without knowing where and when our Burnett ancestors came from Scotland to America. The book details the family and pictures of the family castle, Crathes, near Banchory, exactly where I had pointed!

According to the author of the book, they had searched every port where they might have entered, from Kenny Bunkport, Maine to New Orleans, Louisiana. They had searched ship manifests, tracked colonial records, and could never verify if we actually belonged to that Scotland family of Burnett. All we knew of the Burnetts were the three brothers, Jesse, Thomas, and Joseph, known as the Virginians.

Over the years, I have tried to find more, without success. I have found lots of other relatives. My Aunt Ruth Kelly, who lived in St. Louis, belonged to the DAR—Daughters of the American Revolution. I eventually joined that organization myself. Our ancestor Thomas Bell lived in North Carolina and fought in the American Revolution. Through the DAR, I also discovered that I was a descendant of Colonel Joseph Hayes, of Lauren's County, South Carolina. and Colonel Daniel Smith, of North Carolina. Both are ancestors who fought in the Revolution.

Because of all these connections with the Revolution, when Senator Todd Tiahrt visited my DAR luncheon one day, and asked if any of we ladies would help the SAR (Sons of the American Revolution), finish a monument they were trying to build in Veterans Memorial Park. Of course, my arm went up, just like my finger moved over the globe. The upshot of all this is, that I am on the Board of Directors of the American Revolutionary War Memorial. I worked on it since 2011 and it is completed and was dedicated on the Fourth of July 2019.

One way we raised funds, to build the memorial, was to sell tiles to be engraved with the names of Patriots that fought in the American

Revolution. We also listed the person who purchased the tile. They are $100 each. Between a 3rd cousin of mine and myself, we have five tiles on the memorial. It was through investigating the last two tiles that a remarkable piece of information came my way. Another board member was researching the two Burnett brothers, Thomas and Joseph Burnett, both died at the Battle of Kings Mountain, and their father and grandfather were listed in a document in Ancestry. com. It was called, The Blue Ridge Mountain Burnetts.

Wow! Was I excited! Their grandfather, Phillip Burnett, was born in Scotland in 1688 and immigrated to New Castle, Delaware in 1712. He brought his young son Fredrick Thomas, born 1708 in Scotland, with him. Phillip called Fredrick Thomas, "Son Thomas." They eventually moved to Brunswick County, Virginia, where all three brothers, Jesse, Thomas, and Joseph were born. The family eventually moved to Ashville, North Carolina and that explains why they were knows as "The Virginians." I am a direct descendant of Thomas Burnett, born 1735.

Next, I had to get out my book on Crathes Castle and the genealogy listing in it. I discovered that Sir Thomas Burnett, 3rd Baronet, and his wife, Margaret "Arbuthnot" Burnett, had a son, John, born in 1688. Perhaps that son's complete name was John Phillip? That is my mission. If I can find that out for certain and get some documentation to that effect, I will be satisfied.

I have a hypothesis that (John?) Phillip Burnett, born 1688, called his son, "Son Thomas," because his father was "Sir Thomas." Because family names seem to pass down, I find that my mother's name of Margaret, and my son's name, Thomas, are both good examples. My 3rd cousin's great grandfather, John Frank Burnett, is another example of family naming. John Phillip and John Frank are examples of a saint's name, for baptism, along with a more secular name used more often.

As an aside, if Sir Thomas, the 3rd Baronet, is my ancestor and his wife was Margaret Arbuthnot, she was the daughter of the 2nd Viscount Arbuthnot, Robert. If that is the case, I may even visit Arbuthnot Castle and Muchalls Castle, near Stonehaven, which the 3rd Baronet built. All three are close together. After seeing a photo of Muchalls, I have a feeling my mother has already set herself up as resident ghost there. Sir Thomas was building it for his Margaret when he was called home upon the death of his father. Margaret Arbuthnot's mother was from the family of Keith, another good Scots name.

The good ghosts of all these fine people are swarming around in my head. Yes, I'd better plan on a trip to Scotland and get the rest of the story.

# Always a Part of Me

## Starla Criser

She liked lavish, sentimental cards. I like humorous ones. She liked to watch beauty pageants and silly comedies. I prefer action shows and adventures. It seems we had little in common, and yet we were bound by something powerful—love.

This special person so unlike me, yet exactly like me, was my mother. I lost her twentfive years ago. She left this world, but left me with years of memories.

Over time and healing, I've remembered so many things about my mother and what she did for me. Things that I took for granted.

I grew up with a mother whose cooking skills were limited. But I'll always remember her Bisquick donuts, the cake she made with the brown sugar topping, and her homemade ice cream.

Mom never wanted animals of any kind around her house. Yet I can't remember ever not having a pet.

I remember her concern as she wiped my tears. I can still feel her hugs. I'll never forget her gentle laugh and the way her eyes would sparkle when she poorly told a joke. I'll always recall how she'd never let Dad leave the house for work without kissing him goodbye.

Another thing I fondly remember is the way she displayed all of mine and my siblings attempts at creating works of art. For years the refrigerator was covered with crayon drawings of often unidentifiable objects. The top of the television and the shelves of the upright piano proudly held misshapen ceramic pieces, plaster casts of our hands, and various other items. These "wonderful" creations seemed to stay there forever. I even found a few of those long ago treasures stored away in a bottom dresser drawer after her death.

Opal Mae Wahl Tolliver was my mother. I couldn't have loved her more or be prouder to be her daughter. My hope is that my daughter loves me as much and remembers me as fondly one day.

# On the Shelf

Mary McKay

I'm not sure how they managed to get into my small apartment. They were all having a good time. Everyone was comfortable and enjoying themselves so much that I simply couldn't send anyone home. I didn't want to ask even one of them to leave.

If I tried to describe them all it would be impossible, yet I doubt if such an assembly could have found a more appreciative hostess. Perhaps you will recognize some of them?

There was one woman, her name was Jane, who seemed to be so compelling I was drawn to her at once. A warmth and something of sadness seemed to cling to her. She was so completely cut off from the rest of the group that I followed her gaze across the room and was started to see it was locked with that of one of my most fascinating male heroes—Rochester. They didn't seem to be aware of anyone else in the room.

I checked out the distinguished man standing next to me. He seemed to watch the others with an appreciative smile. He said, "I should be minding the store, but in my quest for the best I wanted to be here." I think he knew we were both in good company. Said he was from Dallas, Texas.

Down the room a little way, I saw a really fascinating character that everyone seemed to have heard of and quite a large group of people were studying him, have been for years, I guess. Someone told me his nickname was "The Bard."

Everywhere I looked they were talking, and I wanted to listen to every one of them. "Hold on here!" I said. "Just one at a time please. I can't listen to all of you at once. If you'll give me enough time, I will listen to each one of you tell your story."

"I'm your Huckleberry!" said the white-haired fellow in front of me. He wore a white suit. A large bushy mustache and wild eyebrows made him seem rather quaint.

One dear thing said to me, "The pride and prejudice, the sense and sensibility that are assembled here is simply overwhelming."

Another lady told me. "You really must hear about my dinner at Antoine's, and also the trip I made down River Road."

One tiny, little lady said she had a secret garden, knew a little princess, little Lord Fauntleroy, and wanted me to meet them, along with that lass of O'Lowrie's. She thought I might also like the head of the House of Coombs, if I would let her introduce him. She confided to me, in a low voice, that she had married one of my ancient uncles, but that the marriage had unfortunately ended in divorce.

One couple looked like they were not getting along very well but the sparks that flew between the two of them seemed to mesmerize everyone around them. "Scarlet and Rhett are here too," someone whispered into my ear, and I realized I was glad they had come to this gathering.

How was I going to make room for all of them to stay with me? Short of putting up a bunch of shelves and stacking some of them in boxes and on top of each other I couldn't find a way to keep them near me and not one wanted to leave.

"I am so glad you're all here," I said to them. "I don't know how my life would have been more enriched than to have met you all and I can't bear to part with even one of you!

"Georgette, I love the banter and wit you use to entertain me, and I know I can't let you go. Or you, Joan Smith, I'll find a place for you. You, too, Agatha, I love a good mystery!"

Before the night was over, I decided they could all stay. I would find a way.

# STORIES FROM CHALLENGES

# Archive/Scrapbook/Biography

Mary McKay

"Look in that top drawer and bring me the scrapbook." requested Sister Mary Walburga. A chest of drawers sat in front of the only window in the small room. A Ludicia Discolor orchid, in a hammered copper planter, was on top of the dresser. The lush, beautiful foliage of its deep green leaves, traced with what looked like bright copper wires, created a pattern on each leaf. It sat on a snow-white dresser cloth, with hand tatted edges, creating a lovely display. Her room was warm and sunny. The only other decoration was the wooden crucifix, centered on the wall above the narrow bed topped with a hand-crocheted bedspread.

I took the scrapbook to her and settled myself on the small, wooden, sewing rocker next to her old overstuffed and comfortable chair. The antimacassar cloth on the top of the back and matching arm covers protected it from soil.

"What a beautiful album cover," I said.

"I did the needlepoint for it with bits and pieces of woolen yarn that were too small to make anything else. I had fun letting the design create itself. I had no idea what would emerge. Divine Guidance brought forth the orange and mulberry abstract design. I used black to fill in the gaps and it came out looking like a stained glass window. We get lots of yarn donated here at the convent. Those two colors were too bright and cheery to be used for anything else. The Sisters like more sedate choices for wearing apparel."

Sister Mary Walburga opened the cover of the scrapbook and it was like watching a pirate's chest of jewelry being revealed in the bright sunlit room. The exquisite illuminated design inside was executed with striking colors. Shaped like the French cross, known as a fleur-de-lis, it had several jewel colors: ruby red, lapis lazuli blue, emerald green, amethysts purple and a rich metallic gold design. It mesmerized me. "Sister Agnes Marie painted this for me. She did illuminated manuscripts for the prayer cards we sell in the gift shop."

"It is truly beautiful!"

"Our little gift shop here at the convent has given us a source of income to purchase those things we cannot produce ourselves here at Saint Ignatius Convent. Some of the Sisters do beautiful needlework, some make soaps, candles and other useful items. Our biggest project is making gluten-free communion wafers. We even have some oil paintings and watercolors for sale. That income buys sugar, flour, salt, coffee, tea, and other essentials, along with a few incidentals."

She turned the page and revealed a display with a small rosary tacked with clear fishing line to the decorative paper that is so popular with scrapbook creators. It had a beautiful filigree cross and the beads of the rosary appeared to be made of animal horns, maybe goat. The daily prayers requested by the many benefactors of the convent were given great priority.

Another page was turned to reveal a two-page centerfold of photographs that told a chronological story of Sister's life from infancy to adulthood.

"You were a delightful little girl!" I said. "Where did your family live when you were a child?"

"Oh, we were all over the place." She adjusted her book and examined it carefully with her sharp, blue eyes. "It was almost like a gypsy's life. My father had a wanderlust, and it seemed like we moved every whipstitch. The grass always looked greener on the other side of the fence to him and his Irish ancestry beckoned him to greener pastures."

I tried to contemplate what kind of life that would have been for a little girl. My parents had lived in the same home my father was born in and lived in until the day he died. Stability vs. instability.

"It gave me a deep appreciation of permanency. The ancient walls of Saint Ignatius Convent represented not only stability, but peace, and tranquility for me. I never wanted to leave it, and from the time I entered its doors, until this day, I have been in this one home and plan to be buried in the lovely, and secluded cemetery that holds so many of my dearly, departed sisters, of happy memory."

"How old were you when you entered?"

"I was twenty-eight," she said. "Too long in the tooth to be eligible for marriage at such an advanced age. My father's penchant for uprooting us all the time, gave me few friends, except for books. As soon as my mother had taught me to read, she began to supply me with literature of every description and genre. Books were the sustenance for my spirit and by the time I entered the convent I had a liberal education far beyond that of most children confined to place and entertained by friends."

"Have you ever regretted your choice?"

"A few times, but God's ways are not our ways. Every time I considered it; He revealed His plans for me. He was always wise enough to make them irresistible to me."

She turned one page after another as I watched her life unfold. She had blossomed into a beautiful young lady and aged into a delightful looking, interesting older woman. It was obvious from her appearance that she had led a pious, productive and meaningful life. One photo showed her up in the limbs of a pear tree, picking fruit. Another depicted the many jars of canned vegetables, as she arranged them in rows. Canned with expert care, they would no doubt grace the tables of the convent all winter long.

"What was the best part of it all?" I asked.

"Being selected as Mother Superior by my peers. I was so excited when the vote came in unanimously in my favor. I had no idea they held me in such high esteem." She pointed to a photo of her in the habit of her order as they gave her a rolled document, tied with a ribbon. I assumed it was some sort of certificate, or confirmation of her appointment. Then she said, "They gave me a little letter of appreciation by the delegates who put me forth as a candidate. Then the entire Congregation voted for me. Afterwards, the Sisters each approached me to promise their obedience of the house rules."

With the gentlest of hands, she closed the scrapbook and handed it back to me to replace in the dresser drawer. It was a true archive.

# Salmon Fishing

Mary McKay

When Captain Meriwether Lewis and William Clark crossed the Columbia River into the Tri-Cities area of Washington State, little did they know they were wading in the river that would one day be a salmon fishers paradise. Few places have a richer history of salmon than the Columbia.

My daughter lives in Richland, Washington and took me to the historical marker that pinpoints a spot where that crossing is alleged to have taken place in 1805.

The Chinook Salmon runs from March through October. In their stubborn determination to spawn, they are protected from any interference. Because a tremendous economy depends upon the success of these fish, the people of Washington and Oregon, both work to protect, give a leg up, and promote salmon.

Standing beside the Columbia can be a spiritual experience. The peaceful quiet is almost like being in a great cathedral. The occasional splash of a fish as it flips along its way, a bird song, or maybe an insect will disrupt the quiet with a whirl of its wings. A frog might croak or flop into the water, but these are about all that will be heard.

There are places where the rush of freezing water and the splashing rapids are almost deafening, but near the Lewis and Clark memorial, things remained calm and quiet. The riverbed is wide, but flat and looked shallow. At least it was the day we were there. I'm sure it can rise and be very menacing.

You can almost imagine the corn being crushed by Sacajawea, their Native American guide, as she made the fried bread so familiar to her culture. Maybe you can even hear the fat sizzle in the skillet?

# Abandoned

## Don Boldea

A windy, black, suspicious looking storm was racing across the Great Plains. The atmosphere was hot and humid. An expanse of wild Kansas Sunflowers was moving like waves of saffron, never ending, never ceasing. Mother Nature was flexing her muscle.

The homestead has existed for over one hundred and thirty-five years. Originally, a grass sod house was the only protection the family had from the elements. As time passed, a grand timber structure with lumber hauled in all the way from Colorado replaced it. I love the land and the families I protect.

Why, I have withstood the wrath of tornados, draught, floods and prairie fires. My walls have served four generations of cattle ranchers and another four generations of wheat farmers. Through all of this history, I stood indestructible and proud.

Then, one day I was abandoned for a bigger, more modern and beautiful home. They built it on a different plot of pasture, nearer to the city, with an irregular-shaped zig zagging creek they called Elbow Creek.

I hoped that one of their children would come and live in me. But no, no one came.

Over the years I fell into disrepair. My roof finally opened to the sky offering no more protection for my once strong but now rotting Colorado timbers. In time, I will collapse into a disarrayed pile of wooden splinters.

Abandoned, yes, but I'm still proud to have lived a long, useful and interesting life.

# Abandoned House

## Mary McKay

We had driven past the old abandoned house many times over the years. I was always curious about it and today seemed like the perfect time to go exploring. Out on our Sunday afternoon drive, to look over the countryside, we were near our home in the Flint Hills of Kansas. I always enjoyed seeing the great expanse of space and the lay of the land. I think it reminded me of some genetic memory of Scotland, where my ancestors were from. The house was built of locally quarried stone on the order of so many houses in the eastern half of the state. It was as close to a Scottish castle as I would likely find.

"Let's go look inside," I said.

"Why not, it's as good a day as any," Alex said, as he turned the car up the weed-infested driveway. Sunflowers and weeds were growing taller than the car on both sides of the hard-packed dirt of the two lanes that straddled the middle of the drive which almost high-centered the car.

"Hang on!" Alex shouted. The car swerved from left to right as he attempted to avoid a particularly large sunflower. He eventually managed to get the left wheels on top of the center of the drive and the right wheels up on the side of the drive's embankment.

"Maybe this was a mistake?" I said.

"No, we've wanted to do this for years and it's now or never." He made a sharp left turn and came to a stop right at the back door to the house. It was an easy two step climb to the porch surface and the back door was standing more than half open. We walked in.

"Hello!" I shouted into the echoing interior. No response was returned, so we advanced into the kitchen of the house. It was a nice sun-shiny day, a bit windy, but the room was cheerful and welcoming. Two long narrow windows on the south side extended from about six inches from the ceiling to almost six inches off the floor. A stone floored porch could have been stepped out onto if those windows had been opened. A plain kitchen table with two chairs sat ready to use. The flannel-backed oil cloth still graced the center of the table along with a salt and pepper shaker. The shaker was lying on its side. The table was littered with bits of broken plaster from the ceiling high above and covered with a thick layer of dust from ages of disuse. A wasp nest was included is the debris.

"Look at this," Alex said. He was holding a very large cast-iron skillet that was encrusted in a chard and flaking coating of grease and grime. The black wood-burning cook stove had the usual fittings and accessories and the old tea kettle was sitting on the back burner.

"Hey, we could clean this up and use it on cookouts!" he suggested.

"Not unless you have some old-fashioned lye soap to soak it in for a week or two."

"What do you think this is in here?" I asked, as I tried to pry open the small wooden door on the north side of the kitchen. The house butted up to a steep incline on the north side of the house and I didn't see how it could lead to anywhere. Suddenly the door gave way and revealed a dark hole that appeared to be a tunnel into the side of the hill beside the house.

"My dad would say, 'It's as black as the inside of a cow's stomach in there," Alex said.

I was immediately suspicious and wanted a flashlight or candle or something to illuminate the interior. "I think it is a root cellar. I am going to go get the flashlight out of the car." I headed to the back door and made a quick trip to the car and back. I pushed him aside with my elbow and flooded the cavity with light.

"It must be twenty degrees cooler in here!" I said, as I circled the room with curiosity. The light revealed many shelves with canning jars draped in cobwebs and dust. The floor was hard-packed dirt and the entire dimensions of the room were possibly twelve feet by twenty feet deep. The ceiling was a reverse flooring of wood and was so low Alex had to stoop over to be inside. The shelves seemed to hold up the roof and several barrels sat about in no particular order. A small table was positioned in the middle of the room and the candle holder was empty. Possibly the candle had been eaten by mice?

I started backing out of the room with the hair standing up on my neck and forearms. Something alerted me to the possibilities of rats, snakes, spiders and other creepy varmints being the residents of this close and oppressive expanse.

"Come on, Sue. You surely aren't afraid in here are you?" Alex asked.

"I just think prudence is the better part of valor. It just feels weird to me."

We both left the root cellar and he quickly shut the door and turned the wooden latch that held it is place. We then poked our heads into the living room and were restored to good humor by the bay window on the west side of the room. Again, the window was close to the ceiling and had a nice window seat built into the bay that would have been a perfect location for all kinds of houseplants. A broken terracotta pot was scattered across the expanse, along with sufficient dirt to fill it.

The stove pipe from the old wood-burning stove lay in a reckless array on the floor and black powdery soot extended from both ends of each piece. It was covered with a good thick coat of dust so that it really didn't look like the awful mess it would be to clean up. The gaping hole in the chimney where the stovepipe should have been connected, appeared to have parts of a bird's nest hanging out into the room. This house had been abandoned for all the years we had lived on our place, so my guess was at least fifteen years. It was obvious that some little critters, possibly squirrels or rats, had tracked the soot about on many various occasions throughout the years.

A stairway led up the north wall and we both headed toward it. "Do we dare?" Alex asked.

"Of course, we do! I don't want to miss anything we can see today," I answered.

We slowly climbed up the stairs and found ourselves in a low-ceiling room that was divided by a wall with a door. The brick chimney of the wood-burning stove downstairs extended through the ceiling. Four fairly small, and rectangle-shaped windows on the south wall were matched with two on the north. They were the kind that opened up into the room on hinges and latched on the opposite side. The window at the end of the room was a full-sized window.

The room was empty except for a few children's toys scattered about on a shelf along one wall. Some Popsicle stick vehicles had been made in the style of military vehicles. An old cigar box that I investigated contained some letters that were from a soldier to his sweetheart. Nestled, as they were, under an assortment of glass marbles, they had been left behind to tell their stories.

Alex proceeded to the second room which was a twin of the one we were in. It had an old-fashioned bedstead with wire box-springs on the slats. The contents of the once stuffed mattress were scattered around the room in clumps and wads. Once again, I got the feeling that small animals were possibly nesting in the mattress innards. I suddenly wanted out of the house completely.

"I'm out of here," I said, and made a dash for the stairs. As I descended them, I could hear Alex's shoes, fast on the treads behind me, and we kept up a brisk pace until we were outside on the back porch again.

"That was a satisfying adventure. I feel like a scientist that has just finished an experiment, or an explorer that has just reached the top of a mountain," Alex said, as he whipped the car around, and we bumped our way down that awful driveway.

# The Middle of Nowhere:
# A Continuing Intrigue Story

## Lois Ann Seiwert

"Oh, my goodness! What time is it and where are we?" piped Julie from the back of the van.

"Well good morning, um, afternoon," Rosie answered. "We're still six hours from Chicago and a long way from Seattle. And we're two miles from a rest stop and convenience center. Tom needs some lunch and a chance to stretch his legs. I will do likewise. You are welcome to join us."

Turning in her seat, Rosie continued, "Tom will take a nap. I will drive as we go on down the freeway into the middle of nowhere. I'm so glad that you will keep me company."

She paused, looking out the window. "Right now, I'm thinking I will get a small bag of ice for the cooler. And maybe some bars in case we need something quick to eat."

\*\*\*\*\*\*

"That was great! Everything was so good, and everyone got to order something that they wanted," Tom said, grinning and patting his stomach. "That double cheeseburger, sweet potato fries, and large dill pickle filled me up good." He grinned even more. "But I couldn't pass up that free soft serve ice cream, especially not a chocolate cone."

He started running, making circles around Rosie and Julie as they walked back to the van.

"What are you doing?" Julie asked, amused by his burst of energy.

As Rosie put the ice in the cooler and closed it, Tom stopped, looking restless. "How about we walk over to the far corner of the rest area and back for a little more exercise?"

"I'm game," Julie and Rosie answered together. Smiling, Rosie closed and locked the van.

Refreshed and eager to get on the road again, they returned to the van and checked the map. With a quick look outside, Julie noted they appeared to be heading into gentle rolling countryside. There weren't any trees or buildings in sight. They were going into "the middle of nowhere," just as Rosie had said.

With Tom settled into the sleeping bag, Rosie filled the van up with gas, washed the windshield, and climbed into the driver's seat.

"It will be good to get back to some things we have going on," Rosie said, pulling out of the rest stop. "There are a couple of gigs in a few weeks. We were working on some new song ideas when the trip to Chicago turned up. It is amazing that everything came together so we could do some things we needed to do and also help you get out of a bind."

Rosie glanced at Julie. "Oh, while I'm thinking of it ... If you will get in the glove compartment, your cell phone is in there. You can keep the other 'communication device' in case something unknown appears on the scene and presents a problem."

Julie stared out the window for a bit before she pulled out her phone. She thought about "the communication device" they had given her, and the bind her friends had helped her with. About how she'd invoked The Plan Code 3, an agreement between she and her friends they had agreed to in order to help her in any dangerous situation. Sometimes her life was so complicated.

Putting those thoughts aside, she turned to Rosie. "Thanks for the phone. I hadn't thought of it yet. I must check later for any important messages."

She took a deep breath. Their current situation made her think back to after their college days. She'd gone to Japan to teach English. Rosie had gone to Africa. "This 'middle of nowhere' stuff makes me think of your African Peace Corps outpost. When you were two hours from the nearest city with train service and some regional government offices. Something about being on the boundary of a wild game preserve and being an outpost for several settlements scattered around the area. Sounds pretty isolated and scary to me."

Rosie took a second before she said, "Gosh, I haven't thought about that for some time. Yes, it was scary, especially for a small-town gal. I had heard about coyotes but had seen nothing bigger than a racoon in the wild."

She smiled at Julie. "Oh, I'd been to the zoo in Chicago but that was different. Everything was in cages or behind big fences. You were safe there!"

Julie's stomach tightened at the mention of feeling safe. After what she'd gone through with Eric, her quick departure from the danger, she was still uneasy. Maybe if her friend kept talking about her past, it would distract Julie from those memories. She offered Rosie an encouraging look. "Tell me about the experience." She'd heard some of it before, but not all.

Rosie focused on the road. "During our orientation they reassured us that in the ten years that the Peace Corps had an arrangement for residents, there had been no serious problems with animals. A couple of old lions, which they scared off with their water cannon, and a young male prowling for territory wandered in and left as soon as he saw strange activity."

She frowned. "There were strict rules for activity and housing. You did not go outside from sundown to sunrise. No food or food scraps in the open anywhere, all doors and windows securely locked at all times. No carousing or loud noise. They cautioned us to always be on alert if we were outside and gave us whistles to wear or carry."

Julie knew she wouldn't have wanted to even think about that much potential danger. "I'm glad I didn't get those kinds of warnings during my time teaching in Japan."

"Most of the time we didn't think about it too much, beyond being cautious," Rosie said with a quick look at Julie. "We had been on site for about six months and things had settled into a nice routine. School sessions in the mornings—learning simple math, craft and construction projects one day a week and a visit from a state cultural coordinator from the city on another. She knew English besides the local dialect. She would bring her set of picture cards and we would do games or exercises to learn the words in both languages."

She smiled. "When we started the sounds of our alphabet, two of the older students got real interested. They wanted to make their own alphabet so they could write words like we did in English. They used some of our letters but had to create others for sounds that English didn't have. It was exciting to watch them figure things out. We also started to have language classes ourselves with the kids teaching us their sounds so we could identify the things in their lives and begin to talk in their language."

"That must have been fun for you," Julie inserted.

"It was fun, encouraging, too. We heard later that several of those students were invited to attend the school in the city so they could work on their alphabet project and learn more language and math skills."

Julie thought about her time teaching English in Japan. It had been rewarding.

"The afternoons were spent helping local people with problems and working on the bedroom addition and storage shed that were being built for the Animal Preserve Patrol," Rosie said, catching Julie's attention again. "The kitchen expansion was just about finished and they were planning a big festival for everyone in the surrounding area to thank them for their help."

She drew in a breath, hesitated. "That all changed late one afternoon. The animal alert sirens came on in emergency mode. The Patrol hit the streets in their secured safari vehicles warning everyone to get to safety, lock down, and stay put until they were contacted. Luckily, I was already at my place. I pulled most of my curtains and flipped on the night light. I parked my chair in front of my peep hole so I could catch any activity."

Julie tensed, remembering having heard some of this story. "I would have been scared to death."

Rosie nodded, looking straight ahead at the road. "I remember being lost in thought about our plans for the next day when I heard the sounds of bird songs. The Patrol used that for a horn, because it didn't startle the animals."

Her fingers tightened on the steering wheel. "I checked my peep hole to confirm that a Patrol man was here to see me. He reviewed my lock down list and reminded me of the rules about staying put until I heard from them about any change. Then he told me what they knew at this point. It wasn't good news."

Julie thought about stopping her friend from telling anymore of the story. But she sensed Rosie needed to get it out.

Rosie continued after a minute. "There was a small group of houses on the south edge of the settlement, mostly young families. One woman whose husband was out of town on his job during the week was having a picnic lunch with her young son who loved to eat outdoors. Her husband had made them a little low picnic table that sat not more than twenty feet from the house. Her son was singing a melody of sounds he was learning to speak."

She stopped to swallow hard. "Not thinking, she went toward the house to get something she had forgotten. Her daughter was standing at the door, unhappy. She had spilled her drink on some pictures she was coloring and all over the floor. The mom hurried to clean it up, grabbed the food she needed and headed for the door."

Julie knew what came next, wanted to stop her friend, but braced herself instead.

Rosie glanced at Julie, horror in her eyes. "The mother screamed when she couldn't see her son. She yelled for her daughter to stay inside and close the door. The neighbor lady, an older woman, came to see what was wrong. They gathered her daughter and a few personal items, checked the surrounding area, then scurried over to the neighbor's house. She was comforting the woman and her daughter when she looked out the window and saw one of the Animal Patrol on the street. Quickly opening the door, she caught his attention and explained the problem."

"I can't imagine how awful it was for them, for the poor mother." Julie touched her friend's arm. "Or for you."

Rosie shuddered from her memories. "I had nightmares about it for a long time. The Patrol reminded me that this was, sadly, a part of the reality of living there. The next day they notified me that arrangements had been made to take all of us to the regional center in a major city on the coast about three hours away. There had been two separate reports of sightings of eight or ten male lions hunting in the middle of the day in a draw in the valley close to our location."

"That situation was when you decided to leave Africa, wasn't it?" Julie hoped to encourage Rosie to cut the story short, for both their sakes.

Rosie nodded, seemed to become less tense. "Yes. Back in the city, life was so different. You could hear the activity in the park, taxis and buses were everywhere, and I saw people on the streets from various countries. It was all interesting, but I just didn't want to do anything. After a couple of weeks, we started talking about what I could do if I went home. There were several openings available where I could join a group in an ongoing project. That seemed like a good idea."

"Hey, ho! It looks like we are still in the middle of nowhere," Tom said as he popped his head between the seats and put an end to the disturbing memories. "That was a good nap. Now I'm ready to find some food. Where are we?"

Rosie flashed Julie a look of relief, then grinned at Tom. "Boy, am I glad to see your face! We're about ten miles from the next rest stop where we can do some walking, get some food and change drivers. I'm definitely ready after sharing some details about my Peace Corps experience in Africa with Julie. It got to me a bit."

"It got to me, too," Julie said, thinking the rehash had distracted her from her recent problems, but had also been disturbing.

Tom gave them an understanding nod, then tried to lighten the moment. "I'll give Brian a call while you girls take a walk. I'm sure he's wondering where we are and why I haven't called yet." He patted his stomach. "But first let's talk food for this hungry boy!"

"You won't starve in the next ten miles so chill out," Rosie said with a laugh.

"Yes, Ma'am, Ms. Chauffer! I'll play with some of those lyrics that have been bouncing around in my brain."

Julie sat in silence, thinking about her relief at having survived her dangerous situation with Eric and reuniting with her friends. She was ready to meet Brian, Tom's friend. He lived in the backwoods in Idaho and would lead them to his place. Tom intended to stay with his friend there, while she and Rose would take a car Brian had stored on to Seattle.

As Julie and Rosie returned from their walk at the rest stop, Tom greeted them with, "Well, things may get interesting."

"I'm not sure I'm ready for more 'interesting,'" Julie said with a sigh.

After they had all climbed back inside the van and Tom sat in the driver's seat, he explained, "Brian said he decided about midafternoon that he would lock up his place, turn the dogs loose and come into town. He had some errands to run and needed to have a couple of things checked on his van. He's hanging out at the big truck stop just off the highway for us to meet him there. He has a permit on file to park there with the campers. He can get one for us with the agreement that we are out of there by noon."

"Okay," Rosie said, sounding confused.

Tom headed out of the parking lot. "Anyway... when he heard a couple of truckers talking about somebody making a scene claiming he was there to shoot the aliens, Brian started asking questions. Seems some weirdo had parked a small semi in the lot at one of truck stops between here and there. He had a 'tank' in the trailer which he used to shoot in all directions. There were a couple of fatalities and the state patrol shut down the traffic, so it is backing up from both directions."

He pulled in a breath before continuing, "We decided it's not worth the extra 200 miles to turn around and come in on the other highway. So, we may be awhile. Good thing I have my harmonica in my pocket and a couple decks of cards in the van. Do we have water and snacks if this turns out to be a long ordeal?"

"Aliens? Some weirdo shooting? Fatalities?" Julie gasped. Life seemed to get crazier and crazier.

Tom shrugged. "Just passing on what Brain said."

Before any more could be said on the subject, Rosie announced, "I see a patrol vehicle with lights flashing down the road."

When they pulled up on the side of the road, a patrolman came to talk to them. Tom asked, "What's going on?"

The patrolman looked serious. "We had a sniping in progress. Three fatalities, and no contact with the perpetrator. We shut everything down." He took a second before adding, "Luckily some truckers that had run the highways in Mexico helped. Now we have the situation surrounded and are escorting people out so they can get on the road. It will be awhile, though, before things here start moving. Please stay in your vehicle, keep it quiet and keep cell phone times to a bare minimum."

"Thank you, Sir! We will certainly do that."

\*\*\*\*\*\*

"That was the darndest game of Spades I've played in a long time. I had some pretty strange hands, and I don't remember ever having the Ace and King of trump twice in a row." Tom glanced out the window. "Hey, I'm seeing movement on the hill up ahead! And here comes someone from the other direction."

He moved back into the driver's seat. "I hope we can get this show on the road. I'm eager to see Brian."

As he crested a hill, Tom exclaimed, "I see lots of lights up ahead! We may have made it safe and sound. Try to spot Brian's van. It has flowers and music notes dancing around everywhere. He said to call him if he doesn't blink his lights twice. We must go back to the 24-hour window as I can show my driver's license and get a one-time permit to park."

Later Brian led them back to the designated area where they gathered in his van. He offered hot cocoa from a couple of thermos bottles, fresh cinnamon rolls, some turkey wraps and a bag 50/50 spinach and lettuce greens. He'd happily greeted them with a big smile.

While Tom and Rosie dove into the food, Julie pressed him about the alien hunter story.

Brian sat down on the big pillow in the corner, looking eager to share his tale. "I was talking with the manager and some trucker when a couple of highway patrolmen walked in and described a real bizarre scenario in the next truck stop. The one that had been between us."

His eyes shone with excitement. "Suddenly the trailer 'doors' of an odd looking semi flung open and a ramp inched out from under the floor. Apparently electronically activated. Then a 'garage' door rose and disappeared inside. Next, a strange, homemade 'tank' came creeping down the ramp and moved toward the convenience store. It was round, domed and encased in heavy metal. With the sounds of gears and air hoses, the top of the dome lifted about three inches, followed by rotation. Someone with a thick accent shouted, 'I'll get those aliens. I'll mow them down!'"

"That's wild!" Tom exclaimed, intrigued.

Julie thought it was far beyond wild. It was creepy and dangerous.

"Bullets started spraying from the dish on the top of the machine. In the ensuing chase several people were hurt, windows in the building were shattered, people were shouting, 'Take cover, now!' Then the emergency sirens began wailing."

Brian stopped to make sure his audience was paying attention. "The manager, who had been on the floor, ducked behind a concrete pillar in the middle of the convenience area. He began shouting, 'Hit the floor and stay low. There is gunfire in progress. Code 3 Employee Shutdown! Code 3 Employee Shutdown! Keep a low profile to proceed. Does anybody need help? You can exit the rear door to access campground vehicles, but no movement is allowed.' He punched the 911 button on his cell phone which was wired to give his location to all available emergency services."

Julie blinked at the mention of "Code 3." What a coincidence.

"Meanwhile, outside several truckers sprang into action. They had previously run the highways in Mexico and had an array of protective gear for themselves and their trucks. One truck was parked just a short distance away. The driver, wearing armor headgear—like Middle Age Crusaders—and sitting behind a steel plate in the side window, moved his truck on one side of the 'tank.' Another truck with plates covering the tires and similar cab protection pulled up in front allowing a third truck to circle around to the third side. They had 'It' contained. This allowed the Campground and Highway Patrol to manage the surroundings. Several people were injured. It killed one elderly man who got confused in the melee and started walking around. And tragically a young, visibly pregnant woman was hit as she entered the building, falling forward."

Rosie gasped in horror.

Brian went on, "Some people pulled her inside, but she was losing too much blood. She began spitting up blood and fell unconscious. There was no way to help her."

"This was a nightmare," Julie said, hurting for the poor woman and everyone else.

With a nod, Brian continued, "One trucker came forward with a slingshot apparatus. It was loaded with ping pong ball sized projectiles filled with some sticky stuff that expanded ten times upon exposure to the air and then set hard in a couple of seconds. He was a good shot and soon had the guns shut down and the dome frozen in place."

He took a second before adding, "Then a trucker who had been sleeping way over on the other end of the lot brought his big caterpillar over. He proceeded to pulling the 'tank' on its top and then gave it a couple of whacks, so part of the shell cracked. There was a loud scream from inside and then silence. They later removed the occupant who had died from a broken neck."

Suddenly Julie sat up straight in her spot on the floor. This wasn't right. "Wait a minute! I was dreaming about this kind of thing this morning. Only it took place on a weird-looking planet somewhere in space. I don't remember the rest of the dream, but the purpose was shooting the aliens. Premonition?"

She drew in a deep breath, shaking her head. "It's all just too weird for me! I'm ready for some peace and quiet."

Brian stood up to stretch. "Well, I think I'm ready for some shuteye myself. I sure am glad that none of us were there. I don't need that kind of dangerous situation. One of the interesting things is that truck stop is the biggest in the area. They have their own water system including a couple of buried tanker units for fire safety, their own water tower, grounds patrol and alarms and emergency systems. They were the best place around this part of the country to handle this kind of situation."

He yawned. "If I don't see evidence of activity by 10:00 o'clock tomorrow morning, I'll call you. We can get the car ready to roll, do some music in the evening, and then get a good night's sleep. That way you girls can leave early and make your way back to some familiar territory in Seattle."

"Sounds like a plan to me! See you in the morning!" Tom answered as he was out the door.

Rosie followed him. "Thanks for the food and hospitality. See you tomorrow."

Julie pulled the door closed behind her, frowning. "I've had enough. I'm ready for some good sleep, something without crazy dreams."

# My Mom on the Farm

## Bonnie Lacey Krenning

When I first became aware of daily life on the farm, I was four years old. It seemed Mom was always in the kitchen cooking. She didn't sit down, except for our meals and in the evening with the family. In early morning, as I came into the kitchen, she was standing by the large, ornate, wood-burning cookstove, cooking breakfast. Close by was the kitchen cupboard where she kept her needed supplies. Starting from scratch on the work-surface of the cupboard, she made biscuits, cornbread, sourdough bread, pie crusts, dumplings and noodles, to mention just a few. She had what she needed in easy reach to cook three meals a day for our large family.

My mom was particular about the kinds and cuts of wood she needed and wanted for the cookstove. Daddy and the boys made sure she had them.  In wood-boxes behind the cookstove there was kindling, split and dry wood and small green logs to keep the heat at the temperature she needed as she cooked different foods and breads. Even with a broken thermometer on the oven door she could control the fire so everything turned out perfectly baked and cooked.

The family always had a big early breakfast. While Daddy and the boys were out at the barn feeding the animals and milking the cows Mom was in the kitchen cooking. She cooked a variety of breakfasts such as biscuits and gravy, rolled oats, rice and eggs and biscuits. On rare occasions she fried stacks of large, plate-size pancakes. Starting with two stacks of pancakes, each six to eight inches high, she continued frying until all of us had all we wanted.

Every Monday, Wednesday and Friday morning, without fail, Mom started a big batch of sourdough bread from the starter she kept active in a gallon crock. She mixed flour and liquid into the dough until she could knead it and let it rise. As the dough raised to nearly overflowing the dishpan, she kneaded it several times throughout the day so it would be light and fine textured. About mid-afternoon Mom made six large loaves of bread in pans of three loaves each and let them rise double for baking. There was enough dough for a large pan of cinnamon rolls.

The yeast bread was not enough to last from one yeast bread day until the next, so Mom made cornbread, biscuits, pancakes and sometimes cornmeal mush—called grits in the south. And for several weeks in the spring, delicious Morel Mushrooms grew down by the creek. She sliced and fried them for breakfast, two or three times a week for several weeks. They made a complete meal and were so delicious.

Mom was known throughout the neighborhood for her great cooking and fine breads. Occasionally one of our neighbors would just happen by at mealtime, hoping to enjoy her cooking. The family welcomed them. There was always plenty of food, even if sometimes there was not much variety, especially in the wintertime.

The family appreciated Mom's cooking but rarely told her. One day in winter, after the noon meal, the boys had finished eating and left the table to run out to play. It was before spring crops came in, so Mom "made do" with whatever she had on hand, probably some kind of beans and cornbread and maybe a fruit cobbler. I was clearing the table while Daddy was drinking his coffee. Mom was sitting close by. I heard Daddy quietly say to Mom, "Annie Mae, you can take almost anything and make it taste good, better than anyone I know." And she could!

Throughout spring and summer Mom cooked fresh vegetables from the garden every day. She had the cookstove fire going all day, even when the outside temperature was over 100 degrees. In the kitchen the temperature was over 110 degrees. There were no fans and seldom a breeze through the screen doors. Her hair and clothes were often wet with sweat, which she wiped away with a 'kerchief' she kept in her apron pocket. She just kept on working.

That summer I noticed Mom going barefoot like the rest of us. When I asked her why, she said, "To save my nice shoes." Her only pair of shoes had high heels. They hurt her feet and the corns on her toes from wearing shoes that didn't fit. She had been told, the rare times she bought shoes, that her feet were short and wide, and she was fit accordingly. Many years later she found that her correct shoe size was a 7A. The wrong shoe size caused the corns and callouses.

Even with the pain, she always kept her shoes close at hand, in case a neighbor stopped by so she wouldn't be seen barefoot by an outsider.

To me Mom was beautiful even when she was barefoot. She had dark brown eyes and beautiful, long black hair that she kept pulled back in a neat bun. When she sat down in the evening and let her thick hair down, it was long enough for her to sit on. I loved combing it. My hair was fine and thin and never grew long. I wished my hair was pretty like Mom's.

Mom was five feet, two inches tall and weighed about 120 pounds when she wasn't having a baby. I noticed she was always neat and clean. She wore a cotton print dress and an apron. She quickly removed the apron if someone stopped by. She ironed our dresses with a flat iron heated on the cook stove. Some neighbor women, at their house, sometimes wore wrinkled dresses and often didn't look clean. Some women, though, had to work in the gardens and fields. With all my brothers Mom didn't have to do that. She felt it was just as important to look nice at home as when she went somewhere.

Most of Mom's and my dresses, except the hand-me-downs, were made from printed feed sacks on her treadle sewing machine. She had a special "fancy dress" that hung in the closet, by Daddy's dress suit, that she wore on special occasions.

I loved being around Mom. She was singing most of the time and had a beautiful, clear soprano voice. She sang hymns, Jimmy Rogers songs and folk and mountain ballads. She learned the songs in better times before the Depression and before moving to the farm. She knew the words to many songs and liked it when we asked her to sing one of our favorites.

Through it all, I don't remember Mom seeming sad or depressed. In the wintertime, however, she would sometimes say, "I wish it wus summer agin!" And in summertime she would say, "I wish it wus winter agin!" Looking back, it is easy to understand her feelings with it being stifling hot in the summertime. And it was so cold in winter, with the cold winds blowing in around the windows and doors that she wore her ill-fitting shoes. And, more than once, the water in the bucket in the kitchen froze solid overnight.

The boys took turns helping Mom in the kitchen. She seldom raised her voice, but she didn't have to. Everyone knew what they were supposed to do and usually did it. When Mom firmly said, "Bonnie Mae," I knew I had better do what I was supposed to do or stop doing what I wasn't supposed to do, or she would "raise her voice" to me.

I can recall the first and only time when Mom physically punished me. Whether it was something I didn't do that I was supposed to do, or it was something I did that I shouldn't have done, I don't recall. She said "Yer gonna have to have a switchin! Go git me a switch!" I went outside and got the thinnest switch I could find from a bush in the yard and brought it back to her in the kitchen.

Mom stood beside me and pulled my dress tight against my bloomers and lightly switched me a few times. It didn't really hurt, but I thought it was such an indignity, so I threw myself down on the floor, sobbing. She kept lightly switching me saying, "Git up! Git up!" So, I quickly got up, and it was all over. It never happened to me again. I don't know whether I learned my lesson or whether Mom was simply not inclined to repeat the "switchin."

Our family worked as a team and Mom was in charge, clearly leading the way, especially on washday. Washday was always on Saturday so the boys could help. They carried many two-gallon buckets of water from the spring below the house and built a fire outside under our large cast-iron kettle to heat the water. They poured the hot water into two wash tubs on the ground and lye soap that Mom and Daddy made was added. In cold weather we placed the wash tubs inside on the kitchen floor. They placed several pairs of overalls and other heavily soiled clothes in the tubs and left them to soak.

When the water cooled enough, we smaller barefoot kids would step into the tubs and "stomp" the clothes to get the worst of the dirt out of them. The boys wore their overalls for a week at a time, so they were really dirty. The overalls were wrung out by hand by the boys working two together. The overalls were transferred to washtubs of warm water on benches in the kitchen. Mom and the older boys did the final scrubbing on washboards After rinsing the overalls, the boys hung them on the clothesline to dry.

Washday in the summertime was usually a fun time for my

brothers and me. The boys went without shirts and underwear in the summer so there were fewer clothes to wash. But in the wintertime, all the washing was done in the kitchen and they hung the clothes out to freeze dry or draped them on chairs around the heating stoves in the front room and dining room to dry.

Sometimes it was just too cold to do the washing. Then we would have to wear the same long underwear and outer clothes for two or three weeks at a time.

Fortunately, or maybe unfortunately, most of the families in the neighborhood went without washing clothes as our family did, so we probably all "smelled" about the same.

The biggest problem may have been in the one-room schoolhouse. It was not easy, though, to keep the room warm, because there was only a wood-burning heating stove in the middle of the large classroom. The room was often cool, even cold. The younger kids sat closer to the stove and the older boys sat farther away. That may have helped to lessen the "aroma."

About two years before we left the farm Daddy bargained for a used washing machine that had a gas-powered motor. It had a wringer and two wooden tubs meant for washing and rinsing the clothes. With the washing machine we didn't have to, or maybe get to, "stomp" the clothes anymore. The washing machine completely changed and improved Mom's life.

Every fall, for several evenings, the family gathered around the dining table. Not to eat, but to help Mom make our denim quilts that were so essential for us to keep warm when the fires burned down at night in the wintertime. Mom didn't have time to do "fancy" quilting, but she had a few nice quilts she used on her and Daddy's bed.

When the boys' overalls were completely worn out, Mom cut squares of fabric from the backs of the legs and sewed them together to make a denim quilt top. She bought dark flannel by the bolt, thirty-six inches wide, and sewed two long strips together to make the outer lining for a quilt. It was spread out on the dining table and an old worn sheet blanket was placed on the lining and a denim top placed on it. Sometimes Mom covered a worn-out denim quilt with new flannel outer lining and a "new" denim top, making a "new quilt." They became quite thick and heavy; that was good!

The older boys tacked through the quilt every few inches with a darning needle and string. They cut the string between where they tacked the quilt and the younger kids tied the string in hard knots to hold it together. Mom sewed the outer edges together all around the quilt at another time. We made and covered several quilts each fall.

In the coldest weather we had to cover ourselves with layers of quilts to keep warm when the temperature dropped below freezing in the house at night. The boys could snuggle together but I slept alone.

Sometimes Mom wrapped a warm lid from the cookstove in newspaper and put it at my feet to help keep me warm. I would often wake up shivering, realizing I had wet the bed. I didn't want anyone to know, because Mom would call me "a peetail." But she found out anyway in the morning when she took the cookstove lid out of my bed.

Mom spent many evenings patching the boys' and Daddy's overalls. She sometimes sewed patches on patches on their overalls and they were often handed down to a younger brother. Daddy and the boys each had a good pair of overalls to wear places away from home. Daddy watched the boys to make sure they changed into work overalls when they got home. Patching overalls was a difficult task, but Mom felt it was important, even necessary. It saved a lot of money that could be used for other necessities. Also, Mom would never have allowed the boys or Daddy to wear "ragged" clothes.

When the long winter was over, the wonder of spring took hold on all of us. Trees started to blossom and leaf out. Daddy and the boys planted the garden and fields. Before that, the mushrooms, wild greens and wild onions grew big enough to eat. We went all winter with no fresh vegetables or fruit. We did well on beans, grains, potatoes, home canned berries, sauerkraut and many kinds of pickles. We had enough to eat but longed for fresh foods.

The spring I turned five years old, I started noticing Mom as she worked. I wanted to learn to do the things she did so I could help her. I was usually at her elbow watching and trying to help. She was so patient with me and showed me how to do many tasks. I learned how to peel potatoes, pick and shell green peas, pick and snap green beans, shuck the ears of corn and cut and wash the asparagus. Sometimes these tasks took me two or three hours, but I was pleased to be helping Mom and we were all happy to have all the fresh vegetables we wanted.

The only thing Mom took charge of outside the house was the chickens. She counted on eggs often for breakfast and for her cooking, to make the noodles, dumplings, cakes, puddings, chocolate meringue pies and other foods that called for eggs.

She had Plymouth Rock hens and roosters because they were larger and produced more eggs than other breeds. We had a chicken house where the nests were about four feet off the ground, so the blacksnakes could not easily reach the eggs and swallow them whole. Occasionally a snake got into a nest and swallow an egg. Sometimes we saw a snake crawling on the ground with a bulge that showed it had swallowed an egg. Mom hated blacksnakes. She kept a hoe by the kitchen door and if the boys told her they saw a blacksnake, she would take the hoe and chase it down and cut off its head.

In the spring, when nesting season started, some hens sat on nests in the chicken house and hatched their baby chicks. Some hens would go into the woods, make a nest, lay and hatch the eggs. The hens and chicks would then come into the yard for the grains we scattered for the new chicks.

When the chicks were grown, they kept the hens for layers, to keep the flock going. Some of the roosters were kept for mating and they used the others for chicken and noodles and chicken and dumplings in the fall. Chickens were our main source of meat.

Each spring Mom ordered two boxes of one-hundred baby chicks from a hatchery in town, one box at a time. She mailed cash in an envelope to the hatchery and the baby chicks were sent out by the mailman to our mailbox. One of my brothers would go to the mailbox every day until the mailman delivered the chicks. He carried the baby chicks the quarter mile to the house. They were raised for fryers for the family or to trade at the country store in exchange for needed groceries.

One summer morning a magazine salesman came walking up the hill to our house unexpectedly. Mom told him that she didn't have any money for magazines. When he saw all the chickens running around, he offered to sell Mom magazines in exchange for chickens. She ordered a year's subscription to The Lady's Home Journal and Good Housekeeping for her and the Jack and Jill Magazine for us kids. She traded four fryers for all the magazines.

With the coming of summer Mom started preparing food from the garden for the winter. She didn't have a pressure cooker, so she canned only acid foods. I picked the gooseberries, and the boys picked the blackberries. I had buckets of gooseberries, but the boys picked washtubs full of blackberries. Mom canned over a hundred half-gallon jars of berries so she could make several berry cobblers often throughout the winter months.

Mom made five-gallon crocks of sauerkraut, beet pickles and cucumber pickles. She seasoned them and knew just when they were ready, to heat and can in half-gallon jars. Along with the sweet potatoes and red-skinned potatoes we were all set for winter. When freezing weather came the canned food and potatoes had to be stored in Daddy's root cellar to keep them from freezing.

My mom liked, even loved, black walnuts. She considered them one of our most important crops. She used them in her baking, but just as importantly, she crushed the nutmeats and squeezed the oil out into small jars for ear drops to treat our earaches in the wintertime. She believed the oil worked better than anything she could buy at the drug store. Mom was relying on "folk medicine" and experience, but she was right. Black walnuts are anti-fungal and have many other health and nutrition benefits.

Every fall the boys gathered bushel baskets of black walnuts, hulled them and set them beside a big rock where I cracked them. Cracking the walnuts was my chore, but I loved it. I cracked them and dug the nutmeats out with a hairpin, collecting them in jars. It took several weeks to fill several half-gallon jars with nutmeats for Mom to use in the desserts she made.

My mom liked doing fun things. It seemed like she even enjoyed her work. She enjoyed having neighbor families in to pop popcorn and make popcorn balls. She laughed and smiled at our family's dancing at home in the winter evenings. And she liked the neighborhood dances. Mom and Daddy did the square dances, waltzes and two-steps together.

Mom knew all the dances. She and her friend Goldie, the woman that delivered me, liked to do the "Schottische Dance." They danced arm-in-arm across the floor to any peppy tune. Everyone else would step back and clap their hands in time to the music while they danced. Mom was one of the best dancers in the neighborhood.

Women and girls in the neighborhood were not supposed to wear slacks, pants or, Heaven forbid, shorts. One day a package came in the mail from one of Daddy's sisters in the city. Mom opened it and there was a yellow linen slack suit for women. Mom put it on. It fit perfectly and she looked so pretty. Daddy smiled his usual big smile of approval, but Mom knew she wouldn't be wearing the suit anywhere off the farm.

One fall day after Sunday dinner, Daddy said to Mom, "If you'll put on that slack suit, we'll take a walk around on the farm." With Mom in her yellow linen slack suit and Daddy in his best shirt and overalls they walked off together, hand-in-hand, out of sight of us kids for a couple of hours.

When they came back, they were talking, smiling and laughing between themselves. I don't recall seeing the slack suit again but that one time was worth it all.

Although Mom didn't have much time to read, she enjoyed reading her magazines, the local newspaper and The Weekly Kansas City Star. Mom and Daddy often discussed world, national and local news, including politics. The older boys checked out books at school for them and for Daddy and Mom to read. They liked Harold Bell Wright's books, western and historic novels. Mom had more time to read in the winter when we were in school and canning season was over.

Mom was adamant about voting. She was twenty-four years old when women won the right to vote. She believed everyone who was voting age should vote in all the elections: National, State and Local. Daddy made sure that Mom had a way to ride to the polls. She would have probably walked but Daddy wouldn't have allowed that.

So that Mom didn't need to walk, Daddy traded for a beautiful old one-horse buggy with a fancy top. It was not big enough for all the family, so it was just used when Mom and Daddy went somewhere by themselves and sometimes with little ones. When not in use, the buggy sat idle by the garden fence and was much admired by our visitors. It gave Mom a chance to let people know she always voted. I don't recall the folks ever missing a chance to vote. I do recall one time when they went in the buggy in heavy snow to the schoolhouse to vote.

I learned early not to ask too many questions, so I usually tried to figure things out for myself. One night in late winter I had been sound asleep but woke up to Mom and Daddy talking in the front room. I kept quiet and listened. I heard Mom say, "We don't have any money. What are we going' to do?" I got up and went in where Mom was standing by the stove and put my arm around her because she looked sad. She hugged me and told me to go back to bed.

I woke up the next morning thinking about what she said. I knew that Mom kept her coin purse in her envelope purse. I opened it and saw there were three pennies in it. I didn't tell Mom I had checked but wondered why she said she didn't have any money. Not knowing the value of money, I didn't understand. I thought maybe she didn't know the pennies were there, but I didn't dare say anything.

I checked her coin purse every few days without her knowing and the pennies were still there. As winter faded into spring, everyone seemed happy and excited with the warmer weather. Then one day I checked Mom's coin purse and there were some nickels and dimes in it. Now Mom wouldn't have to be sad anymore like she was that winter night.

In that remote area I had not heard of slaves or people with different colored skin, except my little negro doll. One day I heard one of my brothers telling Mom that one boy at school said, "Slave mothers didn't care if their babies and children were sold. It's just like Daddy selling our horses and cows." Mom became really upset and started crying. She said, "Don't ever believe that! They love their children just like I love you!"

I didn't realize the full meaning of slavery then but later became aware that neither Mom nor Daddy were prejudiced, unlike many of the people in the community and the county. There was a sign on 54 Highway, just outside our town that said, "NO NEGROS ALLOWED IN TOWN AFTER SUNDOWN." The sign was not removed until 19 48.

In the late 1930s the country was recovering from the Depression. Markets were up and the economy was getting better so there was money for some extras. But I didn't like it when Mom had her beautiful hair cut and got a perm. She said she paid for it by selling some eggs and chickens. She decided I should have a perm in my straight hair, so she saved $2.00 from selling eggs for my perm. Mom's hair turned out nice, but I hated my curly, frizzy hair and was glad when my perm grew out.

I didn't realize it at the time, but I led a very sheltered and protected life in my early childhood. Since I was the only girl among ten brothers until I was nine years old, I got a lot of attention. Often visitors would give me, just me, a nickel or a few pennies. I could see that Mom didn't want that to happen and was sometimes able to intervene.

I didn't have any way to spend the money, so I would save it until there was enough give to Daddy to buy a large bag of candy for all of us. Then there was the time I saved a few coins and gave it to my brother to buy firecrackers. He bought several packages of little Lady Fingers, enough for all of us to have a good time on the Fourth of July.

Mom taught me some pretty songs and poems she learned when she was a little girl in school. They were teaching songs and poems. She didn't want me to be "Tryin' to be fancy." Most of them I have forgotten but one poem she taught me was to let me know God made me and I was where I was meant to be. I still remember the poem:

## DISCONTENT

Down in the field one day in June the flowers all bloomed together
Except one who tried to hide herself and drooped that pleasant weather.

A robin that had flown too high and felt a little lazy
Was resting near a buttercup who wished she were a daisy.

For daisies grow so trim and tall and always have a passion
For wearing frills about their neck in just the daisy fashion.

"You silly thing" the robin said, I think you must be crazy!
I'd rather be my honest self than any made-up daisy."

"Look bravely up into the sky and be content with knowing
That God wished for a buttercup just here where you are growing."

Author: Sarah Orne Jewett (Excerpt Mom taught me from a longer poem).

I am blessed to have had such a firm but loving mom in my early years. She tried to keep me humble. She would say, "You're no better than anyone else." In the same breath she would say: "And, nobody else is better than you." I believed Mom.

# CONTRIBUTORS

# CONTRIBUTOR LIST

Starla Criser

Starla Criser

.